THE BROWNSTONE EFFECT

THE BROWNSTONE EFFECT

ALISON BROWNSTONE™ BOOK FIVE

JUDITH BERENS   MARTHA CARR   MICHAEL ANDERLE

DISRUPTIVE IMAGINATION

THE BROWNSTONE EFFECT TEAM

Thanks to the JIT Readers

Diane L. Smith
Keith Verret
Nicole Emens
Jeff Eaton
Larry Omans
Misty Roa
Daniel Weigert
John Ashmore
Paul Westman

If we've missed anyone, please let us know!

Editor
SkyHunter Editing Team

DEDICATIONS

From Martha

To everyone who still believes in magic
and all the possibilities that holds.
To all the readers who make this
entire ride so much fun.
And to my son, Louie and so many wonderful friends who
remind me all the time of what
really matters and how wonderful
life can be in any given moment.

From Michael

To Family, Friends and
Those Who Love
To Read.
May We All Enjoy Grace
To Live The Life We Are
Called.

CHAPTER ONE

Conrad raised his wand and spoke a quick incantation. Two rows of spaced light orbs winked into existence above the thick stone table and covered the room in soft light. The new illumination highlighted the intricate patterns carved into the stone walls around them, some arcane but most purely aesthetic.

It's almost unfortunate that our enemies will never know to strike us here. Oh, the glories of centuries of defenses layered on this place. I'd like to see them bring their crude tools and machines and come here so that they meet their death with at least the comforting satisfaction of knowing that superior beings destroyed them.

The wizard smiled, satisfied with his efforts. Atmosphere was not as important as blood. Some of the others he worked with didn't always understand that. Their magical lineages might be as deep, but sometimes, they were as myopic as any of the new-blood wizards and witches who had arisen since the opening of the gates.

What separates us is more than power. The blood will tell

1

only if we don't allow ourselves to be polluted both in bloodline and culture.

The last few decades had brought new power and new magic, but it all represented the same thing—a threat to their birthright. The dark wizard families had worked through the centuries to preserve this when magic was difficult and hidden.

Some might have questioned their methods or the type of magic they took advantage of, but the dark wizards deserved to control magic and the Earth. They had earned it through careful effort, not chance historical circumstance, and the flood of magic back onto the planet threatened that.

It was unacceptable. Completely unacceptable.

We shall rule. Not those who spent centuries wallowing in pathetic ignorance or these foreign creatures who neglected this planet for so long. No, it is our right, but we must prove it. We must continue to push past those who would threaten us. If we can't, then can we say we have the right to rule?

Three other robed figures stepped into the chamber from the narrow hallway outside.

"Welcome," Conrad announced. "Everything has been prepared. After our discussion, we shall dine."

The wizard took a seat and waited for the other three robed figures to follow suit. Their faces were hidden, as was his, by a ceremonial mask, all smooth and a solid color. All members of the Seventh Order wore one, despite the fact that they didn't hide their identities from one another. The masks symbolized their sacrifices on behalf of all the ancient lineages of power. They'd been selected to help execute the Grand Plan and now, they needed to deal with the fallout of some its partial failures.

Victories have accumulated, as have our defeats. But a preponderance of advances is sufficient for total victory in the end. It doesn't matter. We're not children and understand that victory is always accompanied by necessary sacrifice.

"Thank you for coming," Conrad offered in his posh English accent. He folded his hands in front of him. "I know we've all seen the reports, but I thought it best if we discussed what occurred two months ago in person, as we've not yet come to a consensus on the best way to handle this situation."

"It's nothing but a failure," hissed a woman in a blue mask, Tabitha. "That's what this situation is. For how many years must we be vexed by that obnoxious half-breed Brownstone? I won't question her power, but she is one girl. I grow increasingly agitated when I hear her name mentioned without the sentence ending in a discussion of her death."

Zachariah shook his head and his white mask gleamed under the light of the orbs. "Let us not misunderstand what has occurred. Yes, the Mountain Strider was neutralized, but we prepared for that eventuality. Even if Brownstone hadn't resealed it, the American military would have eventually destroyed it. Remember, it was only a means, not the end. Don't let Brownstone's interference obscure that."

"The wards to the Great Pillar remain," Tabitha countered. "What do you call that but a failure?"

The bearer of the yellow mask, Jeanne, sighed. "We should have attacked the Pillar wards directly," she replied and her French accent colored the words. "Rather than rely on the secondary disruption caused by the awakening of the Mountain Strider. Even if it had lasted longer, I doubt it would have destroyed the wards."

"The level of power necessary would have led to our discovery if we tried something directly," Conrad challenged. "The necessary rituals are too complicated and long to accomplish if they are disrupted by even a small group of the PDA or others. Our efforts have only been able to proceed as far as they have because our enemies don't understand what we're attempting to do. Secrecy continues to be paramount."

"Perhaps we should still consider alternatives to the current plan. Forward progress isn't enough. We need to complete our goals."

Conrad shook his head. He needed to make the other members of the Seventh Order understand. If they changed course on the plan now, too many variables would be altered and the risk of failure would dramatically increase. Decades of effort would only come to fruition if everyone kept their focus.

Many in the dark wizard families had other concerns, plans, and schemes, but the Seventh Order had worked quietly in the background to prepare the forces and resources needed to execute the plan. The lack of interest from some of the others, while irritating in a certain respect, had worked out better in the long-term. It had allowed the Order to move forward with fewer restrictions. It wasn't as if the dark wizard families could always agree on the best course of action, even if they all had the same overall goals.

No. I will not let frustration destroy our efforts, especially frustration over one girl.

"We have strained the primary wards," Conrad insisted. "And if anything, I'd argue this plan was far more effective because of the interference of Brownstone and Berens. The entire world is focused on the resealing of the Mountain Strider, and they don't have even the faintest idea that we were doing something far more fundamental. Accordingly, I'm not particularly concerned about Brownstone's involvement in that incident, even if she continues to grow into a troublesome irritant."

Tabitha snorted. "Brownstone." Her gloved fingers curled into fists. "While still at that disgusting and inappropriate school, she managed to interfere with the plans. And the younger Berens was there, and our people didn't know beforehand and failed to take her once they did. We need at least two of the Berens for the plan to work—the daughter, mother, or elder Berens. We need access to the power of their line, and we need to get them before another faction takes them. Perhaps the elder Berens would make the most sense. At least we know where she is at any given time."

Jeanne let out a melodramatic sigh. "Do you honestly think you can penetrate that school again? Our allies' earlier forays were fortunate, but they've secured it too tightly since then. Perhaps if Powell wasn't there, we'd have a chance, but he's also survived all our allies' attempts to remove him and continues to help strengthen the school's defenses. Besides, the elder Berens rarely leaves the grounds." She shook her head. "No, the daughter and the mother are our best options despite the fact that they scurry and hide from our power. Their flight proves their ultimate weakness. If they could truly stand against the dark families, they would have already done so."

Tabitha chuckled darkly. "Young Izzie is foolish enough to constantly expose herself out of some feeble belief that she'll be able to stop our long-term plans. She will make a similar mistake again soon. I suspect that if it wasn't for Brownstone, our people would have captured her in Seattle." She cut through the air with her hand. "The solution is simple. We need to remove all possible support for the younger Berens. With no allies, she'll make a mistake again and we'll have her. Once we do, we'll be able to force the mother to come to us as well." She sucked in and exhaled a long, deep breath. "Besides, we can't let Alison Brownstone continue to operate as she wishes. There are other considerations when it comes to her."

Zachariah turned toward her. "Our attempts against her—along with those of others—have cost much in personnel and resources. Is she really so important? We must remember the plan. It doesn't call for her death."

Conrad nodded. "Well said."

Tabitha slammed her hand on the table and the sound echoed around the high-vaulted ceiling. "Don't you understand what she is? Am I the only one who sees the truth? Your cowardice will doom us all."

"It's not cowardice to recognize the truth," Zachariah responded, his voice cool.

"Let us maintain our decorum." Conrad raised his palm, half in command and half in placation. "We all understand that Alison Brownstone has made herself an enemy of the dark wizard families, Tabitha, but Zachariah does raise a point worthy of consideration. Our end goals are paramount over any other considerations. This is why so many have paid with their lives. They sacrifice for what we must achieve."

"If she were merely an enemy, that would be one thing." Tabitha shook her head so hard one might suspect her mask would fly off. "That half-breed of two worlds is a symbol that people look to, one that inspires them. I don't care if she stopped that pathetic man's anti-magic plot. She continues to inculcate inappropriate ideas in the minds of the people. We will never be able to take our rightful place in power while creatures like her operate with such freedom. They will continue to rally to her."

"Are we so sure?" Zachariah challenged. "The love of the masses is fickle. Wait long enough, and they'll no longer care."

"The authorities took her orders in Seattle when fighting the Mountain Strider. That level of influence can't be tolerated. We should have assassinated her at the School of Necessary Magic when we had a chance before she grew into her true power." Tabitha sighed. "If only we'd known she had been weakened, but now, even that window of opportunity has been closed to us."

Jeanne nodded her slow agreement, as did Zachariah a moment later.

Tabitha's passion might blind her, Conrad thought, *but if we can focus this anger, it can be useful to our cause.*

He allowed himself a faint smile under the mask. "If we're in agreement, our discussion should be about the most efficient way to deal with the interloper. I would suggest more misdirection. If Brownstone has a major weakness, it is that she's far too straightforward, much like her crude father. If we give her an obvious and identifiable enemy, she would readily strike and destroy it."

"Perhaps we can attack her family," Jeanne suggested. "If we kill them, she'll be demoralized at the very least. Then we can attack her during that moment of weakness."

Her companions swiveled their heads toward her. Tense silence choked the room.

Conrad cleared his throat. "That would be inadvisable. We don't want to invite the father into this struggle. It's only fortunate that he seems little interested in dark wizard affairs."

"Why?" Jeanne shrugged. "I know of his reputation, but he's merely one man, and the mother doesn't even have true powers. She's only some pathetic non-magical scholar with a few toys she's collected. Neither seems worth that much fear."

His response was a vigorous shake of his head. "You lack the contacts in the American government I do. James Brownstone is only barely kept in check by their efforts as it is, and there is little we could bring to bear that might win against him. His wife is far deadlier than you realize. The combination of the Brownstone family together would be too much. If we attack them in LA and don't succeed, we risk their daughter coming to reinforce them in a way the parents don't assist her in Seattle, if only because of her attempts at independence." He scoffed quietly. "No, we will focus on her and her alone. James Brownstone, fortunately, doesn't like to leave LA much, and our information suggests he will only come briefly to Seattle and leave again. If we time our operations correctly, we minimize our risk to only the daughter."

The Berens and the Brownstones united would be too much, perhaps even with all our resources marshaled. I hope the others realize that.

"A cat's paw," Zachariah suggested. "One that can strike at Alison Brownstone when the time is right. If we combine such a person with another effort to advance our Grand Plan, she might not even realize what's happened until it's too late."

The other three took a moment to consider the suggestion. It was the best plan given the circumstances.

Jeanne raised her wand. A spinning image of the Earth appeared. It stopped once the United States came into view and then zoomed in until an aerial view of Seattle appeared.

"Have we abandoned any thought of disrupting other Great Pillars? With Alison Brownstone based out of Seattle, there is a high probability she will be a threat to any of our future operations there. It might be advisable to avoid her entirely and focus on another area of interest."

Conrad sighed. "The wards have already been weakened by the destruction of the Seattle kemana. It's why the Galbrathians, as crude as they are in their methods and mindset, did it to begin with. They've been a useful tool, even if it has cost many of their members." He shook his head. "I doubt we could successfully destroy another kemana while maintaining the appropriate ritual without detection. If we want to have any chance of completing our plan in the next few years, it will have to be the Great Pillar in Seattle. Once it's disrupted, we can draw on the power we need for the final stage." He stood and gestured broadly with his arms. "Let us rely on our patience to separate us from our enemies and even our allies who would lead us astray. If we move too rashly now, we'll throw away everything we've accomplished in these preceding decades. Remember what we fight for. The deserving few will lead this planet."

"The deserving few will lead this planet," the other three intoned.

"And Alison Brownstone?" Tabitha asked.

"Zachariah's suggestion makes the most sense," Conrad responded, a little more emotion than he wanted in his voice as vicious inspiration flowed through him. "We simply need to give her a reason to believe we have a different plan, and I know one way to do it that will also weaken the younger Berens." He retook his seat. "Symbolism is important, and I think I have a suggestion that will be perfect in that regard."

CHAPTER TWO

Mason scanned the road ahead of his SUV. There wasn't much traffic, but that was only to be expected given the rather lengthy and indirect route they took to the airport and the early hour of the morning. It was hard, even in a city with so many abandoned industrial and commercial zones, to find large areas where no one was at risk, but at least in this area, they had minimized the danger.

Sometimes, I wish A was more worried about herself than everyone else. That obsession with protection will get her killed someday if she doesn't have people like me or Hana to watch her back.

"I still think we should have flown the client directly to the airport," he complained. "What's the point of having the helicopter if we're don't use it for jobs like this?"

Tahir's receivers had connected all of them for the job, excluding the newly hired members of the field support team. The new recruits were competent, even if they lacked magic, but Alison had still not decided how to most effectively utilize them. She needed to give more thought to those times when they were sent out on low-level jobs that didn't require the firepower of a Drow princess, life wizard, or nine-tailed fox decked out in artifacts.

"The point is to not get shot out of the air," Alison responded through Mason's receiver. "I know you're aching to crash another helicopter, but this time, it'd be one I own so I'd be on the hook to replace it."

Mason laughed. "I'll have you know that was the first helicopter I've ever crashed. Will you never let me live that down?"

"Sure. That can be your birthday present."

He checked his rearview camera. His SUV led the front of the convoy and three other vehicles followed, carefully spaced and all with tinted windows.

Protecting an asset was something he'd done for his entire professional life. It would have made him a natural fit for Brownstone Security even if he wasn't dating the owner of the company.

I wish she could have driven with me, but she's right where she needs to be. And it's not exactly like this is a normal body-guard mission.

"What do you have for me, Tahir?" Alison asked.

"I was about to tell you that you have possible trouble coming," the infomancer responded.

Mason's heart rate kicked up. No matter how many jobs he made it through, there was always the tension that settled in at the beginning of a fight. The problem with being a bodyguard or security contractor was that it wasn't only his life on the line. Personal survival wasn't the most important consideration in any given confrontation.

This should be easy, though. We know what's coming, and we're geared up for it. A's plan is solid. Those bastards won't see it coming.

"There are multiple vehicles approaching the convoy," Tahir reported. "I wouldn't have been suspicious of them given that it's a small number and they all approach from different directions, but they all turned toward you at the same time. When I checked on thermal, I found they are jam-packed with men, and judging by the silhouettes, decent weaponry."

Mason tightened his grip on the wheel. "It looks like your plan worked, A. They're all coming to the party."

"Hana," Alison began. "Is everything okay on your end?"

"The package is secure," the other woman responded over the comms. She laughed. "It's so fun talking like that."

"Let's keep our focus."

"Sure thing, boss."

He allowed himself a little grin since no one was in the SUV to watch him. Hana might not be as serious as Alison or him, but when the bullets flew, she kept her calm. For him, that was more important than whatever jokes she might crack along the way.

We all have a different way to be good at our jobs.

"Now, you have multiple incoming tactical drones," Tahir reported. "Rocket-armed."

"Do I need to make an appearance?" Alison responded with slight tension in her voice. "I don't care what the dealer said, I don't want to test the SUV armor against rockets."

"Don't worry," the infomancer replied, as calm as ever. "They will *not* engage you. I guarantee that."

Mason remained silent. No one needed to respond to that. While Jerry and his team of non-magical field support personnel were new, everyone else had worked together for months now and expected competence. They all had their strengths, and when it came to their specialties, they'd proven themselves.

"It's still annoying," Alison complained. "I thought the mercs would be a little lazier, but this ups the chance that those power armor reports were accurate. All right, everyone off the road. The support team will set up around the vehicle of interest. I'll radio them now."

With the recent hire of a small team of support personnel, Mason had pushed Alison for more formal organization, including communication callsigns. That was how he'd worked for most of his career as a bodyguard, but she'd pushed back because she preferred the informal atmosphere. He wasn't convinced that would be practical as the company grew, but it wasn't worth the fight in the middle of a job.

"I see a good spot ahead," he advised them all. "Follow me."

The convoy pulled into an empty side street and slowed to a stop with three of the vehicles positioned around the fourth in a rough triangle. A half-dozen men and women leapt out of the other escort vehicles, all with rifles, body armor, and anti-magic deflectors. They split into pairs and rushed to position themselves behind the parked vehicles.

Mason scrambled out of his SUV and ran around the other side to draw his wand and prepare his basic ass-kicking package of enchantments. He layered shields and body enhancement spells before he holstered his wand and drew his gun. Not every battle could be resolved hand-to-hand so he'd wait until he had his opportunity. Besides, the plan wasn't over.

Explosions filled the sky in the distance, the sounds little more than pops from so far away.

"All enemy tactical drones eliminated," Tahir reported. "The mercenaries on the ground have increased speed. Contact imminent."

"At least these assholes don't have dropships," Alison replied.

Jerry narrowed his eyes as he switched his rifle to burst rifle. "Movement on this side."

Two SUVs roared down the street and men aimed assault rifles from the windows. Another two pairs of vehicles raced toward them from different directions.

"Let's take them down, boys and girls," Mason shouted. "Don't let them get near the asset."

The Brownstone Security personnel opened fire. Jerry and his partner's years of experience as ex-SWAT served them well. Their bursts eliminated the driver of one of the first SUVs, and the vehicle careened to the side and crashed into the side of a building. One of the men catapulted out the front window. The other field support team members pelted the other enemy vehicles.

That's why you wear your seatbelt even during an assassination attempt.

The surviving enemies on all sides returned fire and rapid volleys rebounded off the armored Brownstone Security vehicles. The rounds sparked on contact and bounced off the SUVs, the overlapping clink and ting almost drowned out by the heavy crack of rifles and handguns.

The bullets didn't penetrate the windows, but the glass cracked and spiderwebbed. Alison wouldn't emerge from the encounter without paying for some repairs, but at least the stream of hot lead didn't rip through the vehicles and into the men and women behind them.

"How long until we spring the surprise, A?" Mason sprang up to unload his magazine into an approaching vehicle. His rounds blew a tire, and the unfortunate driver's panicked jerk of the wheel tipped the SUV onto its side with a loud crunch and scape of metal on tarmac.

"Good one, Mason," one of the field support team called out.

A stray bullet struck the wizard and forced him into a crouch. His shield protected him from serious harm, but the sting lingered as he slapped another magazine into his weapon.

At this rate, we won't even need Alison's surprise. I thought these guys were supposed to bring some heavier weapons.

The remaining mercenary vehicles squealed to a standstill and turned sideways so the enemy could unload on the opposite side. The value of cover had become clear for both groups of combatants.

The heavy sustained fire from all sides forced the Brownstone support team down behind their vehicle shields.

"They have us pinned," Jerry shouted. "We'll be shredded if we stand."

Mason squeezed off a few more rounds. "Stay down and let them get close."

Jerry gritted his teeth. He obviously didn't like the plan and Mason didn't blame him. This was the first job they'd worked where things had become a little dicey, but the man needed to trust Alison and the main field team.

"Hana," Alison barked through the comms, "what's your status?"

"The package is almost delivered," the fox responded. "We're close to the eagle."

"Tahir?" Alison followed-up. "What does Hana's situation look like from your side?"

"I see nothing unusual, and the men in the assault against the convoy are consistent with the reports I hacked earlier. That's their entire main force as far as I can tell."

One of the mercenaries dropped into the vehicle out of sight. He emerged with an RPG over his shoulder and lined his shot up.

Mason grimaced. "Everyone down. RPG! A, we're out of time. They took the bait, but we're screwed."

The door to the asset vehicle flew open, and Alison leapt out, covered in a shimmering shield laced with dark lines. She vaulted away from the vehicle as the mercenary fired. Shadow wings grew from her back, and she swooped toward the incoming projectile, her arms folded in front of her. Several yards out, she collided with the explosive.

Orange fire and shrapnel whipped around her as she landed and rolled to her feet. Not a single shot was fired as the white-haired young woman stood and extended a shadow blade.

There we go. Now it's time for some real fun.

Alison aimed a shadow blade toward the mercenary who'd fired the RPG. "Don't you assholes get it? The client's not here. He never was. Now, you can surrender, or you can surrender after we smack you around a little. No one has to get hurt here today, but trust me, you're way outclassed."

"Load anti-magics," shouted a man Mason presumed was the mercenary commander.

"Your choice," she responded. She hurtled toward a nearby wall and turned at the last minute to push off it and soar toward the leader. Mason and the others opened fire and pinned the mercenaries near Alison down.

She dropped her wings and landed immediately behind the enemy squad. Most of the team was still in the process of loading their new ammo and not prepared to face a Drow princess right behind them. A quick thrust with a magic blade eliminated the man who'd fired the RPG, but she cracked her boot against the head of another man nearby as well.

The Brownstone Security squad shifted to once again cover their flanks and felled a couple of mercenaries who had attempted to advance in the distraction. Alison slashed through the bulletproof vest of an attacker before she executed another man at point-blank range with a white bolt from her other hand.

Mason took his opportunity to charge the mercenary squad on the flank opposite Jerry. He rushed forward in a zigzag pattern to avoid fire, unsure whether they had all loaded anti-magic bullets. His movement became almost a blur thanks to his magic but he hissed as an anti-magic round grazed his shoulder.

I guess that answers that.

The wounded bodyguard vaulted over the front of one

of the vehicles to land a dropkick on one man. His warm body reminded him of how many spells he had layered over him, the heat a comforting assurance. He focused to ignore his injury and delivered a powerful punch that hurled a mercenary against the side door with enough force to leave a dent. The man collapsed without a sound.

Two members of the support team rushed in his direction and leveled bursts of firepower at the now engaged enemy. Several mercenaries crumpled with cries of pain.

Alison slashed through a rifle and throat-punched its wielder with her free hand before she knocked him unconscious with a magic-accelerated ax kick, a move Mason had taught her. The man actually seemed to bounce when he landed.

"They're advancing on our flank," Jerry reported between bursts of gunfire.

She flung several light magic bolts at the approaching mercenaries. If they'd had anti-magic deflectors, they might have offered impressive resistance rather than the pathetic display they now presented. Two other men groaned in pain as they fell to her magic bolts but writhed, still alive, and clutched their burn wounds.

Mason ended his flank attack with an elbow strike that crunched violently into a mercenary's chest. With all enemies on his side dead or unconscious, he and the support squad members near him turned and rushed to reinforce the other team.

It was Jerry, however, who finished the fight with a well-placed headshot.

"Targets neutralized," he shouted.

Alison released her shield and looked at their defeated

attackers. About half the mercenaries had died in the attack. "Huh. And the information we received suggested they'd come at us with a lot more than that. I won't say I'm disappointed, but I am a little surprised."

Mason walked toward her and shrugged. "There's nothing wrong with a little overkill from our side. Is everyone else all right?"

Jerry and the support team members all gave their thumbs-up or verbal acknowledgments.

The plan worked. That's good.

The life wizard moved his arm a few times and grimaced at the pain. He fumbled for his wand and a quick healing spell soon took care of his wound.

Sirens howled in the distance from both the ground and the air. The exploding drones alone were enough to assure the prompt attention of the police department.

Alison marched over to a bleeding man propped against a wall. He'd been the one to issue orders earlier. She gestured down the street. "The police are coming. Maybe even AET. I suggest you cooperate fully when they ask you who hired you, or you can simply try to come after my client again if, by some miracle, you get out of jail. I'm sure he'll be happy to hire us again to kick your ass." She shook her head. "I thought you were supposed to have power armor and wizard support. I cracked out the anti-magic deflectors for nothing."

"We had what we needed for the job. I didn't expect you to destroy our drones so easily." The mercenary commander coughed blood and winced. "Why did you do it?"

"Huh?" Alison frowned. "Destroy your drones, or why

did we take you down? Because we're a security company and that's what we're paid to do by clients who like to remain breathing."

He shook his head and managed a pained grin, which looked all the more vicious because of the blood on his face. "It's a damned waste. That's what it is." He nodded toward one of his fallen men. "You're this powerful and you waste it on protecting people. With power like that, you could become the queen of mercenaries. A lot of Oris still aren't in the game on this side of the gates, you know."

Alison knelt in front of him and folded her arms. "I was born in Los Angeles, not Oriceran, and why would I want to be a professional scumbag? Unlike you, I don't like to hurt people. I like to protect them."

"Money."

She shook her head and stood. "I'm already rich. Maybe it wasn't fair. Maybe I should have loudly announced my client across the net so next time, some murderous asshole idiot mercenaries don't risk a bunch of people's lives on a fight they can't win."

"You won't win forever, Brownstone," the mercenary commander lobbed blood-flecked spit at her feet. "That's how this shit goes. When you make too much noise, someone comes to shut you up."

"Probably, but they had better hurry." She nodded at Mason who approached. "Because it's not only me they have to worry about anymore."

The client strode up the portable stairs and into his private jet. The silver-haired man paused and looked over his shoulder at Hana. "Thank you for your aid. This is the first time I've had to deal with this sort of thing."

She shrugged. "It's no big deal. This is actually the easy jogging part of our weekly routine."

He laughed. "I don't know if I should be impressed or terrified."

"You don't have to be terrified unless you don't pay the company the balance of what you owe us." She winked.

CHAPTER THREE

Alison yawned and stretched her arms as she sat at the head of the conference room table. "We shouldn't have stayed out so late last night."

Mason, Hana, and Ava sat around the table near her. Now that the company had a decent number of new hires in both field and building support, they'd established a more formal organizational structure at the business level. In truth, it was mostly Ava who had worked the titles and chain of command out, but Alison had no problem with them.

She served as President. Hana and Mason both had official titles as Lead Investigators. Ava worked as Assistant to the President and Tahir as Head of Information Security. Most of the field support staff had been given some sort of investigator title, and the other small number of building support staff were designated appropriately.

Hana shook her head. "We had to have our victory sushi." She shrugged. "And victory sake."

Ava tapped at the tablet that sat in front of her. "I trust everyone is sober enough for interviews?"

Alison waved a hand reassuringly. "I'm fine. Merely tired. We only have the two today, right?"

"Yes, Miss Brownstone. They are both candidates for your primary field team. I have still abided by your request to delay further requests for additional field support team members."

"That sounds great." Alison looked at Hana and Mason. "Unless you don't think we need any additional magical firepower?"

"You do kick a lot of ass yourself," the fox observed. "But it's your money to spend."

Mason shook his head. "That's the problem."

The women all stared at him expectantly.

"We're overly dependent on Alison," he explained. "The plan worked out today, but if we had to pull off something similar and weren't sure of the level of force, it might be more difficult without her. Sometimes, the client will be an organization or have a family. Trust me, I've had to deal with this a lot in my career. The more depth we have in all our teams, the better the company we'll be."

Alison nodded. "I agree. My dad started his agency with nothing but non-magical gang members, but he quickly added all kinds of magicals—and it's not like he isn't tough enough to beat anyone by himself. It gave him flexibility."

"Yes, your dad," the wizard murmured, a nervous look on his face.

She watched him for a moment and assumed that he was worried about the fact that her father would visit Seattle soon.

Can I really blame him for being nervous that Dad is coming? I'm the one who has built him up as overprotective all these months. But it's important that he meet Mason. What am I expected to do? Wait until next Christmas?

Alison grimaced, suddenly unsure that her dad should be brought anywhere near her boyfriend.

It's not like he'd kill him. I think.

"Miss Brownstone?" Ava's voice cut into her family-related panic.

"Oh, sorry." She forced a smile, desperate to conceal her thoughts. "Um, yeah, the point is that we need to get new people."

Her assistant gave her a cool look of disapproval and adjusted her glasses. "Today, there are only two interviews. The first is with a wizard who worked with a private military contracting firm. He's exceptionally dedicated and comes highly recommended. The second is a Light Elf gentleman. He doesn't have an employment history on Earth, but he did provide an image of a magical scroll of recommendation from various Oriceran nobles." She shrugged.

Hana's eyes widened. "Oh, classy, but did you see the pictures of the guy? Damn, is he one *cut* elf." She laughed. "Don't tell Tahir I said that. I love his body, too, but it doesn't mean I can't appreciate magical muscles."

Ava gave the fox a sidelong glance of disapproval, but it was hard to tell whether she disliked her ogling or lack of focus on the issue at hand. "Oddly, it's been harder than I anticipated to find applicants for the primary field teams."

Alison frowned. "Is what we offer too low? We can discuss compensation increases if we need to."

"No, the pay is very competitive." Ava's gaze flicked to the others. "I think there's merely some intimidation that comes from the idea of working with you, Miss Brownstone."

"And how do I fix that? I'll always be…well, me." She sighed and shook her head. "You'd think the non-magicals wouldn't want to work with me, not the magicals."

Ava furrowed her brow. "There is—at least in some cases, I think—a concern about your background as well."

"Meaning what exactly?"

"Several Oriceran candidates asked me pointed questions about the relationship between our company and the Drow. While they weren't completely forthright, my impression was that some of them are under the impression that this company and your efforts represent some sort of Drow plot." Ava's mouth curled into a slight sneer, and she scoffed disdainfully.

Alison rolled her eyes. "Drow plot? My dad fought the Queen of the Drow so I could stay on Earth. Yes, I trained with them, and Myna's helping me, but the rest of the Drow are more than happy that I chose to stay on Earth and mind my own business. It's always two steps forward, one step back."

Mason patted her hand in encouragement. "Don't worry, A. We'll find a solution, and in the meantime, we have a solid core team. I do think we can use more people, but if we can't get them, we simply have to be a little more careful about the scope of our work."

Someday, I'll grab Izzie and Lily and force them to work for me.

What am I saying? It's not like Izzie can risk staying in one place for too long. But then again, if we were together—

Alison shook the thoughts firmly out of her head. The Berens family had their own problems, and as much as she wanted to help her friend and her mother, there wasn't anything she could do until Izzie contacted her again.

"Bring on the fresh meat!" Hana demanded and slammed her fist on the table. She laughed. "Sorry, I didn't mean to hit it so hard."

"Let's be professional," Alison admonished. "The people we interview today might end up as future team members."

"I hope they're not boring, then."

Who wears a bright white suit to an interview? Alison thought as she scanned the new applicant. The man had—hopefully—finished a long-winded introduction about his time in different private military contracting and mercenary companies.

The wizard at the end of the conference room table set his hands in front of him and a faint smirk settled on his face. "So, yes, I've worked all over the world and have fought almost every type of magical and non-magical opponent you can think of. I'm confident my experience will be an asset to your team. I've faced my share of straight-up monsters, too. So I'm not the kind of man who'll cut and run simply because things get a little freaky."

Alison looked at the tablet in front of her and back to the wizard. Scars crisscrossed his face, which surprised her. He'd have access to healing magic after battles, if not potions. In her experience, a heavily scarred battle wizard had either had to deal with curses or wanted to look that way.

"Thanks for that information," she replied quietly. "Please give us a little more insight into why you are interested in working for Brownstone Security, in particular, Mr. Muldoon."

The man grinned. "You know, I had just returned from some fun in the desert when you first moved into town and made your big splash, Dark Princess."

She kept the smile on her face even though she didn't like how familiar the applicant was with her.

"I mean...Eastern Union, dark wizards..." Muldoon whistled. "A lot of people say you defeated those New Veil in DC around that time, too, but the government kept your name out of it. And things have continued—the Fremont Troll, not one, but two billionaires..." He whistled again. "I'd pay good money to see you fight your dad."

"Excuse me?" Alison narrowed her eyes.

"No offense is intended. Everyone likes to see a strong young woman, right?" Muldoon gave her a lopsided grin.

Mason tensed and Alison caught the slight movement out of the corner of her eye.

"The point is, you have a big rep, Brownstone," the applicant continued. "A big rep for ass-kicking and a man interested in using his skills wouldn't do too badly around you."

"Okay. I won't deny that we kick an ass or two or three around here." Alison shrugged. "The thing is, we do what we need to, but when possible, we do like operations to go off without serious trouble. I'm happiest when people are smart and don't try and mess with us."

He frowned. "You are? I always thought you were the type of woman who liked to show her strength off."

"I like to get things done. It's not the same thing." She leaned back and folded her arms. "Fortunately, I've cultivated enough of a reputation that sometimes, I can persuade people to back off or surrender. That said, *unfortunately,* not everyone is always willing to surrender, and things can get tough and dangerous then. This is a security company with a focus on high-end client work, which means, especially in this city, that sometimes, we'll have to react hard. I don't apologize for it, but nor do I revel in it. Does that make sense?"

Wait. Why should I justify myself to this guy? What is it about him that makes me uncomfortable?

"We dealt with this all the time back in my merc work." Muldoon shook his head. "Don't worry. I'm used to telling people what they want to hear when there's a pile of bodies. No witnesses mean no questions and all that."

What the hell?

Hana blinked and exchanged glances with Alison. Ava pursed her lips in displeasure.

Alison frowned but couldn't bring herself to respond.

Mason cleared his throat. "Look, Mr. Muldoon, you should understand that while death comes with the job on occasion, we don't go out of our way to kill everyone on missions. This is a security company. Our overall goal is protection and recovery, not elimination."

The man grunted. "Yeah, yeah. I get that you have to feed everyone a line about it, but I don't really care. You need someone to kick ass? Then you hire me. I'm simply telling you that I don't worry about the occasional collateral damage, and I expect that you are the same way." He gestured toward Alison. "They have barely finished repairs to that bridge she blew up, from what I heard, and it only got done quickly because some magicals came in and donated some shit."

She sighed and pinched the bridge of her nose. "I didn't casually blow the bridge. My goal was to minimize casualties in the neighborhood by trapping the Fremont Troll. Keep in mind that our general goal in everything we do is protection."

Muldoon looked at the gathered Brownstone Security employees in turn as a frown built on his face. "Are you telling me the Dark Princess is worried about that kind of weak-ass shit?"

Alison glared at him. "Making sure innocent people aren't hurt isn't weak-ass shit."

The mercenary stood and scoffed. "I bet your father is ashamed of you."

She shoved out of her seat but Mason put his hand on her arm and shook his head.

Ava stood gracefully and drew everyone's attention. "I'll escort you outside, Mr. Muldoon. Obviously, you're a poor fit for the company."

"Yes, it seems that way." He strode toward the door with a sneer and stepped out of the conference room.

The assistant stopped beside Alison. "I apologize, Miss Brownstone. He came highly recommended, and I'll make it clear to certain people about the type of people we want. I did not ask Mr. Arain to do any deep background checks because I thought it would be best that we respect his time until we were certain of possible hires."

Alison sighed and retook her seat. "It's okay, Ava. I know how hard it is to get good job applicants. We had to go through several before we found you, and you've done great with the field support team."

The other woman nodded quickly. "Thank you for your understanding, Miss Brownstone." She headed toward the hallway.

"Damn it," Alison muttered. "Is this how people see us?"

Mason rubbed her back. "It's okay, A. He's only one guy. You said it yourself. All the field support team members are all professionals and not psychos."

Hana nodded toward the door. "Yeah, don't let it eat you. We do kick a lot of ass, so we're bound to find people here and there who think that kind of thing. Besides, if people really thought we were super-dangerous, why would the mayor come to that big official opening ceremony for the company?"

"Another thing I should have never agreed to." Alison sighed and stared at the ceiling fan. "We've done business for months now. It seems stupid to host a ribbon-cutting ceremony simply because we've finally put the crap in the building."

"It's good for PR, A," Mason replied with a smile. "And, yes, people are grateful that you stopped the Fremont Troll, but there are many people out there who might worry about the Dark Princess with that kind of power. It never hurts to have a little positive facetime with the public."

Hana grinned. "Come on. It'll be fun. Fancy party and

all that. I've already bought this great new dress—a red strapless thing. Tahir will love it, and I'll look *soooo* elegant and sexy at the same time."

Alison blinked. "Dress? Oh, crap. I didn't even think of that."

"What were you planning on wearing? Jeans and a T-shirt?" The fox rolled her eyes like she had to reason with a child.

"Uh…probably a skirt and suit jacket?" She shrugged. "I don't know. Should I go more for a professional look or more a party look?" She glanced at Mason.

"I'm a guy." He gave her a sheepish grin. "It's easy. I'll slap a tux on, but didn't you look at the itinerary Ava sent out?"

"I haven't got around to it. It's Ava. I'm used to her doing what needs to be done, so it's not like I check everything the minute she sends it to me. Why?"

"Speeches, fancy food." Mason laughed. "Seriously, A, what did you think would happen?"

Alison blinked a few times. "She talked about demonstrating the tactical room. I can't do that in a dress. Or, at least, it'd be more annoying."

Hana opened the message from Ava on her phone and held the device up. "Yeah…in the message, she asks Jerry to select two other people from his team for the demonstration. She specifically notes, and I quote, 'The emphasis of senior staff should be in social interaction with the VIPs. It's important to reinforce that you are 'one of them,' as that will facilitate favorable consideration in the future.'" She read the last two sentences in her best approximation of Ava's English accent.

Alison immediately looked horrified. "Wait. I specifically promised my dad that he would *not* have to wear a tuxedo. It's one of the few things he hates more than flying. I'm still surprised to this day that Mom managed to get him in one for the wedding. Although given what—" She groaned. "You know what? Never mind. Who cares? It's not like anyone on this planet expects James Brownstone of all people to be a beacon of class and sophistication, but I guess I should get something."

Hana gave her a thumbs-up. "Don't worry, girlfriend. I have your back. We'll figure something out. And don't worry about the party this weekend either. That's totally casual."

"Were you serious about that?"

Her friend gave her a look of mock reproach. "When I am ever *not* serious about a party?"

"It's just..." She sighed. "It's a weird reason to have a party."

"A Bad Guy Conviction Party isn't weird. It makes more sense than a Louper World Championship Party." The fox threw up her hands in frustration.

Alison stared at her in confusion. "You were the one who wanted to throw the Louper party."

"I don't even like Louper. People fighting fake monsters and running after a golden token. Weird." Hana's frown turned quickly to a smile. "But I do like parties. Come on, Alison. You need this for closure and stuff."

Mason nodded at Hana. "She's right, A. It's not petty to celebrate the downfall of a man who tried to kill you and your friends."

"Fine." She grumbled under her breath. Sometimes, her

best friend's nature could be exhausting. "We'll have the party. It's at my place anyway, which makes it hard to avoid."

Hana rubbed her hands together in excitement. "That's the spirit."

Ava slipped back into the room with a frown. "Again, I apologize for that. I've already performed a more aggressive prefiltering on the next applicant and sent him away."

"You sent away Duke Elfie McStud?" Hana replied with a gasp. "But he had all those nice recommendations and muscles."

"His first comment to me was about how he was sure that he'd be able to guide the 'Drow girl' along well given his decades of experience." Ava clucked her tongue. "An organization can't function if the subordinates think they are superior to their employers. I'm sure he's a good man with solid skills, but this is Brownstone Security."

"It's not a big deal," Alison replied. "We have a lot on our plate with this apparently much more elaborate event than I realized. We can put off major hiring for a while until we're past the hump."

Ava tapped in a note into her tablet. "As you wish, Miss Brownstone." A few seconds later, she arched an eyebrow. "Much more elaborate than you realized? Did you read the memo I sent?"

Hana and Mason both snickered.

Alison glared them. "Quiet, you two."

CHAPTER FOUR

The stack of pizza boxes Mason carried made Alison glance constantly at him. Her stomach rumbled as the smell of the sauces, meats, and cheeses snuck into her nose and reminded her that it'd been a while since she'd last eaten. "Are you good, or do you need help?"

"I've got this, A. It's only a few pizza boxes." Mason laughed. "This is very far down on the list of things I can't handle."

"Did we go overboard? There are only four people at our party." She shrugged with a sheepish grin. "We could probably get by with one pizza."

"It's good to have options," he replied. "I'm still surprised you didn't go to Maneki for the victory celebration. Are you mixing things up or turning into your mom?"

"No, I still love sushi way more than pizza, but something about this doesn't seem a sushi kind of thing." She opened the condo door and gestured inside. "Maybe it doesn't feel like a victory that we're celebrating. Not fully, anyway. Not until Carlyle's convicted, too."

"Don't worry. It's only a matter of time for that asshole." Mason walked inside and deposited the pizzas on the dining room table.

Alison's sour mood vanished as she moved inside and looked around her condo. A rainbow riot of balloons floated around everywhere, like the happiest deranged dreams of a coked-out preschooler. A huge banner strung in the living room over her TV read. **HAPPY CONVIC-TION, ASSHOLE**. The Costco chocolate birthday cake on the table had a similar message, at least in spirit. **ENJOY THE NEXT THIRTY YEARS IN YOUR NEW HOME, DEREK!**

"You really went all out, Hana," Alison observed through her laughter.

Her friend bounced up from the couch where she sat beside Tahir, who glared at his phone. "I am *so* hungry. Thank goodness you guys finally got here. I was about to inhale that cake or gnaw on the couch. Or maybe even Tahir." She glanced at him, but the infomancer didn't look up. Instead, he muttered under his breath and tapped at his phone.

"Our order was a little mixed up," Alison explained. She removed plates from her cabinet and stacked them near the pizza boxes. "I wonder if I should have invited everyone else from the office. Ava did her standard thing and blew me off anyway, but what about Jerry and the field support team, or some of the new administrative assistants? I don't want to come off like some distant bitch."

"This is more personal than a company thing," Mason replied. "And not everyone wants to hang out with their boss. Keep that in mind."

Hana snickered. "So says the boyfriend of the boss. Hypocrite much?"

"To be fair, I was the boyfriend before I started working here." He winked.

"Whatever you say." The fox loaded slices of pepperoni pizza onto her plate. "But you're fine, Alison. Jerry and the new hires are all cool, but mostly, they have a different vibe than our little inner elite team. I think they're happy to get their paychecks and not hang out in your condo." She looked over her shoulder at Tahir. "What about you, babe? Are you hungry, or are you still busy fighting the good fight?"

"I'm fine. I'll get some in a minute." Tahir continued to glare at his phone.

Alison frowned curiously and glanced from him to the other woman.

Mason waited until Hana was done to select some slices of sausage and pepperoni. "I still think that bastard Chesterton should do three hundred years, not thirty years and some fines. Considering everything he pulled, he got off damned lightly."

"Some fines?" the fox replied. "There are a lot of zeroes in those amounts. How much does a new rocket cost? Can they build a new rocket out of those fines? Or add something to Tranquility City?"

Alison shrugged. "If Derek Chesterton's a problem in thirty years, I'll worry about it then. I'm actually happy he pled. The more this crap stays in the news, the more people bother me about it. At least Chesterton's done and will head to an ultramax soon, but Scott's still giving his big manifesto at his trial. Every freaking news headline is about him." She rolled her eyes. "That guy always did like to hear himself talk. Never trust anyone who likes to hear themselves talk that much."

Hana mumbled something around her mouthful of pepperoni.

"What? I can't understand you."

Her friend swallowed hastily. "From what everyone says in the news, he has no chance of getting off. One legal analyst said earlier…" She laughed. "Sorry. He said, 'There's more chance of King Oriceran dancing naked during Mardi Gras than Scott Carlyle being found not guilty.' So, what's the big worry? He'll go down. It's justice delayed, not defeated."

Alison shook her head. "I never thought he'd get off. The last time I talked to him, even he said that he didn't think that would happen." She picked up a few slices of supreme pizza. "That was never the point. He merely wants to drag it out as long as possible and get his message out there about how everything he did is so self-evidently good for the planet. He thinks this is some sort of ideological crusade he can still win if he convinces enough people to agree with him. I'm worried that a man with his reputation and background will sway at least a few people."

Mason finished a slice of his pizza before he rejoined the conversation. "I'd say no big deal, but after the Fremont Troll incident, people are talking and not in a good way. I hate to say it, A, but he'll wind up as a martyr of sorts for the anti-magic crowd. Even if New Veil never rescues him like they constantly threaten to do, I don't know that this will all go away when he's convicted." He gritted his teeth.

"There's even a publishing company that wants him to write a book about the entire thing."

"You have to be kidding me." Alison rolled her eyes. "'Hey, you created a dangerous virus through illegal magic and genetic engineering and were directly or indirectly involved in the murders of tons of people. But still, let's hear your side of it.'"

Mason shook his head. "I wish it was merely a joke. They've had some pushback. The latest argument is that they want to donate all his royalties to a charity. Carlyle has already agreed to it. But even if one company doesn't do it, I'm sure someone eventually will."

"Martyr, huh? Aren't you supposed to die to be a martyr?" Alison took a seat at the table. "Now, I wonder if I did the right thing when I didn't kill him. He had it coming. Not because of what he did to me, but what he did to so many others. And that's only the crap we know about."

He shook his head. "For all his speeches and arrogance, he doesn't seem to care all that much about admitting who he has worked with. It's helped the government bring in a lot of people. If you had killed him, most of them would have been able to slither away and hide their involvement."

She snorted her derision. "Of course he's talking. It's because he doesn't think they've done anything wrong and should all stop hiding so their grateful public can support them." She shook her head. "I can't do anything about what people say. I can only deal with bad guys when I run into them. The sad part about all this crap is that if Scott really cared, he could have done more to help keep things under control. This stupid-ass plan merely raised tensions all around. If it's not HDL and New Veil on one side, it's dark wizards or other magical extremists on the others."

"That might have been the point." Mason's expression turned thoughtful. "If you think a war is coming anyway, it sometimes makes sense to provoke it when you think your side might still have an advantage."

"A war between magicals and non-magicals isn't a war anyone can really win. Given what happened on Oriceran during their Great War, I don't even want to imagine what might happen on Earth."

"I know, A," he agreed. "And I don't think that way. Carlyle thinks that way."

Hana waved a slice of pizza at Tahir. "Babe, join the party. Please tell me you're not still arguing with that guy about…what was it, encryption algorithms? Is it really that important to win the argument right now?"

The wizard looked over his shoulder and frustration contorted his face in a way that robbed him of his handsome looks. "But he's wrong and an idiot. And people constantly upvote his comments as if they provide any sort of true insight. Can you believe that?"

"An idiot on the internet?" Alison laughed. "But that *never* happens. What a shocking turn of events."

"Some battles need to be fought. Ignorance cannot be allowed to stand." Tahir snorted and returned to his phone. He typed with furious dedication to deliver a deadly rhetorical assault on his enemy.

Alison took a few careful bites of her pizza so she could perform her recent standard activity whenever she ate. This was to pay close attention to the interplay of smell, flavor, and texture while attempting to individually identify every ingredient in the mouthful. A good palate was the key to good cooking. Her skills had advanced in the last couple of months, but she was still a rank amateur and her palate and other abilities were underdeveloped—especially temperature and seasoning control.

"It does make me think," she continued once she had swallowed her food. "About my long-term plans and what I want to do with the company."

"It's like he's not even heard of Kolmogorov Complexity," Tahir shouted. "Why are you such a fool? Were you cursed by King Oriceran to be an idiot? Even magic would have difficulty producing such an obvious deficit in thought."

Hana rolled her eyes. "I'm surprised to see him do this in front of you guys. It took him a while to allow himself to cut loose like this in front of me, and I sleep with him."

Mason laughed. "This is cutting loose?"

"Some people watch sports or movies. Tahir fights with people over obscure computer stuff." She stared at her boyfriend with a loving smile. "I don't understand ninety percent of it, but he seems really relaxed at the end." She turned to Alison. "He's cut down on some of the personal challenge stuff like he did with you, Alison. He doesn't want to draw negative attention to the company, especially since some of what he did wasn't all that legal." She shook her head. "But you were saying something about the company?"

"Yeah," Alison responded softly. "My dad's company is huge, with what is effectively an army in both Los Angeles and Las Vegas. Mom told me a few weeks ago that it turns out the police departments in LA and Vegas have been able to control their budgets a lot more than departments in similarly sized cities because of the Brownstone Effect—or the Brownstone Agency Effect you might say."

"That sounds good to me. Seattle could use a little less crime." Hana leaned over to grab a beer from the cooler. "Want one?"

"Sure."

She slid it to Alison before she retrieved one for herself and popped the top.

"It's called qubit stability, you insufferable moron," Tahir muttered. "And, no, a few spells don't change it that much."

Mason headed over to snatch his own beer. "What is it, A? Does the fact that your dad is coming make you feel like an underachiever or something? I never read anything about him taking down a giant stone troll."

If it wouldn't probably bring the government down on us, I'd love to tell you the kind of things my dad has taken down.

"It's not that," she protested and thankfully, no hint of her thoughts leaked into her tone. "It's that the interviews made me realize that I'm not sure if I want a huge team. My dad gets around this because he rarely does bounties anymore, and even when he does, much of the time, it's on his own. But I work directly with people. It's different."

Hana gave her a warm smile. "No one says you have to solve all of Seattle's problems. If you're not comfortable with a huge team yet, then don't hire anyone else for a while. Grow into it."

Mason stroked the top of her hand with his thumb. "She's right, A. You've done great."

"But what about the need for more coverage for clients?"

"You simply select jobs that don't need them or do what you did with us."

Alison looked at her companions. "What do you mean?"

"We didn't interview with you. We're people you met who ended up being a good match for you and your company." Mason grinned. "Come on. We both know more major trouble will eventually come. If it's not killer Oriceran Giants of Mass Destruction, it'll be something else. I'm sure you'll run into someone who will be good for the team. Organic hiring or whatever you want to call it."

"And that's why ECC fell first, you nitwit," Tahir mumbled.

Alison glanced at the couch. "It's like he's barely speaking English."

Hana laughed. "Isn't it? But I like listening to him sometimes and trying to understand it." She sipped her beer.

"Do you understand what he's going on about, Mason?"

The life wizard shook his head. "No clue. Not only am I not an infomancer, but I'm not all that great with computers in general."

A comfortable lull settled in the conversation as the three friends focused on their pizza and beer.

Dad's proud of me already, so it's not like he expects me to live up to what he's done. I guess I'm really more bothered by the idea that there are psychos out there who think they get to join my company to do what they want to whom they want.

I'm not that much different than Dad, at least not that way. It took a long time before everybody thought of him as something other the Granite Ghost most likely to blow up a building because he's mad.

"You're right." Alison finished her can of beer. "I'm overthinking all of this. The company's less than a year old, and it's not like I don't have enough savings. I'll take things a little slower." She pointed at the banner with her can. "And I'll enjoy and savor each and every takedown of every scumbag asshole that we achieve."

"That's the spirit, girlfriend," Hana replied.

Tahir stood and sneered at his phone. "That's right. Flee, you coward. Flee before your obvious superior. Go and take your sad, sad thoughts on encryption and algorithm design to some preschool so the children there can give you some helpful advice, but maybe their work would be too complicated for you to understand." He turned his phone off and strode to the table. "I'm ready for some pizza now," he explained in a calm voice.

The others simply laughed.

CHAPTER FIVE

Alison hummed to herself as she plated the red snapper on top of the colorful bed of roasted vegetables with a heavy emphasis on peppers and zucchini. She added one last squirt of lemon to both the plates she had prepared before she lifted them and carried them to Mason's dining room table. He watched her as she set a plate in front of him and the other for herself and sat down.

Here we go. A nice meal, and only the two of us. I've pulled this off, but let's see what he has to say.

He inhaled deeply as he poured them both a glass of Pinot Noir. "It smells great, A. And looks great, too."

"I'm improving, meal by meal." She raised her glass and took a sip. "I'm learning to cook far faster than I learned to use my magic. Seattle's inspired me to focus on seafood, even though this particular snapper isn't local. I saw a recipe online and became obsessed with the idea to try it, but it turned out far better than that."

"Speaking of more local stuff, that halibut last week was

something else." Mason gathered some fish on his fork and brought it to his mouth. "You're right. You've improved a hell of a lot in a short time. If you ever decide to give up on the security game, you could always do this instead. Chef Alison Brownstone has a nice ring to it. I know every dinner would be damned delicious."

Alison laughed. "That's ridiculous. Me? A chef? I've spent most of my adult life taking on the bad guys, not cooking."

"Your dad owns a barbecue restaurant and participates in competitions all over." He shrugged. "Is it really that ridiculous? You don't need to specialize as much as he does. And I'm not saying you *should* quit, only that you could. I don't care what you do as long as you feed me delicious meals."

She sipped her wine as she thought the suggestion over. In truth, she wasn't sure about all the real reasons for her father's semi-retirement. His family and life situation had changed, and that was important—along with certain interactions with the government—but the truth was that he was James Brownstone, and no one could make him do anything he didn't want to do.

Did Dad merely get tired of kicking ass all the time? Even without the government breathing down his neck, he had slowed down anyway. When will I be tired of it? Sooner? Later?

Her father had told her many times that he'd thought more and more about focusing on a life away from bounty hunting shortly after he'd first met Shay. Like most things in life, his reasons were complex and multifaceted, and perhaps even he didn't grasp the total truth of why he'd ended up where he had. The most important thing was that he and her mother were happy together.

Dad's got the right idea. Keep it simple. Don't overthink it. Enjoy what you have.

Mason frowned at her. "A, what's going on? You have that look on your face again. The whole Alison Brownstone carrying both planets on your shoulders thing. Trust me, I read the news not all that long ago. There are no giant statue monsters currently rampaging around Seattle."

"There's always something."

"Of course, but it's not always your responsibility. It's okay to take time off and relax. If you don't, you'll burn out sooner rather than later. I saw it a lot in bodyguarding. Many guys get too involved with what it means to protect someone else they consider important and they forget that they're important, too."

"It's not that. I merely thought about things. The past. The future." Alison punctuated her sentence with a mouthful of snapper and enjoyed the earthy hints of cumin and tart undertones of sumac.

Ooh. This is good if I do say so myself. I'm definitely better at my spicing. Chef Brownstone does have a nice ring to it.

"This will be a weird thing to say," Mason began, "but there is such a thing as thinking too much, and you do it a lot."

"And that's what I'm doing, thinking too much?" She raised a white eyebrow in challenge. "It's not like I'm paralyzed with doubt."

He shook his head. "I'm not saying you are. If anything, it's the opposite. I think you're a lot like those other bodyguards I mentioned. You're always ready to throw yourself in front of the next monster. I think that on some level, if you're not planning for that monster or how to arrange your life for that possibility, you feel as if you're somehow failing everyone."

"Planning's not a bad thing, especially in a city like this one. A lot of dangerous crap has happened, and it's good to be prepared. And, of course, that does also make me think about my future. I don't think that's a bad thing."

"Yes, but people can only plan so much." He pointed with his fork toward the open window where the bright lights of the city were visible at night. "Think about everyone older than us. Think about all those people who maybe spent twenty, thirty, or forty years getting up and going to work and *knowing* how the world was and always had been. A world of science, a world where magic was something that wasn't real—or least was so rare that it was something special that most people would never truly see. Then, one day, they wake up and everything's different. Magic's real. Half of what they know about history is a lie. Could anyone plan for that? Who actually did? What good did it do them if they did?"

Alison looked down and considered the possibilities for a moment before she raised her head with a grin. "What about crazy conspiracy theorists? They thought about the possibility at least."

"I guess. It's funny how they didn't change much, though." Mason shook his head and refilled his glass.

"What do you mean?"

"Conspiracy theorists." He shrugged. "Before Oriceran, it was all ancient aliens and abductions and that kind of thing. Now, it's the same, except they claim that it's not only the Earth governments hiding the truth of extraterrestrials from space, it's Oriceran, too." He picked his glass up. "Which goes to show you, that kind of thinking isn't about evidence. It's simply about having a story you believe and sticking to it no matter how different the facts are. If your plan doesn't change, no matter what the facts on the ground are, that's one way to get through life."

She hid her smile behind her glass. There were some secrets she wasn't ready to share with her boyfriend, but the mention of aliens did make her want to steer the conversation away from anything extraterrestrial, especially since she'd led it there.

I'll tell you the truth about some of the things I know someday, Mason. You'd be surprised.

"So you really like the fish?" she asked. "What about the vegetables?"

"I've never been a huge veggie guy, but I like these well enough." Mason speared a few zucchini slices and popped them in his mouth. "I could do without the bell peppers, but that's personal taste. Something about bell peppers has always annoyed me."

Alison eyed him with disbelief. "Bell peppers annoy you?"

"Yeah. They don't taste as good as they look. It's like they're conning you."

"Duly noted. No lying peppers in the future." She deliberately lifted a segment of bell pepper to her mouth. "I wonder when I should try to integrate some spells or potions. There are all kinds of ways to enhance flavor or change the food experience. I've read a lot about them. I'm not an expert at potions, especially compared to many people I went to school with, but I do all right. It helps that I have so much basic magical power, but it'll take a lot of experimentation and refinement."

Mason's face grew concerned. "Don't take this the wrong way, A, but don't you think you should learn to walk before you run?"

"What do you mean?"

"You've only been *really* into cooking for a few months now, not years, and already, you're talking about adding magic." He grabbed another slice of zucchini. "You have to understand what it is that you're modifying before you go ahead and try to do that sort of thing. Trust me, I know this from experience."

Alison set her fork down and folded her hands in her lap. Mason wasn't exactly a closed-off man, but he didn't volunteer nearly as much detail as she would prefer.

It wasn't fair. Half the world knew about her childhood and her unique heritage, if only because of the adoption fiasco and a certain Drow queen who refused to take no for an answer, but there was no automatic reciprocity for her.

"Tell me," Alison invited quietly.

"I went through the same thing with painting." He gestured to a few watercolor landscapes hung on the walls before he nodded to a near photo-realistic oil painting of a smiling blonde woman Alison recognized as his mother. "When I first started, I constantly asked myself, 'How can I use magic to enhance this?' I wasn't interested in mastering my technique but short-circuiting some of that training with the help of spells. It actually held my painting back for a while. I tried to figure out how to do some new trick with my magic when I should have simply concentrated on mastering painting so I'd better understand when to use magic and when not to use magic." He stood. "And on that note, I have something to show you."

She watched him, wondering what he had in mind.

Mason disappeared into another room and emerged a moment later with a gorgeous oil painting of her. In it, her white hair flowed freely in the wind and she wore a loose yellow sundress while walking along the beach.

Alison gasped. "Mason, that's beautiful." Her cheeks heated. "I semi-forgot you were painting this for me."

He held the painting up with a proud smile. "Do you sense anything?"

She tilted her head and focused. He was right. Low levels of magic emanated from the painting. She'd not noticed them at first because of all the background magic from the various wards and other spells he had set up around his home.

"So after that big speech, you're giving me a magic painting?"

Mason set the painting gently in an empty chair. "I wasn't saying that magic and art, whether painting or cooking, don't mix. What I meant was that it took me a while to figure out the best way to combine them." He returned to his seat. "When I first started, I tried all the standard things—moving paintings, interactive paintings, and that kind of thing."

Alison's gaze lingered on the artwork. It was beautiful and not because she was the subject. While far from an expert, she could appreciate the subtle brushwork, excellent attention to color balance, and eye for detail. It was less that he'd captured a photography-like level of detail but more a warm feeling of relaxed happiness.

A memory that wasn't actually a memory. That's what the painting felt like.

Come to think of it, I don't even own a dress like that.

"What's wrong with all the stuff you just described?" she asked quietly as her attention returned to her boyfriend. Her wine had caught up with her and now warmed her face and clouded her mind.

"A painting should be a moment, a slice of time," he explained. "That's what separates it from something like a movie or a novel or a song. It's why I like painting. Food is a particular experience that you'll only have at that exact moment. Sure, you can make the same recipe again, but the whole point is that it ends."

"So if you make a moving painting, you're making... well, a movie?"

He nodded. "Exactly, A. It's why my magic was so useless to help my art in the beginning. It wasn't me trying to make a better painting but me trying to make it into something that wasn't a painting."

Alison narrowed her eyes in playful suspicion—or at least what she hoped came off as playful suspicion. "You never did answer the question about what magic's on it."

"I love you, A."

She blinked and averted her gaze, her face on fire in a way the wine could never spark. It wasn't the first time he'd said it her, but she'd managed to let it float by without engaging it, if only because she wasn't ready to face her own feelings.

Mason laughed. He picked his glass up with a smile and

took a sip. "You're worth waiting for. If you're not ready, I'm fine with that."

"I..." She let her head fall forward. "I do like you, Mason. Spending time with you makes me happy, but I don't know if I'm ready to say I love you."

"Because of Tanner?"

Her head snapped up defensively. "It's not like that." She sighed. "It's hard to explain. I don't..." She groaned. "It's not like we didn't already have our chance to get back together. It wasn't meant to be. I've moved on."

"Have you?" There was no accusation in his tone, only honest curiosity.

"Yes. He'll always be special to me, but I wasn't the same person when he came out of that coma as when he went in. He loves that naïve girl, not the jaded woman." Alison raised her glass to gulp down the contents before she refilled it. "I know I have my issues."

"Like I said, you're worth the wait." Mason gave her a lopsided grin. "And you've not kicked me to the curb." He nodded to the painting. "I love you because you inspire me, A. You make me feel like something more than merely some wizard bodyguard. The painting represents itself— that inspiration. It does change, but not like a movie. It changes slowly with the season, as does the beautiful woman in it. I wanted it to still be a memory and a slice in time but several rather than only one."

Alison drew a few deep breaths and tears threatened at the corners of her eyes. "You're too good for me."

"I could say the same, but I'm willing to deal with it all for my chance, including the most dangerous challenge of all." His face relaxed and a playful smile crept in.

"What are you talking about?"

"You told me your dad is coming to the Brownstone Building official opening, right?"

She jerked as if she'd been shot. "I almost let myself forgot about that. Oh, damn it."

"It doesn't have to be that bad. It's not like I'm a jobless loser who lives on your couch and does drugs all day. I even like barbecue. That has to count for something, right?"

"I'll tell you the truth," she replied. "I don't know. I've tried to tell him about you, but he also seems vaguely annoyed. I think, on some level, Dad can't get past the thought of me as the teenager I was when we first met. I honestly think he's more worried about me going out with a guy than fighting something like that Mountain Strider."

Mason burst out laughing. "You Brownstones can't do anything in moderation, can you?" He waved a hand dismissively. "I'll make a good impression. I promise you. I'm good with people. Part of being a bodyguard is convincing people to like and trust me."

"That sounds so shady."

"Not everyone has a famous family reputation." He winked. "Leave it to me, A. I'll make sure your dad goes back to LA liking me—or at least not folding me up like a pretzel."

"He wouldn't do that." She scrunched her face in thought for a few seconds. "He wouldn't do that I hope."

CHAPTER SIX

Someone pounded on her front door and Alison frowned in sudden concern. Myna didn't portal in anymore without calling ahead, but she also didn't knock like a maniac when she arrived. None of the wards they'd set up had been tripped, which suggested her visitor wasn't magical or anyone else unusual.

Is this trouble?

She strode to the door and activated the entrance camera. There was a thin line between confidence and arrogance, and she didn't want to be assassinated because she was too lazy to see who was there. She hesitated for a moment and considered summoning a shield before she decided there was also a thin line between caution and paranoia.

Neither assassin, terrorist, angry billionaire, nor dogged reporter stood on the other side of the door, merely a middle-aged man in a suit. It was Ryan from 208 downstairs. He licked his lips and rubbed his hands together.

What's he so nervous about? If I didn't know any better, I'd think he was high.

The man glanced back and forth down the hallway before he thumped furiously on her door again.

"I'd better see what's up," she murmured and opened the door before he hurt himself or got blood on the carpet.

"Thank God you're here," he blurted. "I didn't know if you would be."

Alison blinked and her heart rate kicked up. One nightmare scenario that continued to haunt her was the idea that someone would attack the condo building to reach her. She had even considered having an apartment built into the Brownstone Security on multiple occasions so she could move there.

Her father's example provided poor guidance. His house had been destroyed at one point, but it had not been threatened since the initial destruction. Alison wasn't sure if her reputation had advanced to the point where she could skip the whole first step of having her beloved home blown up with a rocket launcher.

In the meantime, she had at least taken precautions. Besides the wards she had set up around her condo, she also placed a few key wards around the building where they wouldn't easily be seen. Unfortunately, there were limits to what she could do in the building without drawing too much attention from the other residents, and not all wards could be prepared without something being visible to non-magicals.

If it's a conventional attack, why haven't any alarms gone off? Wouldn't someone press an alarm?

Alison tried to decide whether she would be able to hear first- or second-floor gunfire from her condo.

"What's going on?" Alison would need to move fast to minimize casualties. Whatever small gems of situational awareness the man could provide would be critical to direct her initial efforts. If the intruders weren't magical enemies and they didn't have anti-magic deflectors, she would be able to eliminate them without trouble as long as she knew where they were.

"I read it on the news," Ryan explained. He frowned and folded his arms. "And you didn't even tell me. I'm a little hurt, but you can make it up to me. I understand that you're busy, but still. Have a little consideration for your neighbors."

"Huh?" She frowned in real confusion. "The news? What are you talking about? Isn't there trouble in the building?"

"They need to do something about the inconsistent heating in the pool." His face scrunched in deep thought. "That's the only major problem I can think of. Why? Have you heard something? This is why I wanted you on the condo board. You always pay attention, probably because of your job." He nodded in self-confirmation.

Alison rubbed her forehead. "Let's take a step back because I'm very confused—as in I have absolutely no idea what you're talking about." She took a few deep breaths. "So, what the hell are you talking about?"

Ryan huffed a little indignantly. "Well, there's no call to be rude, Alison."

She closed her eyes and sighed. "I'm sorry. When you came knocking on my door like that I thought there was an emergency. The kind that normally involves calling AET. Sorry, that's my security contractor instincts at work."

"Oh, I see. I'm sorry." He waved his hands vaguely. "No, no. I was talking about the ceremony—the official full opening of the Brownstone Building." He chuckled sheepishly. "I got really excited, and then I wondered why you didn't tell me. Or—wait, were you trying to spare my feelings? I know the mayor will be there, and the reception is an invite-only even if the public can come to the outside event." He slapped his hands together in a praying position. "Please, I beg you. They said *he* is coming. Is it true? The Granite Ghost himself will be there?"

Why did I allow Ava to make this thing so elaborate? When she mentioned it to me the first time, I thought she was talking about a twenty-minute photo op, and now, we have media coverage, the mayor, and a fancy reception. At least I have a nice dress, although this whole thing has ended up more red-carpet Hollywood than a security company's big debut.

Is that good or bad?

Alison blinked a few times as she tried to respond to the fanboy ambush and still wrap her head around her retreat from the idea she would need to fight terrorists invading her condo.

A few seconds passed before she replied with what wasn't exactly the prime example of thoughtful consideration. "Huh?"

"The articles I've read said that even though he won't participate in the ceremony, your father is coming." Ryan's puppy-dog eyes confused her as much they annoyed her. "Is it true? These were reputable news sites, not random net trash."

She scratched her ear and looked away. "Um, yeah. He's coming alone because my mom's busy with...stuff."

I don't have to tell him all my family's business. He's already obsessed enough with all things Brownstone as it is.

Ryan fell to his knees, his hands still clasped together. "Please, it's your company. You can get me an invite, can't you? I'll do anything. *Anything.* Even if it's illegal."

Alison grimaced. She didn't even want to begin to guess at what that meant. "Fine. I'll give you my assistant's number, and she'll make sure you can come to the reception. Is that good enough?"

"Really?" Ryan scrambled to his feet and salvaged some small shred of his dignity. "And could you introduce me to your father?"

"Sure, but you have to understand that my dad isn't exactly a big conversationalist. In fact, he brings new meaning to the idea of anti-social. You might find the experience less than thrilling."

The man scoffed. "I'll be more than able to talk to your dad. I've memorized the entire Jessie Rae's menu, all the publicly listed class-fours through sixes bounties your dad has apprehended, and all his best catchphrases."

"Catchphrases?" Alison stared at him in bewilderment. "My dad doesn't have catchphrases. Unless 'stupid asshole' is a catchphrase now."

"Well, calling them catchphrases is too much. But he does have interesting things he says." Ryan furrowed his brow. "When I read through *The Granite Ghost, From Orphan to Hero: An Unauthorized Biography*, they talked about so many cool things he said. Like when he fought King Pyro." The man cleared his throat and engaged in a feeble attempt to emulate James' low voice. "This is America, asshole. We don't do kings."

"King Pyro?" Her gaze darted to the side as she tried to remember who that was. Her father had taken down so many dangerous criminals over the years that they'd blurred together after a while—and she didn't even know about many of the ones from before she'd met him.

"Wait. The bank guy, right. The pyromancer." Alison shook her finger. "That guy had a lesson in why you don't threaten a Brownstone's family. I don't feel any pity for what my dad did to him, not to mention that the guy was a ruthless killer."

"Exactly." Ryan bounced a few times. "He was Brownstoned!"

Alison struggled to fully comprehend the evidence of her own eyes—a grown man bounced in front of her like an excited child about to meet his favorite costumed character at a theme park.

"Anyway," he explained, "I've spent years preparing various James Brownstone-related conversation starters with a particular focus on barbecue, so I'm sure I'll be fine. I probably know better how to talk to your father than your mother does."

"Uh, yeah, sure." Her head throbbed from such direct exposure to fanboy worship "Okay, um…so, I'll send a message to my assistant, and you call the main office number. Ask for Ava Garden and tell her your name, and she'll make sure you get an invite. Okay?"

"Thank you, Alison. I'll never forget this until the day I die."

Given the look on his face, she believed him.

I guess I'm lucky he's only one-tenth the fanboy for me that he is for my dad.

She waved and closed the door.

I think I might have just screwed Dad over.

Hana guffawed on the couch and hit her knee. "He actually dropped to his knees and begged? That is the funniest thing I've heard this week, and I saw the latest episode of *Misadventures of Fargo Trolls* this week."

"Yeah." Alison spread her arms wide as she paced her living room. "How do I even deal with that kind of insanity? He'll embarrass himself." She groaned and slapped a hand to her forehead. "What if my dad says something to him that destroys him? I'll have to hear about it every time I see Ryan." Her eyes widened. "I'll have to move. This is what I get for buying this place outright." She frowned. "I guess I could rent it out."

Hana shook her head, a huge smile on her face. "Don't go looking for problems that haven't even happened yet. This guy is obsessed with your dad, right? So he knows that he isn't some friendly, cuddly guy who likes to sign autographs and say how much he loves his fans. Ryan is probably half-hoping your dad will kick him into a wall so he can say, 'James Brownstone kicked me into a wall! I can die happy now.'"

"Ugh. Don't give him any ideas." She sighed as she headed over to the couch to finally sit. "Next time, I should pay a lot more attention to what I have Ava do. Her help with the staff's been great, especially the administrative and maintenance staff. Although I'm not so sure we needed a chef and cooks for the cafeteria yet. We don't have that many employees."

Her friend gasped. "Don't you dare fire them. I'm already too used to eating that food. I'll waste away if I have to go out for lunch again."

"I won't fire anyone." Alison shrugged. "I merely think I let things get a little away from me and want to spin it down so it's more under control. That said, I'm still interested in sourcing another infomancer—or at least a non-magical hacker. Tahir's great, but he's also one man. If he is sick or something, we're screwed. I don't want to bring it up again anytime soon since he reacted poorly when I talked to him about this a couple weeks ago. I forgot how egotistical he can be since he doesn't target it at me anymore." She took a deep breath and exhaled slowly. "Has he said anything about it?"

"Oh, he's still being a big baby about it." Hana rolled her eyes. "It's not even that he thinks you're trying to replace him. It's more this general Tahir arrogance about having anyone else dare to step into what he considers his territory. Fair enough, the man's brilliant—a genius in a lot of ways—but that ego can be a bit much even for me, and I'm his girlfriend." She raised a finger and waggled it. "But I've been working him. A little praise here, a little admonishment there, trying to convince him of why it's so important. I think I can get him to come around, at least a little."

"Thanks." She nodded. "I don't want to drive him away or piss him off. I was lucky to land someone that talented, to begin with, and I'm certain that without Tahir, I would have never been able to find out what Scott was up to."

Hana giggled with excitement.

Alison eyed her friend, taken off guard by the abruptness and inappropriateness of the reaction. "What was that about?"

"I'm sorry." The fox slapped a hand over her mouth as she giggled again. "All this talk about how great Tahir is, just…" She hopped off the couch, a huge grin on her face. "I have news. I think you'll be happy, but I'm not sure. Maybe you won't be." She frowned a little as her grin faded.

"Right now, I'm mostly lost, which seems to be today's theme. Lay it on me."

"Tahir asked me to move in with him. He said that it'd be more *efficient* if I stayed with him, so there's no reason why we shouldn't." Hana's nine tails winked into existence and her eyes turned vulpine, but she didn't extend her claws. She danced around the living room, which included leaping and bouncing off walls. "This is the first time in my life I've had a man interested in me this way and not because I spent weeks conning him or manipulating him with my charm magic." She spun a few times before she stopped abruptly and stared at Alison. "Wait. I'm being a selfish bitch, aren't I? I didn't even ask you how it'd affect you."

"You're dating him, not me." Alison scoffed. "You don't have to ask my permission to move in with your boyfriend, Hana. I want you to be happy."

"I know that." Hana tilted her head as her tails swayed behind her. "But I also know you need someone to pull you back from Brownstone Brooding Land every now and again, and I worry about you."

She groaned. "I'm not *that* bad."

The fox pointed at Mason's painting, which Alison had hung in the living room, not at all bothered if other people perceived it as narcissistic. "He tells you he loves you and gives you magic paintings. Maybe you should move in with him or vice-versa. It's not crazy when you think about it."

"It's a little early for that."

"Do you think it's too early for Tahir and me? It took us a while to get together."

Alison shook her head. "No, it's too early for me. I'll be fine, Hana. It's not like this will be the first time I've ever lived on my own. I'll survive, roughing it in my huge expensive luxury condo."

The fox's tails dropped along with her lip. "Are you sure? You're my boss and best friend. I'm not sure if those add up as more important than my boyfriend, but they have to be close. I don't want to do it if it causes problems between us."

Alison stood and walked over to hug her friend. "I'm fine, and I'm really, truly happy for you. One thing I can promise you is that I'll always be a supporter of anything that makes my friends happy. There's been too much darkness in my life for me to not do that."

"Oh…" Hana crossed her arms and nodded sagely. "I get it now." Her tails vanished, and her eyes transformed to human and brown. "No point in investing too much emotion in someone your dad will tear apart. Is that why you don't want Mason to move in?"

Alison laughed. "My dad won't tear Mason apart. The worst he'll do is mildly threaten him. Mom and I have worked on Dad for years. He has way better manners than he used to have."

"So, let me get this straight. Your father, a world-famous class-six bounty hunter, the Scourge of Harriken, will *mildly* threaten your boyfriend?"

"You're right." Alison hung her head. "This will totally suck."

CHAPTER SEVEN

Tahir relaxed his eyes and took a deep breath as the VR display for the drone activated. His stomach lurched as the vast panorama of Seattle buildings replaced the darkness in front of him.

He didn't attempt direct VR flying of drones much during jobs. It was too difficult to manage multiple drones that way, even with the aid of magic, but there were no dangerous enemies he needed to keep an eye on that afternoon and Hana was shopping with Alison.

A quick turn of his paired smart glove turned the drone. He wasn't alone in the sky as delivery, news, and police drones flew above, over, and to the side of him. The birds had long since lost their dominance of the city skies.

The infomancer wasn't old enough to clearly remember a time when drones didn't fill the sky. Every time he looked at old videos or images of cities, they always seemed so empty to him with only the occasional helicopter or plane.

His drone glided around a corner. Tahir kept it low

enough to avoid any potential legal issues. Even if most of his work had been on the right side of the law in recent months, Alison wouldn't appreciate having to deal with unnecessary trouble, considering how often she ran into major problems without even trying.

I've thrown my lot in with this strange woman, even though she's what I've always thought laughable—an optimistic person who actually believes she can make the world a better place.

But somehow, working for her, I wonder if that might be true. Now who is the greater fool?

Tahir resisted the urge to do a remote hack of a pizza delivery drone, one of his favorite activities as a teenager. He'd grown out of it not because of the illegality but more because he'd accepted how annoying it was to be hungry and have to wait for your food. A man of true talent reserved his efforts for actual challenges, not petty pranks.

He smiled as he buzzed past the delivery drone close enough that the automated navigation system jerked the machine to the side to avoid a collision. Petty, yes, but it retained a certain childish entertainment value, and the customer would still get their pizza.

I feel so alive lately in a way I haven't felt in a long time. Alison's given me a way to use my skills to show the entire world how great I am and earn only their respect. I helped take down two billionaires.

And Hana makes me want to get up in the morning. I never thought a woman like her would move me so.

The infomancer chuckled. If this kept up, he'd end up as sentimental and naïve as Alison. For all her power and battle strength, she was still obsessed with protecting her friends. She'd turned him into her friendly hacker on a leash and Hana from a con artist to a *mostly* law-abiding citizen.

The nine-tailed fox would move in with him soon, although he still hadn't decided why he'd even asked her. He wasn't sure if he understood love in the sense that some people talked about it. But he did know that waking up and going to sleep beside her calmed him, and he looked forward to spending time around her even if it was as simple as sitting on the couch listening to her relate some amusing anecdote.

The old me would have mocked what I've become, but as long as Hana soothes my soul and Alison gives me challenges, I'm happy with this life.

A small drone cut right in front of his. He dove instinctively and barely escaped a collision by mere inches.

He scowled and his gaze darted to the corners of his VR display. Several more camera angles were displayed there.

The small drone twisted and wagged back and forth, a purposeful movement.

Tahir slowed his drone to a hover and slowly circled the other drone.

Is this an attack?

His free hand flew over the keyboard, and he brought up a more detailed status display in one of the smaller windows. If the drone were being hacked, his passive defenses should inform him, but he wanted to be sure.

He found nothing.

What's your game?

Tahir narrowed his eyes. He was the one who should be dominant, not some random person who might threaten him.

I don't know if it's another infomancer or even a hacker. It might simply be some non-magical hobbyist.

A light pulsed rhythmically on the smaller drone. After a few seconds, he smiled. A few quick commands brought up a program he hadn't used in a few years—an optical Morse translator. It was a quaint way to communicate in a world of direct links and magic, but it had its uses.

He waited for a few cycles to ensure he'd received the correct message.

ARE YOU TOO SCARED TO RACE ME? BATTLE RULES.

The informancer scoffed. Drone battle racing? His skill level was above such petty challenges, but the poor, foolish pilot on the other side wouldn't know that.

It wouldn't hurt to prove to this fool how good I am.

Tahir ran his message through his own rapid optical Morse translator.

WHERE TO?

FREMONT TROLL. START IN EXACTLY ONE MINUTE.

He started a countdown. **LET'S RACE.**

YOU WILL LOSE came the reply.

The wizard sneered and shook his hands out. Impressive tricks with infomancy had their place, but sometimes, he needed to prove to others and himself that his skills went far beyond that.

Perhaps there's less tactical utility in my drone-racing skills, but it's not like I'm asking for permission.

Five...Four...Three...Two...One...

Both drones thrust forward. The smaller tried to cut

across his flight path again, but Tahir dove and avoided it effortlessly.

It'd been years since he last participated in a drone battle race, but he presumed the rules were much the same. A racer could win by getting to the finish line or crashing the other drone without crashing his own at the same time.

Typically, battles took place in custom courses—often large indoor spaces—to provide more attack options. From the very beginning of the sport, however, battle racers enjoyed the natural opportunities a city provided as a course, even if other people in those same cities didn't always appreciate aggressive drones flying overhead.

Many organized groups of battle racers even turned their drones into hybrid flying knights with sharp blades and other weapons protruding from them. Few people tolerated projectiles or EMPs in such races, as it defeated the point of testing their control and drone design. It was difficult to survive even as an attacker without good skill, despite the robust strength of modern drones.

Tahir tried to clip his opponent, but the other pulled up and looped behind him. He dodged the counterattack with a grin on his face.

From what he could tell, the small drone lacked some of the power of his but was more agile. Neither his nor the other bore any weapons, which made the battle more challenging.

His smile faded.

Why would a random drone pilot suddenly ask to battle me?

The smaller drone nudged his, which wobbled for a few seconds before it recovered easily.

Pathetic. You won't take me down unless you get me close to a building.

The smaller craft cut between two apartment buildings. Tahir took his chance, angled, and accelerated for a slam against the wall. The enemy shook for a moment as if the pilot perhaps struggled to stay ahead of him. A last-minute dodge saved the smaller machine, but it was hard to escape from that close to the wall without giving Tahir an opportunity.

A bright glyph appeared on the back of the drone, and the infomancer frowned. The smaller vehicle shot up, its movement a blur.

How pathetic. So it is a wizard, then. He misses the true challenge of battle racing, and he's an arrogant fool on top of it.

While he used his magic to supplement his drone flights, stacking permanent spells on a craft only would make it easier for someone to trace his magic back to him. Accordingly, when it came to magic, he kept it to spells that would help him better handle information from his computer at home or in the office.

He brought the drone to an abrupt stop. The enemy zoomed past in an ill-fated dive, a portion of the fuselage sharpened to a point.

So that was the point of your spell? A hidden weapon?

The modification put him on the defensive and his drone banked, spun, and dove to avoid the enemy. His opponent, despite the use of magic, was obviously a rank amateur based on their aggressive stance and limited handling.

Tahir continued to speed toward the Fremont Troll. It might be a race that involved battle, but it was still a race in the end. That meant he could win by reaching the destination even if by the normal rules, he needed to keep generally within about one hundred feet of his opponent.

The infomancer launched a quick feint and charged the other craft before he dropped his machine close to the street and buzzed over the stream of cars and people. He was probably too low, given his speed, and he might need to ditch the drone so the authorities wouldn't complain later. The other drone dropped altitude and kept pace with him.

He banked hard to the right to hurtle down the street before he turned to the left. A few more turns would place him on Aurora Avenue and from there, it was a straight flight to the Fremont Troll.

His opponent seemed to be frustrated given how the small drone constantly rushed him but almost wobbled out of control.

Challenge whomever you want, but know that masters always wait out there, sometimes in the most unexpected of places.

Tahir continued to hug the ground and buildings as he negotiated up Aurora Avenue. The other drone seemed to fall behind for a few moments before it blazed ahead when fire blasted from the back. He wasn't sure if it was a spell or some sort of hidden jet.

The infomancer grunted with real disappointment. He slowed and let the enemy rocket past. This race had become a farce. The earlier magic was forgivable, but a drone battle race was, at its core, a test of flying skill, not tricks. The limits of a game or challenge were what made it interesting, and his arrogant wizard opponent had made a mockery of those limits.

It's not as if I'm not capable of such coarseness. I simply don't choose it.

He left the street to cross the water of the Fremont Cut and closed on the trapped stone monster Alison had defeated and resealed only months before. The other drone floated near the head of the Troll and blasted out more optical Morse.

YOU SHOULDN'T HAVE MESSED WITH ME. I WORK FOR THE DARK PRINCESS. I HELPED SEAL THIS TROLL. YOU SAW MY MAGIC, RIGHT?

Tahir gritted his teeth. He would tolerate some things, but not someone staking their claim to the work of Alison and the company as their own.

The hacker didn't send a message. Instead, he initiated a probe into the drone's feed with the help of a frequency cycler. Someone needed to be taught a lesson.

HAHA, the other pilot sent. **MAYBE I SHOULD HACK YOUR DRONE AND CRASH IT.**

He smirked. This wizard could claim whatever he wanted, but he wouldn't allow it.

A new frequency notification window notice popped up in one of the sub-windows. Tahir entered a command to connect with it.

"What are you doing?" came a heavily modulated deep voice over the new frequency. "You're trying to hack my drone? Don't you know what happens to people who fight Brownstone?"

"Yes, I do," Tahir replied evenly, not bothering to run a voice modulator on his own communications. He'd already accessed the primary drone systems and now traced the signal, although he doubted his opponent was aware of that. "And you claim to work for Alison Brownstone?"

"Of course I do. I bet you don't even know how she stopped the Troll. I bet you're like all these other dumbasses who think she simply used a lot of power."

He chuckled. "Then why don't you educate me?"

"Containment wards. She reactivated them."

"Anyone who reads the news would know that." The infomancer sighed. "If you work for Alison Brownstone, tell me her favorite restaurant."

"Jessie Rae's, you dumbass," came the reply.

"Oh, feeble, quite feeble," Tahir replied. He shook his head, disappointed. "Here's a hint. She's not her father. You're a pathetic liar."

"Screw you," seethed the other pilot. "Do you want to know something no one else knows? Fine. You know that New Veil attack in Washington, DC? She was the one who stopped it."

His stomach tightened. This was all suddenly less amusing. "The news said it was government operatives."

"That's crap for the ignorant masses. I can tell you the server with the Homeland Security report on it where it talks about how she wasted those terrorists, but you wouldn't have the skills to hack it, you loser."

"Identify yourself," Tahir demanded.

The other hacker laughed. "Man, you're pathetic. You can't handle that you got owned, but like I said, don't feel bad. I'm a badass and you aren't."

He remained silent as his trace resolved to Puyallup. That proved the infomancer had some decent skill if they could run such a nimble drone from over thirty miles away.

"Wait," shouted the other hacker. "What are you doing? You're trying to trace me. This crap is done, man. You'll regret this."

The rotors on the small drone cut out and it tumbled to smash into pieces as it struck some rocks.

Tahir continued to work his trace, but with the dead-ended signal, he was at a loss. He activated his drone's auto-return program and pushed his goggles up. He'd not lost yet. His opponent had made one mistake—a surprising one considering that he was a wizard. He'd left a physical object for him to recover.

I'd better call Alison.

Hana made a face as she stared at the Fremont Troll. "I can't imagine what it was like for you to go at this thing when it was larger."

Alison eyed the statue and half-expected it to start moving. She suppressed a shudder. "It wasn't my most fun fight. That's for sure." She glanced at Tahir who gathered fragments of the destroyed drone in a small bag.

He'd called her and explained the situation, and they'd decided to retrieve the fragments together on the off-chance that it was some sort of trap.

"I might have overreacted," he admitted as he dropped a cracked rotor into his bag.

"What do you mean?" She rubbed her shoulders. Something about the magical power of the wards that emanated from the Mountain Strider's prison roiled her stomach in a way her previous visits hadn't. Between what she and the government had done, the entire area reeked of magic in way it hadn't before.

She admired the bridge repairs. It didn't even look like she'd ever damaged the north end.

"My surprise that the person knew your involvement in the New Veil incident was greater than it should have been." Tahir finished his rubble collection. "Although I've secured your systems, there are many government systems that are far weaker. I suppose it shouldn't be a shock that someone found that information."

Alison nodded. "It doesn't hurt to follow up, especially since they seem to be locals, but if you're not worried, we can let this sit for a few days. If I blow up a building or something right before our big media event, Ava will probably put an anti-magic bullet in my head for ruining all her hard work."

Hana waved at the Troll. "Hey, can you hear me? I used to visit you all the time. Spare me in your next rampage."

He chuckled and shook his head at his girlfriend's antics before he returned his attention to Alison. "Something else occurs to me."

"What?"

"This person does at least have some skill, even if they're arrogant and presumptuous."

She grinned. "Yeah, I don't know *any* infomancers like that."

Tahir frowned. "Be that as it may, depending on their overall skill level, they perhaps might potentially be an asset. At least they've demonstrated some useful skills already."

Alison gestured toward her Fiat on the street. "Do what you need to do. Unless you think they'll call in a missile strike or something in the next few days, we can let it rest until we're not so busy."

CHAPTER EIGHT

A lison lingered in front of the entrance to the Brownstone Building. She threw an occasional smirk at the thick red ribbon that extended between two black stanchions. Even it was symbolic and she had trouble getting over the fact that she'd run the business for half a year, but they still called today's function a grand opening ceremony.

Okay. Keep it together, Alison. Ava put a lot of work into this, and everyone seems like they're interested. It'll be good PR, and it's not like I have to do anything other than play nice with a bunch of wealthy and influential locals for a few hours. It's not exactly battling a horde of dark wizards and Mountain Striders.

The mayor stood in the corner and chatted quietly with Agent Latherby and few other men. All wore tuxedos. Her entire staff was present, although none were working.

Well-dressed waiters and waitresses darted in and out of the crowd with silver trays of drinks and food in hand.

Ava ensured that every aspect of the night would be handled by outside contractors so everyone in Brownstone

Security could participate in the festivities. Her people were dispersed among the crowd and rubbed shoulders with the elegantly dressed guests. The bulk of the visitors were human, but a few elves and gnomes were mixed in with the crowd.

Alison offered the occasional greeting as people approached her, but everyone seemed to accept that a quick handshake and a, "thank you for coming," was all they should really expect.

I'm better at this than I thought I'd be.

Every once in a while, she spotted Ryan circulating through the crowd, a laminated menu from Jessie Rae's under his arm. He didn't seem to notice or care about any of the strange looks he received as he continued on his single-minded quest to locate James Brownstone.

She had tried to tell her neighbor that her father hadn't arrived yet, but it was almost as if he believed it was some sort of trick or test of his faith in the Granite Ghost.

Hana stood in the crowd in her bright red, high-slit evening gown. She chatted with an elderly couple, a smile on her face, and gestured widely while she likely related some anecdote about one of their recent jobs. The couple laughed.

She's always fun. Maybe that's why she made such a good con artist. She knows how to talk to people even when she's not using her charm.

The fox's other half wasn't present. Tahir had argued that he needed to work on tracking down the other hacker, so he had stayed at home. Alison suspected it was more about the fact that he didn't like crowds, and she saw no big advantage in forcing the introvert to mix with people he'd probably insult anyway.

Agent Latherby made his way over to her and nodded a polite greeting. "You seem nervous, Miss Brownstone. Is there a problem with the crowd?" He surveyed the assembly. "It's not unwieldy in size but more than a small group, by far."

"Not really. I used to act a little, and you get used to public speaking when you're threatening large groups of criminals on a regular basis."

The PDA agent gave her a tight smile. "Indeed, you do."

"I think it's more the type of event that has me a little on edge." Alison shrugged and felt a little self-conscious in her new blue maxi dress. She'd let Hana convince her to go more aggressive with her décolletage than she normally preferred. The fact that Mason really loved the dress only made her more nervous about it. It was supposed to be a fancy PR party, not sexy time in the club with her boyfriend.

"Don't worry. This is only the mayor's way to honor your recent efforts." The PDA agent moved closer and lowered his voice. "Although, like any politician, it doesn't hurt to be seen with someone people respect. I think this is more for his benefit than yours in many ways, but consider it a favor to him that will ensure he's more favorably disposed to you."

"Respect?" Her gaze followed a reporter who interviewed a young socialite on the edge of the crowd. "Is it respect or fear?"

"The right people respect you. And the right people fear you. Isn't that what's best?"

"I suppose. I hadn't really thought about it that way." Alison scanned the crowd. "This isn't exactly the roughest crowd. Then again, this is the kind of thing Scott Carlyle might have come to. So rough is relative."

"I've always preferred the more obvious type of criminal, but don't worry about someone who will soon be in prison." Agent Latherby adjusted his bowtie. "It's been a while since I've worn one of these. It's not as uncomfortable as I remember."

"I'm glad to hear it." Alison wondered if she should try calling her father, but her phone was in her purse in her office.

If he's not here yet, then he must have a good reason. It's not like Dad would chicken out simply because it's a fancy party. His wedding was fancy, overall, despite some of the other craziness.

The mayor finished his conversation with his other companions and gestured to Alison. He nodded to a small microphone stand set up a few yards away.

You're out of time, Dad.

Alison took a deep breath and made her way over to the official. Several cameramen moved forward and nearby news drones buzzed closer.

Okay, all I have to do is smile, look grateful, and don't say something totally psychotic, and I'm golden.

"Thank you all for coming today," the mayor began. "I'm honored to be present at the official opening of the Brownstone Building, the corporate headquarters of Brownstone Security led by Alison Brownstone."

Polite claps followed from the crowd.

"Since Alison Brownstone has come to Seattle," the mayor continued, "she's made more than a few waves and headlines and had been around more than a few explosions."

This time, laughter rippled through the crowd. She somehow managed to keep a smile plastered on her face.

Just keep thinking what great PR this is. Besides, these people obviously think it's interesting. They don't think I'm a threat or dangerous or they wouldn't be here.

The mayor nodded toward her. "But this special young woman, a woman with dual heritage from both worlds, has chosen to make our great city her new home. She continues, in her capacity as a security contractor, to protect us— not the least example of which is her recent defeat of the Fremont Troll during its rampage two months ago. Let's show her how much Seattle respects her efforts." He clapped enthusiastically, a little too much so for Alison's taste.

Dial it down, your Worship.

Claps and cheers erupted from the crowd. Hana gave her a thumbs-up.

Alison responded with an embarrassed smile and a slight shrug. There were worse things than people who appreciated that you subdued an Oriceran monster of mass destruction.

"Now, she has agreed to give us a small taste of those magical skills she uses on the job." The mayor stretched his arm out toward the ribbon.

I can't believe I let him talk me into his. It's stupid.

She walked toward the ribbon and her heels clicked sharply on the hard pavement. Impressed chatter passed through the crowd when she raised her arm and summoned a shadow blade.

Come on, people. It's not like you've never seen magic before.

She sliced through the ribbon, and the two cut ends fell to the ground.

The mayor applauded once more. "It gives me great pleasure, on behalf of the city of Seattle, to declare the Brownstone Building officially open."

The crowd joined him enthusiastically.

This will be a long afternoon.

Thirty minutes later, Alison escaped from a visiting businessman who tried to persuade her to agree to appear in some commercials for his medical supply company. He'd already even worked out a slogan, "When I am wounded by dangerous criminals, I have only one product I use."

It didn't matter that she used healing magic and potions. He'd even told her as much and didn't seem perturbed about the idea that she would likely never personally touch his products.

She nodded politely to the gathered crowd as she continued her flight from Mr. Medical Products Supply. The guests filled the large lobby and spilled out into the hallways. The most popular spot was the massive fish tank on the wall of the lobby filled with a variety of colorful and glowing fish. It remained the limit of how far Alison was willing to concede to Hana's demand for mascots.

She's moving in with Tahir. Maybe she can get a pet now, but he doesn't strike me as a pet kind of guy.

The guests chatted amongst themselves, snacked on

hors d'oeuvres, and sipped on expensive champagne and wine.

Ava appeared from a side room and hurried toward Alison, her speed impressive considering that she could probably use her current stilettos to slay a dragon or take down a dropship. "Jerry's team is getting changed into tactical gear. They should be ready for the demonstration in the tactical room in about twenty minutes."

"Good." She frowned and looked around. "Did you see where Mason went? I barely saw him outside."

"The last I saw of him, he was speaking to one of the guests. A CEO he used to work for, I believe."

Alison nodded. "Oh, that makes sense."

Mason felt so natural as a part of Brownstone Security that she sometimes let herself forget that he'd spent years as an elite bodyguard before he'd signed on with her.

I don't know if it's a good thing or a bad thing that I have trouble differentiating between my company and my family. It feels right, though, to think that way.

Her stomach knotted. Family could be a problem in its own way.

"Go and find Mason and tell him to make himself scarce," she whispered. "Tell him that on second thought, it'll be better if we handle the family situation in a different context. We're pushing our luck as it is. Make sure he heads out a side entrance."

Sorry, Mason. I'm not sure how this will all work out in this situation. Dad's late, which means he'll probably be tense when he shows up to this room full of polite but still stuffed shirts.

A wry smile appeared on Ava's face. "As you wish, Miss Brownstone. I'll tell him right away."

Yesterday, when Mason and Alison had discussed the two men meeting, she suggested it might be good for him to interact with her father in an environment where the latter would be more comfortable—unlike the reception where there wasn't a single rib or slice of brisket in sight nor any beer. James Brownstone was known for many things but being great in social environments wasn't one of them.

The room was filled mostly with representatives of high-end business and society, not exactly the kind of people her father normally mixed with and not the kind of people he liked to be around. In truth, he didn't like to be around most people who weren't close friends or family.

Ava disappeared into the hallway crowd, somehow able again to combine high speed with perfect elegance.

Bright red drew Alison's eyes to the approaching Hana who still had utter joy painted on her face.

"I forgot how much I love these kinds of parties." The fox twirled once. "There's something about a fancy party, you know? All the beautiful clothes and great food." She winked. "And this time, I don't even have to lie about why I'm here."

She laughed. "That's always a plus."

Surprised gasps spread through the crowd near the entrance. She frowned and turned toward the door and her hands twitched. Several police officers in uniforms and plainclothes men were at the event because of the mayor's presence, but she wouldn't put it past someone to try to attack her when they knew there would be a lot of witnesses.

If you know what's good for you, you'll turn right now and get the hell out of here.

The crowd parted and allowed the interloper through.

A tall, heavily-muscled man in jeans, T-shirt, and boots stepped past them. His face had dragged into a dark frown and his eyes were narrowed. Tattoos covered his exposed arms. His mottled face was far from handsome. In truth, most would say he was ugly with the face only a mother— or perhaps a daughter—could love.

Even Mason, who filled a shirt out well in her opinion, would look like he needed to hit the gym more compared to the new arrival. The man's light jacket didn't do much to conceal his holster, and a slight bump in the center of the T-shirt revealed the presence of an amulet beneath his clothing if a person knew what to look for. Everything about the man radiated menace.

"Is that him?" someone murmured in the crowd.

"It's James Brownstone!" Ryan yelled from the corner and almost squealed like a cheerleader.

James looked at the man and grunted.

Her heart suddenly lighter, Alison hurried to the door and threw her arms around the man's neck. "Dad, where have you been? Why didn't you text me that you would be late?"

"Shit happened. Don't worry. The cops thanked me for my involvement."

"Shit happened?" She regarded him dubiously. "The cops thanked you? What exactly happened?"

"Merely some asshole at a gas station." James shrugged. "It was drug smuggling shit, I think. It wouldn't have been a big deal, but he tried to take some woman hostage. All the commotion held the traffic up, so I beat his ass. I figured you'd be busy with all this party shit, so I didn't text you."

Alison raised her finger to chastise him, but it wasn't like she hadn't ended up in similar situations. "Anyway, I'm glad you made it."

Her father looked back and forth and grunted "Where's the *man*? You said I could meet him if I came." He frowned and scanned the crowd. "I don't see him anywhere. I've seen enough pictures of him."

That was the problem with the internet, social media, and a father with a near eidetic memory. It was a good thing she'd already had Mason get out of there. If her father kicked off with these kinds of question, unpleasantness was definitely in her future.

She groaned. "Don't start, Dad. You'll meet Mason, but he had a few things to take care of. If you don't see him tonight, you'll meet him tomorrow when we go out to lunch."

His face darkened. "A few things to take care of? This is important, and that asshole is out doing his dry cleaning or some shit?"

"Um, I'm very certain it's not dry cleaning."

This is backfiring. Damn it. Would Dad have been more likely to stay under control if I'd had him meet Mason here?

Alison chuckled nervously. "Look, Dad, it's stuff *I* asked him to take care of, okay? He's not disrespecting me. He's actually putting my needs above attending a fancy party. Just because you don't like this kind of thing doesn't mean he's the same way."

"He likes fancy parties?" James asked and his tone hinted at lowered esteem rather than understanding.

Is he determined to hate Mason no matter what?

"I won't leave Seattle until I meet him." He glared over his shoulder like he tried to catch Mason in the process of escaping. "He can't hide from me. Shit, I'm a bounty hunter."

She rolled her eyes. "Come on, Dad. This is kind of a semi-fancy party. Try and keep it in check."

James shrugged and looked around again as irritation lined his face. "This is me keeping it in check. Shay told me to tell you again that she's sorry she couldn't come. She feels really bad about it."

"It's okay. She already came to visit me, and I know how busy she is with things at the school and home." Alison smiled. "But you made it. Your insane quest to gut my boyfriend aside, I'm happy to see you."

"I don't want to gut your boyfriend. I simply want to meet him. I don't think that's such a big deal."

Ryan couldn't restrain himself anymore as he nearly knocked a woman off her feet as he virtually charged father and daughter.

Alison pinched her nose and her cheeks heated in embarrassment. Her father frowned at the approaching man.

"Mr. Brownstone," the interloper began and fanned himself with the laminated barbecue menu. "It's such an honor to meet you. Let me say that you are even more impressive in person. The Granite Ghost. Scourge of Harriken. The Council Killer. The Anti-Five. The Grand Slayer. He Who Kicks Chaos' Ass."

His own daughter hadn't even heard of some of those

titles, and she wasn't sure if it was something people actually said or something the man had made up.

"Who the f—" James glanced at Alison and back to Ryan. "Who are you?"

"My name is Ryan. I live in the same building as your daughter. You should be super-proud of her. We are all so impressed. I keep trying to get her on the condo board, but she refuses."

"Condo board?" He looked at her and she shrugged. "It sounds complicated and annoying."

"It can be," Ryan replied blithely and his grin widened.

"Do you need something?" James' gaze dipped for a moment. "Wait. Is that...a Jessie Rae's menu?" Surprise dripped from the last few words.

The other man held it up. If he smiled any wider, his jaw would detach from his head. He whipped a permanent marker from his pocket with a flourish. "I go there every time I have a business trip to Vegas. Unfortunately, I've yet to have a business trip to LA so I haven't been able to visit your restaurant." He held out the marker and menu. "I wondered if you'd sign this."

"But Jessie Rae's isn't my restaurant," Brownstone replied. His voice was still a low rumble, a thunderstorm mixed with an earthquake, but most of the hostility had bled away.

Ryan was right. He does speak Dad's language.

"Oh, I know." Ryan smiled brightly. "But I wouldn't have even known about it if I hadn't followed your career. It is obviously the best barbecue in the country. Of course, you would know."

"Sure, I'll sign." James grabbed the marker and scribbled his signature.

"Thanks, Dad," Alison commented. "Ryan's a big fan."

"Yeah, I remember I signed something for him a few months back."

Ryan bobbed his head in agreement. "You did, Mr. Brownstone." He ripped his phone out of his pocket so fast he tore the jacket, but he gave no sign that he even noticed, let alone cared. "I'd be greatly honored if you'd take a picture with me. I know it's annoying and I'm sure people bother you all the time, but it'd be the highlight of my night."

James rumbled a low growl of irritation but his fanboy seemed oblivious. He looked at Alison.

He's holding it together fairly well. At least this isn't some woman trying to get him to sign her breasts.

She mouthed, "Please."

"Fine," he muttered.

The younger man rushed to his side and held his phone up. He took several pictures before he stepped aside, opened his mouth to say something more, and shut it as his eyes widened. "It was great to meet you. Sorry, I have to go." He turned and rushed toward the exit, the menu clutched against his chest, and smiled the entire time.

Several people glanced at him with mixed looks of disdain and surprise.

James stared at the man as he fled. "What the fuck was that about? Is that guy high?"

"No. It's like he said. He's a Scourge of Harriken fanboy, Dad." Alison chuckled. "I think it was too much meeting his idol in person. You're too used to people in LA who are afraid to approach you half the time."

"I didn't think Seattle would have more freaks than LA. Consider me surprised."

"James Brownstone's signing autographs," a woman murmured nearby.

"Did you hear that?" a man repeated. "James Brownstone is signing autographs. Does that mean Alison will as well? I need one—for my daughter, of course. It's not like *I'm* interested in something like that."

Oh, crap. Here it comes.

Her father glowered and grunted his disgust. "I feel like I'm about to be ambushed by this entire room."

She smiled as Ava gave her a confirmatory nod in the distance. Mason had escaped. With what was about to happen and her father's building irritation, Alison was even more sure of this plan.

"Our adoring public awaits, Dad."

CHAPTER NINE

After a line of autographs and selfies, Ava called for everyone's attention and led them to the tactical training room. Inside, Jerry's team waited with stun rifles on the ramp on the second floor of the training structure in the center of the room.

The guests crowded near the entrance and murmured amongst themselves.

James leaned toward Alison. "You don't have suits and rifle simulators? I thought you told me that's what you would do?"

She grinned at him. "Originally, that was my plan, but I decided to put some more money into this until I ended up with something that's kind of a combination of your tactical training room and Fort Shorty. You'll see. I had the idea after talking to Myna about Louper about six weeks ago. We can't pull off that level of immersion without a lot more background magic and we obviously don't have that here without a nearby kemana, but this is still impressive. I can at least produce some instant enemies."

Her father grunted. "It also still needs more mud."

"Not all training needs a lot of mud." Alison pointed at Jerry. "Besides, I started differently than you. Most of my people already have law enforcement or military backgrounds. We don't have OGs here, only old soldiers."

Brownstone snorted. "It still needs more mud."

"Ladies and gentleman," Ava announced and her voice cut loudly and clearly through the din. "I must ask you to stay near the door for the duration of the exercise. Although our personnel are well-trained, stray shots can occur. However, I can assure you that if you're struck, no permanent harm will come to you. That said, stun bolts aren't pleasant."

Ava had been the one to suggest the tactical demonstration, and Alison only agreed on the condition that she wouldn't have to participate. Her assistant had also been the one to recommend that the guests be present in the room as much as possible to give them a palpable sense of danger. Most of the people—including the mayor but excluding Agent Latherby and some of the security staff—hadn't been any closer to a fight than what they had watched in movies.

The line of guest stretched along the wall a few rows deep.

The announcer lifted her tablet. "Besides the multistory tactical training maze you see before you, this room has been equipped with technomagic emitters that our president and owner, Miss Brownstone, has charged with a large amount of magical power." She typed commands into the tablet. "They can provide convincing and non-lethal simulations of threats, which allows our personnel to train dynamically against a large variety of potential enemies. As you can imagine from the recent incident with the Fremont Troll, we never know what sort of enemies Brownstone Security might have to deal with."

A dozen images of muscle-bound men with pistols appeared at the far end of the room. The crowd stirred and some gasped, while several people shifted away from the fake thugs.

"Don't worry," Ava assured them. "Stay close to the door and these simulations will not attempt to engage you. Let me also clarify that these are not alive in any sense. They are simply images that can take and deal force to provide a valuable training experience to our personnel. Similar systems are currently in use by military Special Forces."

That produced an excited murmur in the crowd.

"Three," Ava announced. "Two…one…start."

Loud gunshots echoed in the tactical room as the simulated thugs rushed for cover and opened fire. Several people in the crowd yelped in surprise or covered their ears.

It's funny how loud guns seem the first time you hear them fired up close, huh? Even if these are fake, they sound damned real.

Jerry and his team eliminated two of the insurgents before they had to take cover themselves. The simulated attackers twitched and groaned before they collapsed as convincingly as a normal man struck by a stun bolt.

James folded his arms, approval in his eyes. "Huh. It seems complicated and shit, but so is the thing down at

Camp Brownstone. What happens if your guys use normal bullets?"

"We have rifle simulators for when we don't use stun rifles or something else that will dissipate easily," Alison explained. "Normal bullets will pass through the fake thugs. Think of them as little bundles of forcefields, basically."

Jerry and two other personnel executed a quick point-to-point movement maneuver while under fire. They successfully vanquished a few more of their opponents while the rest of their team swept around the opposite side.

"And if one of these fake assholes hits you?" Brownstone asked as he watched the fight unfold intently.

"It's like getting stunned," she explained. "I tested it out. It doesn't hurt as badly as the system you use at Camp Brownstone, but it's enough to keep you down if you're a normal man."

Her father snorted.

A few more quick bursts from the Brownstone Security team brought down the last of the fake thugs. Ava entered a few commands and the bodies vanished.

The crowd clapped and cheered. Jerry and his team rushed to the top of a ramp to bow.

"Let's see the Brownstones fight," a man shouted from the corner.

The mayor smiled and clapped. "Yes, that would be a treat."

All the guests' pretensions to elegance and self-control vanished as a chant of, "Brownstones," arose.

Jerry and his team hurried down the ramp and toward

the crowd. They all grinned expectantly at Alison and her father.

Ava looked her, her chin raised and her eyes filled with a question.

Alison sighed and shook her head. She wasn't exactly dressed for a fight, but if they kept it under control, it wouldn't be so bad.

"I only need to remind myself that it's good PR," she muttered.

Hana bounded over. "Oh, let me in on this, girlfriend."

Alison looked at her dad. "Maybe punch a few fake thugs, Dad?"

James grunted. "Fine. I would have liked to have seen *the man* do this shit, too, but whatever helps you."

She waved and nodded to Ava, and the crowd exploded in loud cheers.

Eight power armors appeared.

She kicked her heels off and summoned a shield by reflex before she extended a shadow blade. The crowd roared at the appearance of her signature weapon. She moved her hand and chanted a quick spell to pin her dress to her body. There really was no reason to flash the crowd in the middle of the fight.

With a shake of her head, she turned toward Hana and cast the same spell. The fox looked at her dress and then at her with a questioning expression.

James, Alison, and Hana headed up to the top of the platform. The whole situation was absurd now that Alison thought about it. Two women in evening dresses and her dad in his T-shirt and jeans were about to take on eight simulated power armors in front of a mob of well-dressed rich people baying for blood, simulated or not.

"I won't do anything that'll cause trouble," her father promised and cracked his knuckles. "Nothing more than what you see now."

"That's fine, Dad," she replied. It'd be more than enough.

The power armors came to life and their fake bullets blasted through the chamber in a deafening cacophony of noise.

Hana ducked. Her tails and claws appeared. "No fair. I don't even have any of my artifacts." After a few moments, she grinned. "Then again, that'll make this more fun."

"I wonder what the best way to make a good sho—" Alison began. She blinked as her father leapt off the structure.

The power armors opened fire and peppered him relentlessly. He grunted as the bullets flashed into arcs of energy as they struck him, but he didn't go down.

"Damn!" Hana yelled. "When we tested this out the other day, one of those shots without my ring or the pendant was enough to knock me on my ass. Your dad takes them like he doesn't even notice."

Alison couldn't tell her friend the truth about the powerful amulet her dad owned and how much it'd changed him. Even years before, stun attacks had barely worked on him.

She decided to join the fun and spun around the corner to launch an energy bolt at one of the simulations. The armor staggered back. The enemy group split into different teams to lay down suppression fire against Hana and Alison while two of them continued to direct a stream of magical bullets into Brownstone.

With a roar, the Scourge of Harriken surged into the attack. The cheering crowd fell silent as he slammed into one of the armors and catapulted it back. He grabbed the rifle away from another and used it as a bat, but the object broke in his hands.

Huh. This system's even more realistic than I thought. It's not quite full magical VR like Louper, but it's decent.

Alison launched upward, dodged a few shots, and took a few, but her shields deflected the high-intensity stun blasts. Hana scrambled down a ramp. Her tails fluttered behind her and her speed became almost a blur.

James knocked another armored figure down and punched it until the helmet cracked and the simulation slumped to its side. Alison released her wings, swooped down directly behind her father, and sliced through another opponent. The illusion faded from existence.

Good, Ava thought ahead. I don't want to freak people out with a bunch of body parts lying around.

Hana lunged onto one of the attackers and yanked his weapon away before she clawed at weak points in the joints of the armor. Another tried to shoot her but James kicked him and the figure rebounded into a nearby wall. A loud clang echoed through the room, and the crowd cheered.

Alison rocketed forward with a quick burst of magic and sliced and diced along the way. She had to admit that in a real fight, it might have been more challenging, especially if the enemies wore anti-magic deflectors. Still, the display would serve its purpose judging by the thin smile on Ava's face and the engaged crowd.

Father, daughter, and best friend made short work of the enemy. The whole fight was over in less than a minute.

Crowds, cheers, and whistled filled the room.

Alison released her spells and waved. Hana sauntered beside her friend with her tails still out.

James walked toward his daughter and scratched his cheek. "Yeah, that shit's pretty cool. Maybe I should get one of these for Camp Brownstone."

"You need to charge it with a high level of magic, but you have a decent number of magicals working for you these days."

Ava walked toward them and watched the crowd. "There you have it, ladies and gentleman, a special bonus. How many people get to see Alison and James Brownstone in action together?"

Alison almost snorted. Her dad taking the equivalent of stun bolts and punching some people around wasn't even remotely a display of his true power, nor was her slicing a few simulated armors with her shadow blade.

Then again, that's a good thing. Dad can live a reasonably peaceful life. I can't imagine what would happen if most people knew exactly what he was capable of.

Her father nodded, a satisfied look on his face. "We should do more shit like this when you visit instead of going to shows."

"Father-daughter bonding through ass-kicking?"

"Exactly."

Ava pointed toward the exit. "Now, if you'll accompany me, dessert will be served in the lobby."

Alison shook the hand of a guest before he headed out the door. "Thank you very much for coming. We look forward to your business if you have any security needs."

The elderly gentleman nodded. "I almost want to threaten the Eastern Union so I'll need your help." He departed with a smile.

Yeah. I'm sure the Eastern Union would go running these days if they knew we were the ones protecting you.

With the man's departure, all the guests had finally gone. The waiters and waitresses moved around the room and cleared stray trash that had fallen on the floor.

Hana yawned and patted her mouth. "That was fun for a while, but I forgot how boring rich people can be."

"My dad and I are rich," Alison pointed out.

"Yeah, but you're *fun* rich."

James chuckled. "Nice moves during the fight earlier, Hana."

"Thanks, Mr. Brownstone." She smiled. "Too bad Mason wasn't here. I think you would have liked him. He has a similar direct style to yours. Punch-punch, kick-kick."

The man's gaze shifted to his daughter. "Yeah, too bad *the man* wasn't here."

Alison shot a dirty look at her friend, who winced. "Well, he'll come to lunch tomorrow, Dad. Unless you plan to go home early?"

"Nope. Kingdom of Pork has some great reviews for a new place. I have to always try new barbecue wherever I find it."

Hana clapped. "Then we'll all have fun together."

"Yeah," Alison murmured and eyed her father dubiously. "Fun."

The wizard started the car and eased away from the curb across from the Brownstone Building. He'd wanted to try to enter, but some of the wards he sensed concerned him. It was obvious that in some cases, Brownstone intended for magicals to know that she and her people had enchanted the location. Even her building threatened her enemies.

Your arrogance grows tiring, Brownstone.

He retrieved a small crystal and intoned the activation incantation. Using non-magical technology would put the dark wizards at a disadvantage, so they avoided it. In addition, every spell they used continued to prove the superiority of their cause and bloodlines.

"Report," Conrad's voice boomed from the crystal.

"It's as you thought, sir. The whole night was less a display of power than it was a cocktail party, other than some brief examples of their combat training. I wasn't able to enter without raising suspicion, but I was able to pose as a reporter and talk to some of the departing guests. From what they described, Alison Brownstone must think she has no threats or worries at all." The wizard scoffed. "If I had other people with me, I could probably have at least made a decent display of power and made her look weak."

"That is doubtful. Throwing away our people on pointless strikes on Alison and James Brownstone would be foolish. Were you able to confirm whether the father is leaving?"

"Yes, sir. The day after tomorrow, apparently. I overheard them talking."

"That's fine," Conrad responded. "I'm not so impatient that a few days concerns me. That said, you need to prepare. We'll make our moves soon, and we need forces available to make the critical strikes in all relevant locations. Do I make myself clear?"

"Yes, sir. Thank you for this opportunity, sir."

Conrad didn't respond for a few long seconds. The wizard thought the crystal had died, but it maintained the characteristic glow of activation.

"You're welcome," the other man replied. "Your family has served mine well throughout the centuries. Don't think that will be forgotten when the time comes. The deserving few shall lead this planet, and the loyal will be rewarded."

The crystal's glowing faded and the wizard returned his gaze to the Brownstone Building. The dark wizard families would indeed take what they had earned, and all who opposed them would be destroyed.

Continue your smug plans, Brownstone. Soon, people will know you're nothing but a weak little girl.

CHAPTER TEN

Alison shook her head at Mason. "Don't worry about ordering yourself. Dad basically ordered everything before you arrived."

"Yeah," her father rumbled. "I didn't want to wait around since you were late."

"That's Seattle traffic for you." Mason shrugged.

"LA's not exactly easy driving," James replied.

The younger man chuckled. "Yes, I'm sure that's true."

They sat together at a simple plastic table with a checkerboard-pattern tablecloth. The small number of other tables in the dining room of the Kingdom of Pork barbecue restaurant was the same, albeit empty. Several people had collected to-go orders when Alison arrived, which made her think the restaurant was more popular for dine-out.

That didn't come as much of a surprise. Her dad had taken her to a lot of barbecue places like that, including his own.

James took a sip of his beer and smiled stiffly at Mason, a too-hungry gleam in his eye as he stared at the other man. Fortunately, he'd been in a better mood when he'd signed autographs for the owner of Kingdom of Pork and the people who'd picked up their barbecue. That gave her some small hope this lunch wouldn't turn into a ridiculous implosion of embarrassment and pain.

Hana had pulled out at the last minute. Tahir wasn't interested in going without her, and Ava, as always, was busy with something else. That left Alison, her boyfriend, and her father.

She'd hoped to have at least one other person there to act as a buffer.

I guess we're about to see the true test, then. Hana probably set this up on purpose. I'm not sure if I should be mad at her or grateful. We need to get this crap hashed out, but it's like I've set Mason up here as a big target for Dad to annihilate.

Mason raised his beer to sip it slowly and glanced at Alison every now and again with an implied question in his eyes.

Don't look at me like that. It's not like I know what to say. At least, I don't know what to say that will defuse my Dad other than to tell him I'm kicking you to the curb.

Fortunately, the waitress—a weathered woman with an irrepressible smile returned with a huge tray of ribs. "To start you off." She set the tray down.

"Thanks," James rumbled. "I appreciate it."

"Anything for you, Mr. Brownstone." She smiled and departed.

A few minutes passed in awkward silence as everyone

ate the admittedly delicious ribs. Alison might not have been the barbecue addict her father was, but it was hard to be James Brownstone's daughter and not gain some appreciation for the fine glories and nuances of grilled and sauced meat.

Is that why I never want to cook any barbecue?

Brownstone polished a rib off and set it on his plate. "So, we should talk and shit."

"Probably," Mason agreed.

The corners of her father's mouth curled up in an almost sinister smile. "Let's start with me learning a little more about you. I know what Alison has told me, but she's left out a lot of shit."

"Sure. I'll let you know whatever you want, Mr. Brownstone."

James leaned forward and studied the other man intently. "Here's an easy one. How many three-headed dragons have you killed?"

Mason blinked. He laughed once before he realized that James wasn't joking. "Excuse me, Mr. Brownstone? Did you just ask what I thought you asked?"

"Yeah. How many three-headed dragons have you killed?" He shrugged. "It's a simple fucking question."

The wizard shrugged at Alison, and she scrubbed a hand over her face as embarrassment burned her entire body.

Come on, Dad. Please don't do this. I know you think you're helping me out, but you're being ridiculous. Oh, what I wouldn't give to have Mom here right now to set you straight.

"Uh, zero, I guess." Mason managed a nervous chuckle.

"I'm certain, actually, that I've not even killed a dragon with one head. If I had, he did a good job of pretending to be something else."

James held up three fingers. "The first one was out of nowhere. It involved this annoying shit in a Romanian forest. The next two were years later—I can't even get into it for bullshit government reasons." He grunted and ripped some meat from a new rib. "They aren't so hard to kill, though, if you rip their stomachs open. The bigger they are, the more fucking guts slide out. Chopping their heads off works great, too."

Mason nodded with a mix of confusion and surprise on his face. "I'll take that under advisement, but we don't exactly find a lot of dragons in Seattle. Most of our threats are more two-legged and don't breathe fire."

Brownstone finished his rib and wiped his hands with a napkin before he responded. "Massive-ass stone giants have two legs and are a lot worse than dragons. Don't act like there's not a lot of weird shit here and you don't have to worry about it."

"I'm not saying that, Mr. Brownstone." The younger man smiled firmly. "I'm merely saying my background and training is as a bodyguard, not a bounty hunter. I'm used to enemies who tend to be less monstrous or whom I have to go looking for, I guess you could say. There are simply not many three-headed dragons plotting to assassinate corporate CEOs or witnesses, at least around here. I don't know about LA." He managed a grin, but the other man didn't laugh.

Good one, Mason. Stand up to him. If you push back enough, he has to see that you're a good man.

"Yeah, bodyguard. The way I hear it, you were gonna work for that fucker Carlyle." Her father narrowed his eyes. "That says something about your judgment."

This is getting out of hand.

Alison rolled her eyes. "Dad, doesn't it also say something about mine?"

"Taking a job or two and getting hoodwinked is one thing. It's kind of like the time your mom and I—" The older man grunted. "Never mind. The point is that it meant Carlyle thought he could use him. Turn him." He pointed at Mason. "And a guy like Carlyle probably knows what he's doing, don't you think? That's how he became a billionaire."

She glared at him. "Dad, that's way over the line. Mason—"

"I killed men to save your daughter that night, Mr. Brownstone," the wizard snapped, his head high and his shoulders squared. "More than a few, actually, and I'd gladly do it again. I didn't know Carlyle was what he was, and I didn't fly a helicopter in under fire because I wanted to help him out."

"How do I know it's not some sort of fucking trick?" James demanded.

"Because some assassin would have killed her already." Mason scoffed. "Why don't you give Alison a little credit? She's a good judge of character."

Alison looked from one to the other, unsure whether she should interfere or if her boyfriend did a good job of defending himself.

"Shit has changed for her." Her father shook his head. "Things are different than they were before."

"What do you mean? Because she doesn't have her soul sight anymore? Big deal. Are you saying that you can't be trusted to judge people yourself because you don't have a special power by which to judge them?" Mason scoffed. "Give me a damned break. Alison wouldn't have such a good team if she were a bad judge of character, and it's an insult to suggest otherwise."

Damn, Mason. I don't think I've seen anyone other than my Mom or me go at my dad like that in a long time.

James' nostrils flared. "I need to protect my daughter. She can kick ass all day and all night, but some little fucker might be able to get past her defenses with a painting and a smile. She's had a lot of shit happen to her, and maybe she trusts certain people way more than she should. If I have to be a son of a bitch on her behalf, that's fine by me. I'll make that sacrifice."

Alison slapped her hand on the table. "Dad, that's enough. You stop right there."

He grunted and glared at the other man.

The wizard took a deep breath. "She's not that little girl who brought you your dog anymore, Mr. Brownstone."

"What do you know about anything? You haven't even known her for a year."

"I know enough." Mason shrugged. "Do you think a grown-ass woman who is so tough the underworld calls her the Dark Princess needs her daddy to come and tell her who is okay to date? If you think you and your wife have done a good job, then you should trust that. Because this shit—" He gestured to himself and his adversary. "Between you and me? It's fucking ridiculous and you're embarrassing yourself."

She slumped forward, her face in her palm, and wondered if it were possible to die from embarrassment.

James' lips curled into a sneer. "It could be this has nothing to do with her then. It could be that I don't think you're good enough for her. That's enough for me to feel okay about this."

Mason leaned forward and locked eyes with the older man. "I'll be honest, Mr. Brownstone. It would be nice if you liked me, but the only person at this table I have to prove myself to is Alison. I've already done that, not only when we took Carlyle but in every fight since then. I have her back, and I'd sooner die than let anything happen to her. So, honestly? I don't give two shits what you think as long as Alison wants to be with me."

Alison blinked at Mason, surprised by the quiet assurance in his tone.

Her father didn't respond for a long while and instead, returned his attention temporarily to his first love—ribs. He ate another two before he finally broke the silence. "Describe an epic fucking proposal."

The anger on Mason's face vanished, replaced by confusion. "What?"

"You heard me." Brownstone aimed a half-eaten rib at Mason's head. "Alison doesn't need some asshole who's merely playing around. If you want to be around her, I need to know you're serious."

She groaned and threw her hands up. "Seriously, Dad? If we want to get into it, let's discuss how long it took for you to come up with a proposal for mom. You are probably the last person on this planet who should lecture other people about coming up with proposals ahead of time."

He grunted and took a bite of his rib. "That wasn't my fault."

"I love her, Mr. Brownstone," Mason announced quietly. "That's all I can do. That and beat the shit out of anyone who threatens her on a job or even when we're walking around. I don't know what the future will bring, but I'm not playing around here. I can promise you that much."

I wonder if you can choke to death on too much testosterone in the air.

Both men stared at each other, their faces hard. Alison worried that Mason was about to challenge her father to a fight. As powerful as her boyfriend was, he was no match the older man. Brownstone had single-handedly fought and defeated the Drow Queen and he'd grown even more powerful since then.

Most of my top-level magic wouldn't even do much to him at this point.

James' frown slowly ebbed and he offered Mason a tight smile, a faint hint of respect in his eyes. "You have some balls, at least. I'll give you that. I half-suspected I'd come up here and find out you were some sort of vegetarian who hates Fords."

"I love meat." Mason chuckled. "But I don't have a strong opinion on Fords one way or another."

"Better than nothing." Her father smiled, this time with a hint of actual warmth as the waitress approached with a tray of brisket. Alison wasn't sure if his changed expression was about Mason or the damned barbecue.

"I don't have any dragon-killing stories to tell you," her

boyfriend began, "but let me tell you about one of the most ridiculous jobs I had."

Alison glanced at the two most important men in her life and hoped the change in the conversation also signaled a shift in her dad's attitude.

CHAPTER ELEVEN

It took over twenty minutes after they'd returned to her condo before Alison dared to broach the question. After purposefully giving Mason a long kiss, she sent her boyfriend on his way, still worried that her dad would kick him through a wall.

The rest of the lunch had gone more calmly, and the two men had exchanged war stories from their respective careers. Despite this surface affability, Alison still sensed an underlying tension between them.

Maybe I should have let them punch each other to get it out of their system.

No, I need to stop running. This is as much about me as it is Mason, and I need to make sure Dad understands that.

Currently, the Granite Ghost, Scourge of Harriken and Overprotective Father of the Decade, sat on the couch and watched television. He'd found barbecue-related programming after less than a minute of searching, in this case, a documentary on the history of spices and their impact on different barbecue sauces.

Alison wandered over to her recliner, took a seat, and folded her arms. "So, let's hear it. I want to get this crap over and done with before you leave."

James muted the TV and looked at her. "Hear what?"

"Whatever it is you have to say about *the man*." She rolled her eyes. "That whole display earlier was annoying, Dad. Seriously, the only reason why I'm not furious is because you stopped being a complete jerk for the rest of the meal and actually acted like a normal person and not a magical asshole machine."

Her father snorted. "If a man can't take me busting his balls a little, then he doesn't deserve to be with you. It's as simple as that. If you think about it, I was fairly nice."

Alison took a few deep breaths. "I knew it was a bad idea for you to come without Mom, but it didn't end up as the complete mess I expected it would. I won't break up with Mason, Dad, because you don't think he killed enough Romanian three-headed dragons or whatever. This doesn't work that way. You don't have veto power over my love life."

James grunted. "I didn't say you should break up with him, and I'm not saying I get to pick who you can be with."

"What did all that mean, then?" She narrowed her eyes. "You like him?"

"Of course I don't like him. He's dating my daughter. But he's not a complete piece of shit and he actually seems to give a damn, so that's at least a start. I might learn to like him." He shrugged. "What can I say? He impressed me. I figured he'd wet himself the minute I got a little in his face." An evil grin followed. "If I can't use my rep to test your boyfriends, what good is it?"

"It's annoying. That's what it is." Alison lowered her hands to her knees. "He's right about what he said, you know."

"About what exactly?" Her father looked confused.

"I'm *not* the same girl I was when we first met." She leaned back in her chair and her stomach churned. The last thing she wanted to do was upset the man who had done so much for her, but he also needed to accept the situation. "Sometimes, I think you understand that, but at other times, I still think you want to lock me in my room at home and line the walls with anti-magic deflectors and motion-sensitive autocannons."

"I'm not a great man or even a good man," he responded quietly. "But one thing I can do is protect the people I care about." He peered at her with an almost oppressive intensity. "And I know you don't believe it, but I understand that you've changed. It's just…"

"Just what?"

"You did all that dangerous shit at that school that I didn't know about, and you've done everything afterward. It's not only about how you were on bounty hunts with me but the dark wizards and the company, too." James scowled. "I know I've been a dick. I know I've been over-protective since I first started taking care of you, but I also see things differently now."

Alison nodded. "You do?"

"Yeah. Seeing you here in your own element and with your own company—shit, your own tactical room that's better than mine—and with your boyfriend, I do see how much you've changed. You're not even close to that confused little girl who used to get upset that all her magic hadn't come in." He smiled. "But that's not a bad thing. I'm proud of you, Alison. Proud of the woman you've become and how you're already a better person than I can ever hope to be." He patted the amulet underneath his shirt. "But I'll always be there for you if you need my help. I don't care what the fucking government says. If I need to go full on, I'll go full on. Whispy would love that shit. In the end, I care because you're my daughter, and I'll do whatever I need to do to protect you, no matter what the fucking cost."

She left her chair to give her dad a tight hug. "Thanks, Dad. I'll keep that in mind, but you saw it. I have good people around me now, but if I ever run into anything I can't handle, I'll call you. I love you, and thanks for understanding."

"I love you, too."

Alison released him and stood. "We can go back to Kingdom of Pork for dinner if you want."

"Nah. Go ahead and take me to Maneki. You always go on about it when you talk to me or Shay. I might as well see what the big deal is. I doubt I'm gonna suddenly like sushi, but I might as well give it a chance."

Her face brightened. "Really?"

"Sure, but only you and me. Leave Lover Boy at home for one day."

She laughed. "Okay, Dad. I'm sure Mason's already tired after having to deal with you earlier."

The next morning, Alison exhaled a long sigh and waved as her father pulled away in his vehicle, a well-maintained non-electric ancient Ford F350. The vehicle had been damaged and all but destroyed several times, but he continued to dump piles of money to keep his old partner alive. In a sense, that truck was as much his revered child as she was. It was also older than her.

Loyalty. If there was one thing that defined James Brownstone, that was it, and she accepted that the same applied to her as well.

It doesn't matter if I'm not a Brownstone by blood. He's helped make me into the woman I am today, and I'll always respect him for that.

Alison turned to head into the condo lobby when her phone rang. She pulled it from her pocket, surprised to see that the call was from Senator Johnston.

"What can I do for you, Senator?" she answered warily. "Or is this simply you trying to pump me for campaign cash?" she joked.

The old man laughed. "You know what the strongest magic in the entire world is?"

"Money?"

"No. Incumbency. At this rate, I won't leave the Senate until I die. No, I don't need your money, but I do need your help. There are some issues that have arisen recently concerning the gentlemen behind that unfortunate incident in Seattle. These are things I'd like to discuss with you in private and face-to-face. I think I could use your help to deal with some of these incidents preemptively."

Bile rose in the back of her throat. They'd killed many dark wizards a couple of months earlier, but she wasn't naïve enough to believe that meant they'd never be a problem again. The bastards' tentacles reached all over the world, after all, even into the US government and the PDA.

"How soon do you need to talk with me?" she asked, her jaw tight.

"Sooner would be better, but it's not a matter of immediate need." Senator Johnston coughed. "Don't think that I have a line on something they intend to try anytime soon. This is more about me marshaling all available resources in the aftermath of a high-profile incident. You know how the government is. They won't spend five cents to stop a problem before it happens, but afterward, it's easy to convince people."

"Okay, then, I'll stop by in a few days. How does that sound?"

"Excellent," Johnston replied and the earlier faint tension that underpinned his voice had gone. "Let me know when you're on your way. And thank you for your understanding."

"You're welcome," she said cordially.

The sound of shuffling papers came over the line "Oh, I've met that friend of yours from your school days. Interesting fellow."

"My friend?" Alison replied, confused. "Who are you talking about?"

"The shifter fellow," he clarified. "He has a good head on his shoulders despite how young he is. I don't care much one way or another that he's a shifter, but he's so damned young, and that made me a little curious. I can see him making the jump to the Senate in the future once he learns to swim in the swamp a little more."

"Oh, Luke." She smiled and warm nostalgia floated from her memories. "He's always been a leader, even in school. I wasn't surprised that he ended up in the government."

Senator Johnston chuckled quietly. "Most great leaders are like that. I don't know him well. I've only met him in passing at a few functions, but now that he's living here in DC and you're coming this way soon, it'd be a shame not to look him up. Feel free to get that out of the way before talking to me. Like I said, I need your help, but it's not too urgent. And it wouldn't hurt me to curry a little favor with you and someone in the House."

"I might do that," she agreed. "Thanks for the suggestion."

"I live to serve," the old man replied, amusement threaded into his tone. "See you soon. I know we'll both be able to help each other considerably."

Alison ended the call and wondered what the dark wizards might be up to. It had to be something bad enough that the Senator wanted her help, but not so bad that it couldn't wait for a few days.

If I'll be in DC anyway, maybe I should try to contact Luke. It's been over a year since we last talked, and that is as much my fault as his.

She lowered her phone slowly into her pocket. While she'd made such good friends at the School of Necessary Magic, many of them had gone their own way, if only because of circumstances, but that didn't mean they couldn't reconnect.

It'd be nice to see Luke again. I'd better tie up all my loose ends over the next few days.

CHAPTER TWELVE

Alison looked up as Myna stepped through her office door. She'd expected the ancient Drow, as Myna had texted her an hour earlier with a request to talk. For once, she'd suggested they meet at the Brownstone Building and instructed Ava to let her through.

As cryptic and stubborn as the old woman could be, she'd been nothing but helpful since they had met, and she owed Myna a debt she might never be able to repay.

"Hello, Myna," she said with a warm smile.

The old woman studied the office slowly and her gaze moved back and forth. "This room is too small for a woman of your station. You had this place built. Why would you not give yourself a more imposing room?"

Alison gestured to the chair in front of her desk. "I won't do much royal entertaining here or anything even remotely like that. A larger room would be nothing but wasted space."

Myna scoffed lightly and settled herself in a chair. "I do

worry about that sometimes—this attitude that you're more the functional kind of princess."

"Oh? Why? We've been over this. I won't involve myself with Drow politics. I appreciate everything you've done for me, but the last thing the Drow need is some girl who grew up on Earth to stick her nose into things, especially since I don't even want to."

"It's less the Drow than what your attitude represents."

"And what's that?"

"Ignorance of your true potential. A lack of mental flexibility." Myna pointed to the computer on Alison's desk and then to a clock on the wall. "You've lived your entire life on Earth. You didn't even know about your true magical potential until you were almost an adult."

Alison nodded, unsure where the other woman was going with this. "That's all true. So what? I've improved my magic now, haven't I?"

"You've only spent a small amount of time with the Drow." The old woman narrowed her eyes.

Is she bound and determined to force me back to Oriceran?

"Yeah, that's true, too, but it's not like I exactly fit in with the Drow. I'm grateful for what they showed me, but there are too many cultural differences for me to ever feel comfortable there, and that's before we get into all the weird Drow politics left over from what my dad did." Alison folded her arms. "As you won't let me forget, I'm the Princess of the Shadow Forged. If I were to live among them, that would bring with it certain obligations I'm not prepared to meet. If they simply needed another woman to hang out and deal with bad guys, that's one thing. But I want to make this as clear as possible. I will never willingly try to become queen of the Drow."

Myna sighed. "It's not that I think you should live among the Drow, but I worry about your potential. Even if you don't care about becoming queen, you should care about that."

"What about my potential? Isn't that what you're doing —helping me live up to my potential?"

Her companion shook her head. "I'm not sure that you can reach your maximum potential if you're so fixated on only living on Earth. The gates have barely opened, my princess. It might take centuries before the level of magic on this planet is truly comparable to Oriceran. Even what can be accomplished with the help of kemanas pales to what can be accomplished on Oriceran." She frowned with what might be concern. "That means you've already started at a disadvantage. At the minimum, it not only means your ability to draw on magic is more limited, but you also lack appropriate flexibility, and that will hold your magic back. You will develop bad habits born of these restrictions. Your ability to draw on different types of magic gives you one advantage, but it's not all-encompassing."

Alison leaned back in her chair. "There are a couple of things you need to understand. First, I accept that I'm half-Drow, but that doesn't change the fact that I grew up on Earth, and I don't intend to move to Oriceran anytime soon. If ever. Perhaps, if I end up living longer than a normal human, there may be something for me there in the future. For now, though, I'm not even all that crazy about the idea of living in another country. So, if you harbor some grand plan to convince me to tour Oriceran, give it up. I run a security company, and I have friends and family here on Earth who depend on me." She sighed. "I want to be clear that I thank you from the bottom of my heart for what you've done for me, but I want to live the life I want, not the life you want for me."

"Understood." The old woman's mouth twitched. "And what is the second thing I need to accept?"

"I'm already damned powerful as is. Yeah, I get that I have to continue to work on technique to improve my application of power. But it's not like I'm the weak girl who started at the School of Necessary Magic and could barely even do magic. I can defeat almost anyone I run into directly, and the Fremont Troll proves I can do things that don't require brute force."

"So you seek no improvement?" Disappointment filled Myna's eyes, and Alison was surprised with how much that hurt.

She shook her head. "That's not it. I'm merely saying I'm not obsessed with a desire to constantly improve my power. And quite frankly, as far as Oriceran goes, I need to master Earth before I think about trying to walk around a place that I'll only barely begin to understand. The gates might be open, but most people stay on their home planets for a reason."

Myna stood. "Master Earth, you say? Perhaps there's more wisdom in your impatient young mind than I realized."

Alison nodded. "Maybe Earth doesn't have as many intelligent species as there are on Oriceran, but it has many different cultures and languages. It provides a wealth of opportunity of me to learn mental flexibility if that's what you're concerned with. I'm not all that long out of college, Myna. I've had a lot more experiences than the average college graduate, but I do know that I have a lot to learn."

"Acceptance of one's ignorance is the first step toward true wisdom."

"You sound like many human philosophers."

"Earth does have its brilliant representatives," the old Drow replied. "I now better understand what your intent is, and I can help you with that if you trust me."

"I might not always like what you have to say, but you've more than proven yourself."

"Good. Then let us dispel a small fragment of your ignorance." She raised her hand and half-closed her eyes before she rattled off an incantation. Magic soaked the air before a portal swirled into existence.

Alison frowned and shook her head. "I don't want to go to Oriceran."

"This isn't for Oriceran." Myna nodded at the portal. "I'm hungry. Let's get something to eat."

"Okay." She blinked as she rose from her chair. "We can simply go to the cafeteria."

"There's something I want to show you." The old woman nodded at the portal again. "It is as I said. I want to help cure some of your ignorance. Don't worry. It's not a portal to Oriceran."

"Fine." She sighed and tapped a quick message to Ava.

Going somewhere with Myna for lunch. Probably out of the country. Be back soon.

She decided not to ask for further clarification. There was something fun about not knowing, and Myna would never lead her into a dangerous situation.

Alison stepped through the portal and emerged onto a city street in front of a large cart where a Chinese man cooked noodles. She blinked a few times before she turned her attention to her surroundings to identify their location. The heavy concentration of Chinese people who walked up and down the street and Chinese writing everywhere at least narrowed down the possibilities.

Several people stopped and stared at her.

Yeah, when two Drow step out of a portal, it's still weird wherever you go.

Myna emerged from the gateway and it closed behind her. She rattled something off in Cantonese, and the various gawkers nodded and smiled before the continued on their way.

"You speak Chinese?" Alison asked.

"No, I have a spell that allows me to translate, but it's something you're not yet capable of because of limitations in your technique." The old Drow grabbed a stool in front of the cart and ordered some noodles.

The owner smiled and gave a lengthy reply as he prepared her meal. He gestured a few times and laughed as he finished talking.

Alison sat beside her. "Do you eat here often?"

"Often enough, but not as often as I'd like. I came to this place when I first returned to Earth. Do you know where we are?"

"Not exactly." She looked around carefully once more. "I can guess, but it's hard to say for sure."

"Hong Kong. Thugs accosted this noodle vendor when I walked around the city with the help of a lovely and helpful young girl. I took care of the bullies, and it's earned me friendship and free noodles when I visit him."

Is this what she does with her free time? Portal around the world earning free food? That's actually awesome.

"Thugs?" she asked.

Myna nodded. "They are called Triads, I believe. I haven't put much effort into learning the nuances of human criminals. It's of little interest to me."

"They don't have as much penetration in Seattle," Alison explained. "But my dad and mom have both dealt with them in California."

"The violations of human law worry me little." The ancient Drow gestured to a passing bus. "But petty applications of strength and power are beneath all who claim to be strong."

Alison smiled. "You always surprise me. It's not that I had a bad time with the Drow on Oriceran, but hearing you talk, it makes me wonder what could have been."

"What might still be. Being a warrior doesn't mean one lacks any standards of behavior. And gaining true strength means testing yourself against others who are truly strong."

The cart owner placed a bowl of noodles in front of Myna. She grabbed her chopsticks and slurped some with happiness in her eyes. The man looked at Alison and said something, but she didn't understand. He pointed to the bowl, then her.

She shook her head and held her hands in front of her chest. "No, thank you."

The man nodded and seemed to understand.

This woman's centuries old, and she likes to hit noodle carts in Hong Kong. I don't know if that's cool or weird, but she takes joy in such a simple pleasure. I can learn more from her than merely better ways to use my Drow magic.

"I'm glad to know you still get around and see some of the world," she commented. "You're not exactly an open book, so I worried that you sat around waiting to train me. I don't even appreciate most of what Earth has to offer, and I was raised here, so I'm sure you can find nothing but delicious vendors and interesting people by traveling all over."

"I do many things in the time between our visits, and I understand you have your own life, my princess. Don't worry about me." Myna quieted to consume more of her noodles.

Alison turned her attention to the scene. It was interesting to her how she could be in a place where even the signage reminded her that she wasn't in her own country, but the cars and buildings weren't radically different. In a sense, Hong Kong was far less foreign to her sensibilities on this first visit than the kemana near the School of Necessary Magic had been.

All my magic and I still think like a human girl.

"So we traveled all the way to Hong Kong so you can give me a lesson on appreciating other cultures?" She smiled softly. "I'm not complaining, but we could have gone to the International District in Seattle. There's a great ramen place there you'd like since you're such a fan of noodles."

"I told you before," her companion replied after another

generous mouthful. "Some of this was to help you, but I was hungry. I really like these noodles. I find them invigorating." She nodded politely to the cart owner. "But this is a useful lesson. I've told you before, and I will continue to say it and demonstrate it to you. You're powerful—very powerful—but raw power is not enough. Technique is important, and your work and your power can easily blind you to the abilities you could develop if you fail to keep an open and flexible mind."

Alison nodded. "It's not like I don't get that. I only beat the Fremont Troll because I accepted that I wouldn't be able to win against it using massive force."

"Good." Myna tucked in for a few moments. "My efforts aren't in vain. You can learn the translation spell sooner with enough effort, but much more shadow compression is necessary before you can freely portal. Right now, you're an excellent weapon, my princess, but you could be so much more than that. What is the human saying? When you have a hammer, everything is a nail?"

"I get that." Alison smiled. "And you know what? If I've come all the way to Hong Kong, I might as well try the noodles." She waved at the man and pointed to Myna's bowl.

He beamed a smile at her and began to prepare her meal.

Myna waved to Alison as she opened a new portal. She'd successfully delivered the princess back to her office after they'd finished their noodles. The lesson was sufficient for now, and the old Drow needed to leave before she raised the girl's suspicions.

She stepped through her new portal and arrived in the living room of the home she used. It was abandoned and without human power or heat, but a careful and judicious application of magic had made it livable enough. She'd lived in far worse places during her exile.

Her entire body throbbed as she headed over to the couch. She trembled as she sat and a hacking cough wracked her body. When she moved her hand away from her mouth, blood stained her palm.

The old woman sighed. Her plan to save her princess had worked beyond her wildest expectations despite the strange curse germs the hideous Scott Carlyle had created. The transfer ritual had successfully moved the entirety of the infection to Myna. Her advanced age meant that it ravaged her even more aggressively than it had Alison, but centuries of developing skill and technique allowed her to use her magic to a decent level without the princess knowing what had happened.

It doesn't matter. I was dying anyway. It's not at all certain that this cursed disease will kill me any quicker. Even if it does, I've saved the future of my princess.

Myna didn't dare tell Alison. The girl wouldn't understand. She thought of herself as an adult, but she was a child really, an infant who simply played at maturity.

The Princess of the Shadow Forged had a vital role in the future of not only the Drow but the two worlds. That was clear to Myna, even if Alison failed to see it. But the girl needed time to develop that maturity and the power necessary to get entire kingdoms to heed her words.

She stared at the blood in her hand. "I gladly sacrifice what's left of my life to give you yours, my princess. Perhaps someday, I will tell you the truth, but if it is my fate to fall without you ever knowing, so be it."

CHAPTER THIRTEEN

H er phone rang with a call from Tahir while Alison was on her way to the office. She put it on speaker.

"What's up, Tahir? Is something about to blow me up?"

"Probably, but I've called because I've located our mysterious technomancer," he explained. "I already knew he was in Puyallup, but I've located the exact apartment building. Even if I can't refine it closer than that based on what I have right now, I'm sure I can detect his magic if we go there. I also think if I approach him directly, he will be impressed with my skill and it'll give me an opportunity to evaluate him directly as a potential hire."

Alison smiled. There was no reason to press him on his earlier reluctance to additional computer help. She was happy he was finally willing to bring someone else in.

"It's worth a shot," she replied. "Do you need me to come with you? If he's half as good as you, he'll see you coming."

"I'll bring Hana," Tahir suggested. "If I show up with you, he might react in panic. No one who is potentially still on the more criminal side of things would be comfortable if the Dark Princess showed up on their doorstep. You do have a certain reputation."

She scoffed. "You didn't seem intimidated by me when I tried to hire you."

"Because I'm me." His tone made it sound like it was the most obvious conclusion in the world.

Alison rolled her eyes. It wasn't like he could see it to be annoyed. "Fine, take Hana. Swing past the office first and visit the artifact vault. I don't want you to go without defenses in case this turns messy."

The infomancer sighed with real annoyance. "Very well then. And if he turns out to be a good candidate?"

"You can do a deep dive on his background and we'll go from there."

"Your guy doesn't like living large," Hana murmured as they stepped out of her car. "I understand the need to keep a low profile, but this is…sad. It isn't like there aren't nicer neighborhoods in this town to live in."

"Perhaps he has a reason to keep a low profile," Tahir replied.

I probably shouldn't have brought such a nice car, Hana thought. *I need to talk to Alison about some nondescript vans.*

The two-story apartment buildings that comprised the complex clustered tightly together, and the cracked and potholed parking lot separated the two main rows of buildings. Peeling paint and termite lines were the norm, along with more than a few missing windows covered by sheets of plastic. The stench of rotting trash lingered in the air from the overflowing garbage cans, exacerbated by the fact that the landfill was separated from the apartment complex by only a fence.

A few suspicious eyes peered through blinds at the new arrivals.

Hana glanced at the crystalline ring on her finger and then at the bronze pendant around Tahir's neck. Before, she'd not been that concerned, but they might have to survive a few bullets.

I grew accustomed to living with Alison and now Tahir. Even before that, I usually charmed my way out of living in crapholes like this.

The infomancer frowned as he looked around and his gaze lingered on a man in a tank top passed out in front of his apartment. "I'll admit I'm surprised, given the talent on display, that he'd choose to live here. One would think he'd at least live in an area that involved less risk of being mugged."

Two men emerged from the narrow space between two nearby apartment buildings and strutted toward them with arrogance in their step.

"I haven't seen you around here before, hot thing," one of the men stated lasciviously as he looked Hana up and down and licked her lips. "Nice outfit."

She'd chosen a short black sequined miniskirt and a matching long tube top.

Hana smile while she tried to decide between charm or violence. "I'm already taken, boys."

The men sneered and glanced at Tahir. "By this asshole?"

Two drones rose in the distance behind a nearby building.

Hana's eyes widened as she immediately identified the rockets on the bottom of the crafts. "Incoming!" She tapped her ring three times and her tails appeared behind her as her claws extended.

Tahir grabbed his pendant and shouted the activation incantation.

The two men stared at Hana's claws for a moment before they sprinted away.

"Fuck this," one of them shouted. "I don't need this shit."

The rockets launched from the drones a second later. The fox leapt aside but the rockets exploded and knocked her back. She landed hard, rolled, and hissed at the pain. While she had been singed with minor burns, her shield had protected her from serious injury.

She pushed onto her feet and frowned at some of the burns on her clothes. "That wasn't fun. And I bought this only a few days ago. Son of a bitch."

Tahir whipped out his wand and quickly chanted an incantation. One of the drones elevated abruptly and crashed into the rotors of the other. They both spiraled downward behind the building. He yanked his phone out and tapped something into it before he connected an adapter that could hold his wand.

A dark shadow in a humanoid shape sprinted down the stairs of a building across the parking lot. It was as if someone had dipped an entire person in pure shadow. The shadow man raised a wand, also cloaked in darkness, and a white bolt blasted out.

Hana and Tahir leapt behind a car.

"Your guy is a real asshole, babe," the nine-tailed fox complained. "I'm really starting to dislike him."

He shrugged. "You do have to admit that a test or two can be useful to evaluate people."

The fox rolled her eyes. "I forgot about all the crap you pulled on Alison when she first tried to hire you. It must be an infomancer thing—being dicks to your future bosses."

The shadow wizard fired off another few bolts, but they struck the car and dissipated into smaller arcs. After a few more attempts, he rushed around the corner.

"There is no damned way I'll let him get away after all that. If anything, he needs to pay for a new skirt." Hana vaulted on top of the car and bounded down before she raced toward the building. Her full fox speed took her there in seconds. She drew her gun and swung around the corner.

A man in a lawn chair glared at her. "What the hell is going on? First, weird shadows and now whatever the hell you are." He stared at her. "What are you? A nine-tailed werewolf or something?"

"Brownstone Security," she said crisply. "It's a very hush-hush thing. Don't worry about it."

"Brownstone Security?" He looked around, excitement on his face "Is she here? Alison Brownstone?"

"No." Hana kept her gun raised but didn't aim it at the man. "She's not working this job."

"Oh," he replied, visibly deflated. "Then this shit ain't worth getting shot over." He stood and opened his back door before he disappeared inside, muttering under his breath.

She looked back and forth and sniffed cautiously. Even

accounting for the shield around her, the air was thick with the scent of magic.

There's too much here. It's not like a trail, though. Did he portal out? But there's no way someone with that level of magic would live somewhere like here. Unless—crap. A dark wizard?

Hana holstered her pistol. She paced a little while she sniffed with intense focus. No, there was something there.

Tahir emerged from around the corner. "Where is he?"

"I smell something—strong magic." The fox shrugged.

"I do sense a high level of magic." He raised his phone, the wand still embedded in the adapter, and tapped in a few commands. "Let's see."

A dark shadow appeared and then resolved into a young teenage girl with short blonde hair. She was probably thirteen or fourteen at the most in jeans and a loose hoodie with headphones wrapped around her neck. Her fingers clutched a white wand, her eyes wide with panic behind her square-framed black glasses.

Hana folded her arms and nodded to the girl. "Is this your guy, Tahir?"

He frowned at the teenager. "If you try to cast another spell, it won't go well for you."

"I hit you with rockets, and you're still walking," the girl stammered. "H-how the hell does that happen?" She looked off to the side as she spoke.

The infomancer pointed to his pendant and then Hana. "Note her red skin. That's not natural, even if the tails are."

"I know her. I've seen her mentioned on the net. She's Hana Sugimoto." The girl groaned. "Damn it. You really are with Brownstone Security. Oh crap. When I saw you get out that car that was way too nice for the complex, I figured you were those mobsters I screwed with a few weeks ago."

"No," Tahir responded with a slight frown. "But don't you think it's advisable to identify your targets before you blast rockets at them?"

Hana rolled her eyes.

So now he's upset that he was attacked when before, it was simply a nice test? Is this simply about him getting punked by some teenager?

"I-I'm sorry, man. I screwed with these guys last week. I acted like I would leak a bunch of stuff to the FBI, and they said they would find me and kill me. I blew it off until I saw your car and figured the Mafia had come to do it." The girl lowered her wand slowly, resignation on her face. "But I've heard how it goes. If you screw with Brownstone, she messes you up bad. I heard she destroyed an entire building of Eastern Union because they stole her cat."

"Alison has never had a cat." Hana laughed. "It wasn't because they stole her cat. It was because..." She frowned. "It was a much better reason than that, and she doesn't hurt people unless they have it coming."

The girl hung her head. "I'm sorry, okay? I panicked."

"Were you lying when you told me you hacked a Homeland Security server?" Tahir asked.

The girl looked up. "How do you know about that? *You* were the other racer?"

He nodded curtly. "Your statements about my boss are what got my attention and brought us here."

"I'm so screwed." She groaned and rubbed her temples as she leaned against the rear wall of a nearby apartment. "I was only having fun and tried to look like I was big, man."

"You didn't answer my question," the wizard snapped.

"Dial it down, babe," the fox suggested. "She's only a kid."

The girl swallowed. "It wasn't like I looked for stuff on Brownstone. I only tried to hack the server and stumbled across the Brownstone stuff. All I wanted was to have a little fun."

"Interesting," Tahir said as his only response.

"What's your name?" Hana asked.

"Sonya." The girl shoved her wand into her pocket.

Her stomach rumbled and she looked down and blushed. "Sorry. I'm hungry, is all."

The other woman smiled softly. "How about we take you to lunch then?"

Sonya glanced at them, suspicion on her face. "You won't hurt me or kill me?"

Tahir snorted. "Brownstone Security isn't in the habit of killing or hurting children, but perhaps we should speak to your parents."

"Good luck. I live alone."

CHAPTER FOURTEEN

Tahir and Hana waited until the girl had stuffed a few fries into her mouth and taken a bite of her burger before they asked their questions. On the ride over, she had sat quiet and pensive in the backseat. She barely made eye contact and often flinched if they looked at her.

I've seen girls like her before, Hana thought. *I don't like what I think it means.*

"Where are your parents?" she asked and suspected that she already knew the answer.

"I don't know. I don't even know if they're alive," Sonya replied between bites. "My dad was a wizard. When I showed some talent, he decided to train me. He specialized in infomancy so that's what he started to teach me, but he split about a year back. The jerk barely even showed me anything. I had only a couple of months of training before he jetted." She shrugged. "I figured he pissed the wrong people off and they dropped him into the bay."

Tahir frowned. "And what about your mother?"

"Mom thought the same thing. She blamed it on the

magic but she wasn't a witch, though. She forbade me to use my magic and slapped me around if she caught me using it. I had to hide my wand." Sonya's expression darkened. "She used to tell me that maybe the New Veil were onto something, and if I wanted to be on the right side, I needed to give up my magic."

"The New Veil are psychotic terrorists," he replied, his tone filled with barely concealed disgust. "They murder innocent people without remorse. The only thing they are good for is dying."

"I know. That's why I looked into the thing in DC and that's when I stumbled on the stuff about the Dark Princess." Sonya gobbled down a few more fries. "It was so cool to learn that she saved all those people. I don't know what to think of her half the time. Some of the stuff I read makes it sound like she'll blow your building up if you disrespect her, and then I read stuff like her stopping terrorists."

"Alison only wants to protect people," Hana explained. "She tries to give everyone a chance, but she also doesn't worry about eliminating people who prey on others."

The teenager nodded, a degree of disbelief still on her face. She still rarely made eye contact.

"But enough about Alison. Where's your mom now?" the fox asked, her fists clenched under the table. She'd been orphaned, but this poor girl had been a victim of someone who should have protected her when she needed her most.

"Who knows?" The girl shook her head. "She disappeared six months after my dad. I didn't care because at least it meant she'd stop hitting me and trying to take my wand. I practiced my power more and tried to train myself.

I looked stuff up where I could, and I was already a halfway decent hacker. My dad had shown me that stuff since I was about seven. He always said I had a natural talent. I tried to keep it low-key, but every once in a while, I wanted to show off."

"Why didn't you go to the police?" Hana sighed. "They could have helped you. Found you a family."

"Some teenager from a crappy neighborhood? No, they'd throw me in a group home. I've known a lot of kids like that. I already had the crap kicked out of me by my mom. Why would I want others to do that? Or worse?" Sonya sneered.

Hana gave her a shallow nod. She'd gone through a similar thought process when she was younger and understood the girl's position completely.

Tahir folded his hands and leaned forward. He tilted his head as he stared at Sonya.

She shuddered and lowered her gaze. "Stop it. You're creeping me out, man."

"You don't know me well, so some of the importance of what I'm about to say will be lost on you." He took a deep breath. "You're very impressive."

The teenager raised her head. She made brief eye contact before she averted her eyes again, open hostility and suspicion on her face. "What are you playing at?"

Hana patted the girl's hand, but Sonya yanked it away and frowned.

"He paid you an honest compliment, Sonya," the fox explained quietly. "Trust me. It's rare that Tahir says someone's impressive."

The infomancer nodded. "You need to understand that

although my skills vastly exceed yours, I'm also considerably older than you and have had extensive training in both non-magical computer skills and infomancy. For you to have already accomplished what you've done at your age, especially magically, is beyond impressive. Your intelligence must be incredible, as well, for you to be able to handle hacking at such a level. It pains me to admit it, but your non-magical skill exceeds what mine was at your age."

"I know a few tricks, but as for the magic, it's not as impressive as you think, man." Sonya drew her wand out and set it on the table. "My dad gave that to me when I made a toaster explode by accident one day. I was so excited, but he barely showed me anything in the end. I can do a lot of stuff through the computer, but most of anything else I can do, you saw. I'm good at a few spells, but I can't seem to pull others off, no matter how hard I try."

She finished her fries and licked the salt greedily off her fingers before she turned her attention to her burger.

Tahir rubbed his chin. "It's because you need additional training. The raw potential is obviously all there."

"Well, duh. I didn't need you to tell me that, man." She rolled her wand back and forth between her two hands. "But like I told you, if I go to anyone, they'll send me into the system. Screw that."

"What about school?" Hana asked.

Sonya shrugged. "I stopped going a while ago."

"And the school hasn't checked on you?"

"I changed their records to make it look like I'd moved away—barely in time, too. They were probably about to start looking." She grinned for a second before the smile disappeared as if drained by the haunting pain in her green eyes. A little discomfited, she adjusted her glasses. "It's not special compared to you guys with your fancy artifacts. You even work for the Dark Princess and she can fly." Her gaze flicked briefly to Hana. "He's a wizard. That's easy to get. But what are you? I've never seen magic like those tails."

She smiled. "I'm a nine-tailed fox. I can also turn into a fox."

"Huh? I've never even heard of that kind of shifter."

"I'm not really a shifter." She kept any anger out of her voice as she suspected the girl would react poorly. "And it's not like there are too many of us around here."

Sonya finished her burger and wiped her hands with her napkin. "So now you know the deal. I'm sorry about everything. If you don't plan to kill or hurt me, let me go back home."

Hana sighed. "It's not that simple."

The teenager's hands curled into fists. "Don't send me into the system. I'm begging you."

"Would you be averse to me training you?" Tahir interrupted. "That would present us with an alternative."

She blinked. "What?"

"I thought the question was rather clear. I can't think of another way to phrase it." He looked annoyed.

"Why? What do you care about me?" She rubbed her hands together and fear and suspicion returned to her eyes.

This poor girl, Hana thought. *She really doesn't trust anyone anymore. Not that I can blame her. Did I really trust anyone before I met Alison?*

The infomancer turned his wrist so his palm was up. "Talent found should be encouraged. It's rare to find this level of potential in someone who isn't already being polished by someone else. It would be an interesting challenge. Your parents are no longer a factor, by your own admission. In addition, Alison needs more infomancy depth among her personnel, and you could serve in that capacity, especially under my guidance."

Sonya's eyes widened. "Let me get this straight, man. You want to train me, and on top of it, you want me to work for the Dark Princess?"

"Yes, that's an efficient summary. We'll have to make arrangements for your education, but given your obvious intelligence, I'm sure we can set something up online with ease." He shrugged as if the solutions were self-evident. "Alison is wealthy. Many things become easy when you're wealthy."

The girl stared at him, one of the first times she'd made sustained eye contact. Her mouth hung wide with shock. "This has to be a joke."

Tahir smiled tightly. "You picked the right person to challenge to a race."

Hana patted her boyfriend's hand. She knew he'd claim this was simply about exploiting a useful resource or something like that, but he now offered to do for Sonya what Alison had done for Hana—give her a chance at a better life where she didn't have to prey on society. She'd never been prouder of him.

Alison smiled warmly at Sonya, who sat across from her. The girl constantly rubbed her hands together and refused to make eye contact. Tahir and Hana sat on either side of Alison.

"Sonya," she said quietly. "I'll cast a truth spell. It's nothing fancy, and it'll simply change colors if you lie."

The teenager swallowed. "Do you think I'm lying?"

"In my business, we run into a lot of dangerous people, so it doesn't hurt to check."

She didn't want to explain that she was not all that good at truth spells, and an experienced witch could probably still get away with lying to her, despite her strong basic power level. She'd spent most of the last ten years able to tell when people lied simply by looking at them. The truth was that she'd never needed to develop the technique, but she doubted this girl was some hyper-sophisticated dark family spy.

Sonya nodded. "Fine. Do it."

Alison summoned a small white orb which hovered in front of her.

"Let's test this out. As long as it stays white, it means you're telling the truth, understand?"

The girl nodded again.

"Is your name Sonya?"

"Yes."

The orb remained white.

"Answer the next question with a lie," she instructed.

Sonya frowned but nodded.

"Are you an elf?"

"Yes, I'm a Light Elf."

The orb turned black for several seconds before it reverted to white.

The girl's eyes widened. "Wow. Cool."

Alison continued with a series of question to verify everything the girl had told Hana and Tahir about her life. She uncovered no lies.

"Thank you for answering all those questions," she stated finally.

"No problem." Sonya looked at all the adults at the table. "Now what?"

"A good question," Tahir commented. He looked at his boss. "You could easily gain guardianship."

"I could." She flicked her wrist and dispelled the truth orb. "But we need to make sure Sonya understands her options. Whatever happens, I don't want her to go back to some apartment alongside a dump by herself. That's ridiculous."

"It's not so bad, you know. As long as I keep the door locked, I'm good. I can hide with the spell, but I've only had to do that once when someone broke in. He stole some crap and left. I have stuff delivered, mostly drones. The only thing that sucks is that is some companies won't send their drones into the place because too many people take them out."

The infomancer frowned. "Where did you get rocket drones, by the way?"

"I...uh, took those from the Mafia guys, too." She smiled but it was a little uncomfortable.

Alison looked directly at the girl and her heart went out to her. She knew all too well what it was like to feel alone and not know what to do. She'd been lucky to have James Brownstone interested in her after her mother's death. Without him, she could have ended up in the system as her power manifested, and she could only imagine how badly that would have gone for her. Not every manifestation of rogue power gained a young magical a trip to the School of Necessary Magic.

"One possibility, Sonya," she began with a nod at Tahir, "is for you to agree to what Tahir's suggested. He could train you, and we'd supplement your education with online classes. It seems clear that you don't want to go into foster care or a group home. And you don't have any other relatives?"

"I do, but they're all garbage." Sonya snorted. "I'd rather be on the street than live with them. They're worse than my mom."

"There are other options." Alison raised her hand and chanted a quick spell. An image of smiling students who added ingredients to small cauldrons appeared in front of her. "I went to a magic school, the School of Necessary Magic. Since I am an ex-student, I'm sure I could get you in if you wanted to go there. Of course, there are other magic schools as well, but that school is the best in the United States."

The girl made a face. "I didn't even like normal school. I don't think I'd like magic school. Do they have a bunch of rules?"

"Yeah. It is a school."

"Do you have computers in your room?"

Alison chuckled. "There's not a single computer on campus. Part of the way they keep the school safe is to minimize its exposure to the outside world. It's a little old-fashioned in a lot of ways."

Sonya winced. "No offense, Miss Brownstone—"

"You can call me Alison."

"Well, no offense, Alison, but I don't want to go to some place with a bunch of rules," the girl stated quietly. "I'm not great with rules. And no way will I go somewhere with no computers."

Tahir snorted. "Rules are what small minds use to constrain greatness."

Sonya laughed and pointed at him. "What he said."

Alison smiled. It was one of the few times the girl had actually made sustained, direct contact.

"There's only one other matter to figure out then," she said finally.

"What's that?" the infomancer asked.

"She has to live somewhere."

Hana's face lit up with excitement, but Tahir blinked once and his jaw tightened.

You didn't think that part, through, did you? Alison thought. *You want to train her, but you don't want to have to be responsible for her. Or maybe you simply don't want a kid to get in the way of your girlfriend living with you.*

She didn't bother to stop her chuckle. "I have an idea for that. There is space in my apartment since Hana will move out. Sonya can stay with me for now while we get a feel for all this."

The girl gasped. "You want me to move in with you?"

"Yes, but I have to take a trip to DC." She turned to Hana. "I know you want to move the rest of your things to

Tahir's soon, but can you stay with her when I'm away? I think she'd be most comfortable there."

The fox nodded. "Sure thing, Alison."

Sonya harrumphed and folded her arms. "I'm not a baby. I don't need a babysitter."

"It's not like I'm suggesting you need to be watched twenty-four-seven," Alison replied. "But you've been neglected for six months. It wouldn't hurt to at least have someone there when you go to sleep."

The teenager looked down and the defiance drained from her face as she gave a shallow nod. "Sorry," she whispered.

"It's okay, Sonya. Like I said, I have space, and we can't send you back to that ratty apartment." Alison forced a stern look on her face, even as the idea of helping the girl delighted her. "This is all a test, though. You said you're not big on rules. Fine. I've broken more than my share, but if you live with me and receive training from Tahir, you need to listen to us."

"You're the Dark Princess," she replied and her voice suggested that she still didn't believe she was even having this conversation. "You're...basically pure power. I think I can listen to you, Alison."

"Then it sounds like we have an arrangement. I'll have my assistant look into all the paperwork."

CHAPTER FIFTEEN

Hana hummed quietly as she carried another box into Tahir's living room. Her boyfriend stood there, a slightly pensive look on his face as he looked over the growing mountain of boxes they'd hauled inside.

Ha-ha. This is what it means to ask someone to move in. Fear my wardrobe!

"You certainly have a lot of things," Tahir observed. "Far more than I realized or estimated."

"Babe, I'm in a different outfit almost every time you see me." She winked and set the latest box down. **FLIRTY SKIRTS** was written in large letters on the top. It sat beside another box labeled **SERIOUS SKIRTS**. "Did you think I would show up with a toothbrush and a pair of shoes?"

She gave him a warm smile to let him know she wasn't mad. She understood how much of an adjustment this was for the man, but she also couldn't help wanting to tweak him a little bit.

Tahir sighed. "It's not that. I'm still getting used to the idea."

Hana walked over to him and threw her arms around his neck. She gave him a quick kiss and smiled. "It's okay to feel weird. This is the first time I've really lived with a guy I actually cared about, so this is new to me in a way, too. You managed to snag me despite the fact that I didn't want to be snagged."

He raised his head and cheekiness returned to his smile.

"Don't get too cocky." She kissed him on the cheek before she pulled away. "But this does mean that I'll need more space in the refrigerator and that sort of thing, you know. Moving in together means mixing minds and styles, not me simply adding some clothes into your closet."

"I understand that, Hana." He ran a hand over a box labeled **FUNNY T-SHIRTS**. "You're a quirky and curious woman. I don't know what to make of you half the time, which is why I suppose I find you so refreshing."

"It helps that I'm so sexy it hurts, too." Hana ran a hand down her thigh, but her baggy gray sweats didn't do much for her attempt at alluring. "I am normally, anyway. Stupid sweats."

"Your physical charms are duly noted." Tahir cleared his throat. "That said, I do have one or two things of concern. They are minor things, but I think it's best I mention them now."

"Of concern?" She raised an eyebrow and folded her arms. "Way to harsh the vibe."

"It's not a big deal, but please try to keep the singing in the shower to a reasonable volume." He shrugged. "It's one of the reasons I'm so tired when you stay over."

The fox poked him in the chest. "You could not sleep in so late, babe. It's not like you always have to wait until the middle of the night to do your work."

"I don't wait. It's merely that I find it's an excellent time to concentrate." The infomancer shrugged and looked at her as if he thought her a little crazy.

Hana laughed. "I'll do my best not to wake you too often—unless you'll get something *special* out of it." She grinned and sashayed away but was again stymied by her decidedly utilitarian choice of clothing.

Damn it. I should get my quality flirt on, but I screwed it up. I should have simply slapped on my yoga pants and one of my sparkly sports bras.

"We haven't talked much about the girl, you know," he mentioned with something approaching uncertainty in his voice.

She studied him, surprised by the change in his demeanor. "What about her? She's staying with Alison. Sure, I'll spend a few days with her, but you don't have to worry about that."

Tahir shook his head. "It's not that. I was curious whether you think my idea to train her is foolish. I'll admit, I'm not one normally given to such concerns, but I can't help but be fascinated at the potential and how I might help shape it."

Hana dropped onto his couch and crossed her legs. "I'm not a wizard or a witch, babe. I don't know what it takes to train someone in magic. Alison's taught me about fighting and fitness, but I don't think it's the same thing. So I don't have much advice to give you."

"I wasn't talking about technique training." He sat

beside her. "I meant the more general sense of what is going on with the girl. I pushed forward on this idea without even discussing it with you."

"It did surprise me a little." She fluffed his hair affectionately. "I don't care that you didn't discuss with me, and you're more of a softy than you let on."

He frowned. "Soft? No. You misunderstand. It was more about e—"

"Efficiency," she finished for him. "Sure. Whatever you have to tell yourself to get to sleep at night."

"Be that is it may, it's true." Tahir pointed at this computer desk. "I've been convinced by these last several months that I will work for Alison for a long time, which means I'll need competent assistance. Isn't the best way to achieve that to personally assure it through training someone who already has a high level of natural ability?"

"Why is it so hard for you to admit that you wanted to help the girl? She makes it easier because she has real talent for you to work with, but it's not like it's a weakness to want to help her." Hana sighed and laid her head on Tahir's shoulder. "It's sweet. I know you think that's not rational or whatever, but I don't, and I'm your girlfriend. So you doing something sweet that I like means you score points with me, and that works out for you, so it's good."

"It isn't that I think it's bad. I merely want everyone to understand my motivations." He stroked Hana's hair.

"Here's the thing, babe. Even if efficiency and training someone who might be your replacement one day are a big part of why you do it, it's not a big part of why Alison and I want to help her. We're both orphans, even if she landed a second set of cool parents. We know what it's like to need a helping hand in this messed-up world that still doesn't know what it wants to do with magic and the people who have it."

"I know," he replied softly. "But I wanted to be honest. I don't think I've achieved the natural level of altruism that you two have settled into. I won't deny some desire to help others, but I also don't want you to resent me because I'm interested in her as an apprentice for practical reasons."

The fox exhaled a contented sigh. "There's nothing wrong with a little win-win. It'll be fun getting to know her while Alison's in DC."

"You aren't worried about her trip at all?"

"Nope." Hana lifted her head. "If this was some big emergency, Senator Johnston wouldn't have told her it was okay to wait. I'm sure he'll simply tell her something general and ask that she spend more time whacking dark wizards. No big deal."

"There's a certain logic to that," he responded. He felt in his pocket and pulled out his phone. "It's been a relaxing couple of months. Our jobs have been easy to handle, and although I do enjoy a good challenge, it wouldn't be awful if we were allowed some time to settle in together before any new major crises arise."

She grinned and stood quickly before she clapped and fixed him with a stern look. "One crisis we do need to handle is that we still have more boxes to bring in."

Tahir stood with a smirk. "Ah, yes. I'm sure we're missing the most valuable box filled with T-shirts with witty sayings for holidays."

"That's a good idea." Hana snapped her fingers. "I wish I had thought of it."

CHAPTER SIXTEEN

Alison stepped out of one of the many Starbucks in Washington DC, her suitcase in hand. She ignored the expressions of a few curious people and knew exactly what they thought.

I didn't see that woman with the suitcase come in, so where did she come from?

She wondered how long the magic train would remain a secret. It was barely one at this point, given that it was hard to continue to conceal fundamental secrets about the world thirty years after the gate opened, but the magical community still acted as if it was dangerous to talk about it.

There was no advantage for non-magicals to know about the train anyway given how they risked being vaporized if they attempted to use it.

Of course, there was also the possibility that should it become well-known, groups like the New Veil or HDL might attack it. A small amount of plausible deniability was helpful to ward off danger. As in the decades past, such worries might not be warranted.

They are using magic to help build moon bases now, and the gates continue to open. What will Earth look like in a couple of centuries with all that technology and magic side by side?

Alison waited at the curb and checked her phone. She'd already sent texts to her friends to inform them of her safe arrival, not that problems with the magic train were common.

Hana and Sonya were settled in without issue, and Ava had already initiated all the necessary legal documents with her standard preternatural efficiency. Still, a little discomfort lingered over being away from her team.

When I was last in DC, I was focused on doing everything by myself, but now, I miss my team after being here for only a few moments.

Alison's Currus was on its way. The self-driving car would take her to the car rental company where she would collect a vehicle. As it was planned as a short trip, she might have been able to rely on taxis or rideshares, but she didn't like the idea. Flying also wasn't always practical, especially for long distances. When trouble arose, she needed to be able to deal with it quickly. If there was one lesson her father had drilled into her, it was that you could never know what might happen.

One example stood out. When she was younger, James had taken her to New York to see *Wicked*, and he stumbled upon a bank robbery during the trip. Dangerous incidents seemed to be drawn to people with the last name Brownstone.

She brought up the Currus app. The car was still five minutes away so it wasn't a terribly long wait.

Even if I don't master portals for years, I will eventually manage them. How different will things be then? Myna goes all over the world for noodles with hers.

A plump pixie flew up the street and lines of light streamed from her fingers and around five plastic bags all bigger than her.

I don't think I've ever seen a pixie that big before, but she seems like she's flying okay. That answers the question of whether the wings are more for show than to actually keep them in the air. Or wait, maybe she uses a spell to help counteract her weight but her wings still do most of the lifting.

Alison frowned as she worked through the various physiological and magical permutations that might explain the pixie's continued flight.

A gnome walked beside the pixie in a fedora and T-Shirt that read, **Go BIG or go home.**

"You'd starve to death if it wasn't for me," the pixie admonished him. Her voice was deep and gravelly as if she'd sucked on cigarettes all her life. "But what appreciation do I get? Absolutely none."

He shrugged. "We all appreciate you, Madge. Everyone says so all the time."

She scoffed. "Do they, hon? They're trying to make me pay for my own magazines."

Magazines? Does she have some sort of tiny e-reader? I don't remember if I ever saw any of the pixies at school reading magazines.

"We've worked together for ten years now." The gnome pointed a thumb at his chest. "You should know by now that honesty is part of the Big Gnome brand. You followed me after we moved on from all that craziness. You had a reason."

Madge chuckled. "I was bored and you look good in a fedora, hon. It's hard to resist a gnome in a nice hat."

The strange pair continued up the street. Their conversation faded with distance as it transitioned into something about the relative merits of particular donut shops in the greater DC area.

Alison couldn't help but laugh. A half-Drow princess stood on the street and waited for a car that used magic to drive itself while an overweight pixie who sounded like a chain smoker walked up the street debating appreciation with a gnome.

Sometimes, I love life. Plus, it's good to be reminded that Hana, Ava, Tahir, and Mason are pretty damned normal compared to what I could have.

She smiled as the waiter led her deeper into the restaurant. Her heart rate kicked up as she spotted a handsome blond man in an immaculate suit. She'd not been sure where they might eat, so she was glad she'd brought a nice cocktail dress that worked for their evening meal at the bistro.

The waitress gestured to the table. "Congressman Shephard's table, ma'am."

Luke stood and gave her a tight hug. "It's been too long. I know you're busy saving Seattle, but you had to run away right before I moved to DC. It's not fair, Alison."

The waitress departed with a polite nod.

Alison pulled away with a smile and took a seat across from Luke. "I didn't try to do that, and I should have visited with you more often when I was here. You were so close, but I just…"

"Got busy?" He flashed a charming smile. It had never been hard to understand what Izzie saw in him.

"We both did." She traced a finger over the rim of the glass of wine already in front of her and picked it up. "How were your first months of public service? I think I'd last exactly two days before I threw someone through a window."

Luke chuckled. "I've thought about that a few times, but if I had to sum it up, I'd say frustrating, annoying, fulfilling, and glorious."

"Not at all contradictory." She laughed.

"I have some nice committee assignments, but I'm still a junior congressman. I make a noise and push where I can, but it's an uphill battle. Not that I mind." Luke raised his wine glass. "I also know there are many eyes on me, so I try to be careful."

"You always were a fighter."

"How about a toast to old friends?"

"To old friends."

He clinked his glass against hers and took a sip. "I forgot to tell you. It's a tasting menu." He pointed to a small plate in front of her with two soup spoons filled with a small amount of smoked salmon coated with cream cheese. "Appetizer."

"Oh, that's great. I've kind of thrown myself into cooking these last few months," she confided.

"Really?"

Alison nodded. "It's a hobby between fighting Mountain Striders or megalomaniac billionaires."

"It's good to have hobbies."

She sipped at her wine before she popped the salmon in her mouth and carefully analyzed the flavors and textures as she chewed. "This is delicious."

"I've hit a lot of high-end restaurants since I started this job." Luke gave her a playful grin. "I've gone native and turned fancy."

"There's nothing wrong with a little self-improvement."

His smile seemed too forced, and it didn't reach his eyes.

Alison blinked and set her glass down. "Is something wrong?"

"How is she, Alison?" He sighed and gulped his wine. "I don't get letters like you do. I try not to think about her, but it's hard."

She averted her eyes. "It's not because she wanted to hurt you. But her situation is complicated. They're still hunting her and her mom."

"I know that, but it doesn't make it less hard. Sometimes, I lie down at night and close my eyes, and it's like I'm back there. We're all teens at the school." He shook his head. "Good memories and bad memories."

"For all of us," she whispered.

He sighed. "Yes."

"Izzie's doing well, Luke," Alison confirmed. "Yes, she's still on the run, but she's taken the fight to them more."

Luke leaned forward, his gaze penetrating and his eyes narrowed. "It's not only a letter for you, is it? You've seen her and not a year ago."

She took a deep breath. "Yes. We did some stuff together recently. It wasn't planned. I basically bumped into her on a job, and we were both doing the same thing."

"Fighting dark wizards?"

Alison nodded.

Luke gulped his drink again. "I'm not surprised. The minute I heard about all the dark wizard activity in Seattle, I thought to myself, 'I bet Alison and Izzie are up to their eyeballs in this.'" He set his glass down. "It makes me angry."

She sighed. "Luke, don't be like that."

Luke waved a hand. "I'm not angry at Izzie. How could I ever be? I'm angry that she has to live like that while these scumbag dark wizards continue to plot and undermine everything good that people work to build. They forced Izzie on the run, and they robbed Tanner of years of his life." His eyes turned yellow for a few seconds. "That's one of my pet issues in the House. I've reached across to the Senate, too, and tried to make everyone aware of the dark wizard threat. It's not easy, though. Some people are worried that too much emphasis on dark wizards will lead to a general anti-magic backlash." He snorted. "And others think it's merely an old shifter vendetta that I'm pushing."

"That's not fair." Alison frowned. "They are a threat."

"I don't care what people think my motivations are. I only care that they listen. I understand the anti-magic sentiment concern. After all that garbage you uncovered, many people on all sides are scared that something terrible will blow up, but we can't sit around and pretend there's no threat." He scoffed. "This is one time when the conspiracy theory is real." He sighed and shook his head. "Sometimes, I don't know, though."

"Don't know what?"

He looked up as a waiter arrived with plates of steamed mussels and set one down in front of each of the diners. "Thank you."

"Of course, Congressman." The waiter departed.

Luke turned back to Alison. "I don't know if I picked the right way to make the world a better place. Sometimes, I want to do what you do—kick ass a little more directly, especially when the moon's full."

"But without people like you, the overall situation will never change." Alison narrowed her eyes as another waiter glared at them while he refilled someone's wine glass. The wine soon overflowed and the woman in front of him frowned.

The waiter sneered at her and threw the bottle on the ground. It shattered and spilled its contents everywhere.

Why the hell did he do that?

Alison blinked as she looked up from the mess. The waiter had a wand out and pointed it directly at Luke's back.

"Luke, watch out!" she yelled.

The shifter pushed up, spun toward the source of Alison's concern, and knocked his chair over. The wizard fired a bright crackling blue orb toward him.

Luke threw his hand up and caught the orb. He grimaced, and his eyes turned yellow as he tightened his grip around the magical attack. A low growl escaped his mouth, and the energy orb disappeared in a shower of sparks.

People shouted in confusion and the diners nearby scrambled out of their seats and edged toward the exits.

He shook out his lightly burned hand and winced. "That might actually have hurt if it had got me in the back. Too bad. What's the problem?" he asked his attacker. "Did you want the other guy to win?"

The wizard gritted his teeth and held his wand pointed at the Luke. "Shifter scum. We should have hunted all of you down once you were no longer of use to us."

"Dark wizard, huh?" Alison stood and extended a shadow blade. "Surrender right now before someone gets hurt. There's no way you can win against both of us."

"Alison Brownstone." The man spat on the ground. He jerked his wand back and forth between Alison and Luke before he yanked a small tarnished bronze pyramid out of his pocket. He held it up with a grin. "You lose, Brownstone. You lose, Shephard."

Her jaw tightened. She'd seen a similar artifact used to annihilate a dark wizard safe house she'd raided after college. It was a nasty little explosive.

"If you set that thing off, you'll kill yourself, too," she commented.

"As long as I take one of you with me, I don't care," he shouted.

A thin glow streaked across the room and struck the man in the chest. Electricity arced through his body, and he collapsed, twitching, and the explosive slid out of his hand.

A woman screamed nearby, and the remaining customers and staff stampeded for the exit.

Alison spun toward the direction the knife had come

from. A pale woman in a black cocktail dress not all that different from hers stood beside a table on the other side of the room. She held a wand in her left hand and another glowing knife in her right. Their rescuer was around Alison's age, and they were similar in that they both had unusual hair. The other woman had shoulder-length black hair with blue stripes and prominent bangs.

"Are you all right, Congressman?" she called.

Her accent sounded odd to Alison. For a second, she thought it was Scottish before she decided it was English, but that didn't seem right either.

Luke eyed the knife dubiously. "I'd feel much better if you put that down."

"Of course." She slipped the knife into a purse on the table and set her wand down. "Is he dead? My friend over there?"

Alison crept toward the wizard and her gaze flicked between the man and the witch. "He's not breathing."

"From what you said, you understand what that little artifact was, right?" The woman nodded toward the body. "I couldn't take the chance that he'd kill all these innocent people. I think it's a tidy job I've done to save people's lives."

"Who are you?" Luke asked.

"My name is Drysi Jones." She blew out a sharp breath. "I won't lie to you. This mess is my fault. If I'd done my job, that fool would never have gotten near you."

"Your fault?" Alison frowned. "Why?"

"I'm what you might call a magical fugitive recovery specialist—the best in Wales, actually. I normally operate my firm out of Cardiff." Drysi gestured toward the dead man with disgust on her face. "That, right there, is a nasty dark wizard I've been hunting. I tracked him to this place, and I've had stupid meals here every night for a week while I waited for him to show his face. That gets expensive after a while."

"Magical fugitive recovery specialist?" Luke echoed with a smirk. "You're a bounty hunter."

Drysi looked pained. "Don't call me that. Bounty hunter sounds so American. It sounds like I'll get my six-shooter and meet you at high noon." She shook her head. "That doesn't matter. What I don't understand is why he suddenly decided to try to assassinate you, Congressman? Do you know him?"

He looked at the dead wizard and shook his head. "I've never seen him before in my life."

"That's unfortunate." She snatched her purse up and walked to the body where she knelt beside it. "I wanted to take this one alive. I hoped he could give up some of the others. With these dark wizards, where's there's one, there are always more. Nasty pieces of work."

"We've both tangled with dark wizards in the past," Luke admitted.

Drysi stared at him. "That might explain it then." She turned and peered at Alison. "And if I'm not mistaken, you're Alison Brownstone? I have to say you look taller on the news."

Alison shrugged. "Sorry?"

Sirens closed rapidly outside.

"It's no bother." The woman pulled her phone out of her purse. "Let's exchange numbers. I assume you two will get away from the local police sooner than I do because I'm the one who killed the man, and I've found your American police don't always trust foreign…recovery specialists. Given your recent dance with the dark wizards, Alison, we might be able to help each other."

Alison alternated her glances between the witch and the dead wizard. "So much for my low-key reunion."

Is this what Senator Johnston wanted to talk to me about? It can't be. There's no way he would have blown off an assassination attempt as not being important.

She fished her phone out of her purse. "Yeah, let's exchange numbers."

CHAPTER SEVENTEEN

Drysi's prediction proved correct. The police whisked Luke off for more questions and to arrange a security detail and released Alison within twenty minutes once they realized who she was and the fact that she hadn't been the one to actually kill the wizard. The Welsh bounty hunter, by comparison, seemed to take the long road to freedom, so Alison drove back to her hotel room.

Perfect. Just damned perfect. Johnston made it sound like it was no big deal, and that's what we already have to deal with? Why the hell wasn't someone guarding Luke?

Alison kicked her heels off once inside and dialed Senator Johnston. Someone needed to deal with her frustration, and he was the one who brought her to DC after he'd suggested she leave to begin with.

The old man answered with a laugh. "Good evening, Miss Brownstone. I was about to call you. I was just informed about the unfortunate incident. I'm pleased to hear that Congressman Shephard wasn't injured during the attack and that you prevented a major incident. The

PDA is checking the area carefully, but they haven't found anything other than the artifact that was on the dead man. Things could have been exceedingly nasty even with that, though."

"Why didn't you tell me dark wizards planned to assassinate Luke?" she demanded. "I've tried to convince myself that you didn't know, but you called me to DC to talk about dark wizards. The minute I show up, assassins blast magic at my friend and try to blow a restaurant up. A little more forewarning would have been appreciated."

"Calm down a moment, Miss Brownstone," the Senator replied, uncharacteristic concern in his voice. "I think you need to back up a minute and consider what you're saying."

Oh no, you don't. You won't politician-talk your way out of this, not after what just happened.

Alison snorted. "If you had told me this was their plan, I could have brought the whole team and we would have shaken down this whole damned city until we found them. We could have taken them out before they actually tried an attack." She paced furiously. "If I hadn't paid attention, Luke would be dead. And if that bounty hunter hadn't been so quick, a lot more people might have died."

She was tired of people yanking her chain.

"I understand all that." The senator cleared his throat. "Now, I have one question for you, and it's very important that you be as clear as possible because it will potentially affect many things going forward."

"What?" She frowned. "I'll take these dark wizards down. You don't have to ask that."

"No, that's not it. It's a more basic question. When did I allegedly call you back to DC?"

"What are you talking about? You called me a few days ago and told me to come here. You alluded to it being dark wizard related, but also said it wasn't an immediate concern, so I didn't have to rush." She stopped and glared at herself in the mirror so she would at least have somewhere to direct her ire. "I don't understand. Is this where you claim you don't have any recollection of that for when they make you testify before some committee?"

"I only wish that were the case, Miss Brownstone." He sighed. "Son of a bitch. I never called you."

"Yes, you did. It was your number in the caller ID. The same contact number you gave me when I left DC and it was your voice."

Alison's stomach knotted.

Oh, crap.

"No, I didn't," the Senator replied flatly. "And I guarantee you, if I were to call on you because I thought you could help me with dark wizards, it'd be when I'd exhausted my other resources and I thought there was an urgent need for you. I would have thought you understood that from my dealings with your father. I value the Brownstones as a resource, but you are all very disruptive to the status quo and you tend to make certain people nervous. If you recall, that's why I suggested you leave DC, to begin with."

She rubbed a hand down her face. "I can't believe it. I let the dark wizards set me up."

"It looks like that way. I'm concerned that your phone had my call identification, but I'm sure there are all kinds of ways to do that with magic."

"But why?" Alison furrowed her brow. "I don't even

think that wizard wanted to kill me. I think he tried to kill Luke."

"It is true there has been unusual dark wizard activity according to our sources over the last few weeks, and law enforcement are doing their best to keep an eye on them, but I never planned to call you about it." Senator Johnston coughed a few times. "The one thing that does puzzle me is that if it was dark wizards who pretended to be me, why would they have called you in? It'd be easier to assassinate Congressman Shephard without you here. To call in the world's best bodyguard is downright stupid. Maybe something went wrong or they were supposed to have more people."

She drew a few deep breaths and sat on the edge of the bed. "I should go back to Seattle."

"I know you're probably not inclined to want to listen to me given that the last man with my voice misled you, but I don't think that's a good idea," he replied. "If you don't believe it's me, feel free to come to my office and I'll tell you this face-to-face."

"If the dark wizards want me here, it's for a reason, and I doubt it's good." Her hand tightened around her phone. "Doing what they want is probably a bad idea. With my luck, it'll turn out that the Washington Monument is a prison for some ancient demon they're trying to free."

The man laughed. "To the best of my knowledge, it's only a monument, Miss Brownstone." Some of the mirth left his voice. "That said, this city has been here a while, and there are more than a few magical secrets best left in the history books. I have no idea if they are targeting any of them, but the PDA and the FBI can keep an eye on that. We can use you in a different way."

"Use me?" Alison scoffed. "I didn't agree to stay."

"I'd ask you if you would. Now that I'm sure the dark wizards want you here—and we also know they want to kill Congressman Shephard, but they had their big chance and failed—here's the thing, Miss Brownstone. If they want you here, it probably also means they'll try to kill you. They probably hoped to kill Shephard first, even if it cost their man his life."

"But why? I don't understand the plan."

Senator Johnston sighed. "I can't say for certain, but given their goals, this might be as much about terrorism as power. Killing a freshman congressman won't lead to them taking over the government but think it through. To kill a friend of yours right in front of you might have been about working your nerves before they finish you off later."

"They're welcome to try to kill me if they want," she exclaimed. "And they obviously don't understand what happens when people threaten my friends."

"That's the enthusiasm I hoped to hear," Senator Johnston responded and a thread of happiness worked its way back into his voice. "We need them to believe they still have the upper hand. We both know you're more than capable of handling yourself, and if you stay in DC, you'll make—and I'm sorry to put it this way—tempting bait for the dark wizards, a nice focus. That will help to provide the FBI and PDA more time to up their investigations and figure out what the hell those bastards' end game is."

Alison wrestled with her conflicting options. She wasn't sure if the dark wizards wanted her in DC or out of

Seattle. As a congressman, Luke now received personal protection, and as a shifter, he was hardly defenseless. But if there was even a slight chance that he might be killed, she didn't want to leave the city.

I won't let dark wizards take anyone else from me.

There was the possibility their adversaries might assault the Fremont Troll again. Even if she took the magic train, that might give it more than enough time to rampage.

The government has strengthened all the containment glyphs and Latherby says they have the site under constant surveillance. If that's their big plan, it'll be stopped with ease even if I'm not involved.

"What am I supposed to do if I do stay?" she asked.

"It would be nice if you minimized active investigation," the man explained. "I understand how that might chafe, but we have well-funded government agencies to check into this now."

"So you want me to simply sit in my hotel room and wait for someone to try to kill me? That sounds like a fun few days."

"I'm sure you'll find something to occupy your time other than dying," he replied affably. "Now, Miss Brownstone, I won't be too forthright because certain restrictions hold me back. However, I will note that if more incidents occur and certain people committing terrorism are stopped by you, most of us in the government won't exactly cry about it—even if, overall, it'd be best if these people were caught by law enforcement personnel."

Alison thought it over for a few seconds before she

sighed heavily. "It wouldn't hurt to stick around for a few days."

"That's the spirit. Now, if you'll excuse me, I need to push certain people to look for our favorite cockroaches. I'm sorry you were dragged into this, but I'm also grateful. Have a good evening, Miss Brownstone."

"Sure. I'll try."

The Senator ended the call.

She stared at her phone. Despite what he suggested, spoofing a phone call didn't even require magic. Imitating someone's voice—especially a high-profile public figure with decades of public experience—was also something that could easily be accomplished through either magic or technology.

I need to be more careful, but if the damned wizards want me here, then they have me. They'll regret bringing me here. If I have to end the dark wizard threat by killing them all one by one, I'll do it.

But I can't ignore the possibility they've planned something in Seattle. I've got friends. It's time to involve the team.

She dialed Mason.

"I knew I should have come," Mason muttered after she finished her explanation. "And probably Hana, too. Ava's still sorting through some of the recent new client offers, but from what she told me earlier, most of them could be handled by Jerry's team. Tahir might not be able to pull off his biggest infomancy stunts from home, but he can still work drones and remote support."

"No, you should stay in Seattle." Alison nodded firmly. "All of you. I need you to stay there."

He grunted his displeasure. "And let dark wizards take potshots at you, A? They already tried to blow you up."

"Technically, I think they tried to blow Luke up and I happened to be sitting close to him."

"Because that's so much better," he responded sharply. "The dark wizards are on the move in DC, which means we should be on the move there too. This isn't only about protecting you, A. It's also about using our resources in the best way possible."

"I understand that, but we have to be careful." She sighed. "We still don't know their plan. If it was to get me out of Seattle and we now pull everyone else, who knows what might happen?"

Mason chuckled. "The AET and PDA are still here, A. It's not like we're the only ones who fight bad guys in the entire city. Did you plan to never allow anyone to take a vacation ever again?"

"Again, I understand all that, but I also trust my gut. Whatever this whole plan is about, it didn't end with one dead dark wizard killed by a bounty hunter. Too many more of them are out there, and since they went through all the trouble to drag me into it, I take it personally. Tahir can check on things around there, and you guys can stay on standby in case he finds some nest you can raid." She threw the closet door open. "I'll stay here for a few days until I find out more."

"What's your plan?"

Alison grabbed some jeans she'd hung up earlier before she'd left for her dinner with Luke. "Tonight? Nothing. I'll ward this hotel room with the help of some of the glyphs Myna taught me and wait. Tomorrow, I'm not sure if I'll do much more than meet Luke and see if he has any leads. He might have something I can act on more quickly than the FBI or PDA."

"That sounds good. We'll push from our end and see what we can knock loose."

"Be careful."

He laughed. "Says the woman who is acting as dark wizard bait."

She snickered. "We all have our roles."

CHAPTER EIGHTEEN

Mason pushed into the darkened bar. Loud rock music blasted from the speakers as people huddled over the shoddy wooden tables to chat with one another over their beers. Low-level magic hung all around him, some obvious—such as the occasional glyph on a wall —and others less obvious, their source the patrons. He wouldn't have been surprised if everyone in the bar was a magical.

If I didn't know better, I would think they used magic to make that stench.

Extra warmth spread throughout his body from the enhancement spells he had cast prior to entering the bar. If tonight went well, he wouldn't need them, but considering whom he was about to visit, there was a good chance he might have to punch a few people.

This was probably a bad idea, but I might as well take advantage of the available resources.

A bouncer approached Mason. The man was a wall of muscle with a surprisingly good tailor given the excellent fit of his dark suit. "Have I seen you somewhere?" Faint magic emanated from his body. "You look very familiar."

Shield spell? Strength spell? I guess that's why he doesn't care about all the magic he must sense from me.

"I have one of those faces." Mason grinned.

"You think you're funny, asshole?" the other man snorted.

"Occasionally." His grin faded. "But that's not why I'm here."

"Then why are you here? I don't like the look of you, so maybe I'm gonna ask you to leave."

"But I hear that ravens like to collect shiny things on Tuesday," he replied evenly. "I have many shiny things to trade."

Last I heard, that was the passphrase, but maybe I should have checked first. The person he wanted to talk to was at the club, but he needed to find her and that would require the bouncer to get out of his face and send him where he needed to be.

The man stepped forward and did his best to loom over the other man.

Mason resisted the urge to laugh in his face. He'd stared down the Scourge of Harriken not all that long before and some club bouncer wasn't in the same league, even if he was a magical.

Come on, asshole. I don't have time for this crap. Let me through.

"Turn right at the end of the hallway, then the last door on the left," the thug muttered. "If you can't get in, don't come crying to me, and if you try anything..." He leaned forward to whisper into Mason's ear. "They'll never the find the body."

"You're a really happy guy, did anyone ever tell you that?" Mason stepped around him and headed toward the hallway. A few people glanced his way but no one appeared to pay him close attention or had their wands out. He saw no obvious Oricerans, but the dim lighting might conceal an elf or two in a corner. Of course, it was also possible that a few patrons used disguise spells.

The blaring rock music quieted slightly as he stepped into the hallway that led to the bathrooms. Following the bouncer's directions, he walked all the way to the end and turned into a narrower corridor lit by only a single bulb that hung from a chain in the middle. A faint tingle passed through his body. Someone had set up a detection ward and would know he was coming. The hallway dead-ended, with worn unmarked wooden doors to both the left and right.

It's the same as the last time I paid a visit, although it was a good thing that I asked around about the combination.

The wizard readied his wand and made several quick movements. A series of glyphs appeared on the door to the left. He pressed them in a particular order, the door clicked open, and he stepped inside.

Small light orbs illuminated the room but left deep shadows in several places. A single quartz stood in the center of the room with dozens of small differently colored vials arranged in neat rows atop it.

Different building, different room, but the same shit. Too bad. I'd almost hoped she'd changed.

A lithe, olive-skinned woman lounged on a white

leather couch in front of the table. Her body was covered by a loose orange dress, and a small diamond piercing adorned her nose. A jeweled choker highlighted her slender neck.

Two men stood on either side of her and both scowled and pointed their wands at Mason.

The woman gave him a coy smile, a hint of amusement in her eyes. "Now here's someone I never expected to see again, especially after the rather rude and hurtful speech you gave me when you left me."

"Hello, Raven," he replied.

She gestured to the table. "I would ask if you're here to buy something, but we both know you think you're too good for these." She sighed. "Which is unfortunate, as someone who's so fond of personal enhancement might get a lot of use out of them. You shouldn't be so closed-minded."

"I trust my own magic more than unstable potions made with questionable techniques and ingredients." He shrugged and offered her a lop-sided grin. "I make no apologies for that."

"Questionable techniques? How rude." Raven sat up and crossed her legs before she folded her hands in her lap. "But my, my, my. You have no idea how surprised I am to see Mason Lind stroll into a place where I sell my wares. I doubt you've come to throw yourself in front of me and apologize for your overly dramatic departure."

He shrugged. "That's an easy no."

"Of course it is," she scoffed. "Why are you actually here?"

"I have a few questions for you."

"A few questions?" She released a low, throaty laugh. "Did the little Drow bitch send you to me?"

Mason's face twitched and his smile vanished. "Don't call her that."

The woman's two guards glared at him as their fingers tightened on their wands.

"Oh, did that strike a nerve? Do you whisper all the things in her ear you used to whisper in mine?" Raven licked her lips. "And I'll call her what I want. I should have known you'd end up with someone like that. You're so predictable that it's pathetic."

"And what's that supposed to mean?"

He didn't care that much that the woman insulted him, but he wasn't sure he was willing to stand there while she insulted Alison.

"She calls herself a security contractor, but she seems to spend a huge amount of time eliminating gangsters and dark wizards." The woman smirked. "So you think I've forgotten all those drunken rants of yours about what you'd do to Galbrathians if you ever got your hands on them?"

"Those assholes blew up the kemana and killed a lot of people," Mason replied, his voice cold. "If you want to play the moral relativism game, fine, but don't act like I—or even you—are on the same level as them. They are damned psychos."

"Is that what the Dark Princess offers you?" Raven asked. "A chance to live out all your little fantasies of being a defender of justice? Too many years of working for the self-absorbed captains of industry left you feeling empty. We both know not every client you've protected has been a good person, but now, here comes the cute little half-Drow who runs around saving the city and hobnobs with the mayor. It's everything you always wanted." She sneered. "It's perfect for the man who left me simply because he refuses to face the dark truth of how broken our world is."

He narrowed his eyes. "There are lines people shouldn't cross. You didn't merely step over them. You backed up, sprinted, and jumped as far as you could and laughed the entire damned time."

The woman leaned forward and picked up a white vial, her movements languid. "Everyone knows the risk that comes with one of these. I don't force anyone to take them. I simply provide a product they tell me they want."

"And no one forces you to use dark magic when you make them, either," he replied. "I bet you don't tell every new client that."

"Even if I don't, do you think anyone believes my creations are pure? And dark magic?" Raven sighed dramatically. "You make it sound so sordid, Mason. I'm not taking over the world or blowing up kemanas. I simply take advantage of all the available tools to produce a product that other people will offer a lot of money for." She shook her head. "What's the point of you even stopping by tonight? To track me down and get past the door, you had to ask around for the combination. Or have you kept track of me? Does your heart still miss me?" Her gaze dipped. "Or does something else?"

Mason snorted. "Don't flatter yourself. A few people owed me favors. I didn't come to you before because I didn't need to. You and me will never happen."

"Never happen again, perhaps." Her cold smile made Mason's hands twitch.

"Don't screw with me if you know what's good for you."

The two guards grunted and raised their wands.

"You assholes had better put those down," he warned. "I'm tired of you pointing them at me, and I'm seconds away from knocking your asses out."

Raven grinned. "I'd like to see that. You always were ferocious. I appreciated that about you."

"Ferocious?" He ducked to the side. Two fireballs launched from the men's wands but his enhanced speed pulled him out of the line of fire in an instant. The attacks exploded against the brick walls and left scorch marks although they didn't start a fire.

Mason leapt over the couch and tackled both guards. All three men landed hard but his two strengthened punches knocked the guards unconscious as their heads smashed against the hard floor. He stood and kicked their wands away with a frown.

Raven hadn't moved during the entire altercation but now, she clapped lightly. "You didn't kill them, did you? It's hard to find decent help."

He stood and shook his hand out. "They're still breathing."

"Will you kill me now, Mason? For playing around with forbidden magic?" She gave him a thin smile. "Is that what your Dark Princess commands? I imagine she can't satisfy you like I used to."

"Shut up," he snapped. "If you don't want her to come sniffing around you, help me out and give us both a reason to believe you're not actively helping the dark wizards. I know you don't give a shit about what they are doing, but after the Fremont Troll, I'd figure even you would realize that they can't be allowed to do whatever they want. It's not like that thing was careful about what it destroyed. Nihilism won't prevent you from dying."

Raven lay on her stomach on the couch and batted her eyelashes. "Have you ever thought about it, Mason? One night. To feel some of that old passion?"

Mason scoffed and shook his head in disbelief. "Are you kidding me?"

"It's a valid question."

"And the answer is no." He glared at her.

Raven's smile only grew as if she enjoyed his anger. She always did when they were together.

What did I ever see in her?

"I'd never betray Alison." He scowled. "And I left you behind a long time ago, so stop with this crap and listen to me. Right now, I'm trying to figure out if there's some tiny part of you that still cares about something or someone other than yourself. Or at least cares enough about yourself to help us stop another dark wizard plot that might lead to many people getting killed."

"And what am I supposed to tell you? Hmm? I find dark wizards as dreary as what you've become. Delusions of power and glory and a foolish belief that they can control the path of the future." Raven sat up slowly and ran a hand up her thigh and over the side of her chest. "All we can hope for is what we have in the here and now. You're right, Mason. To destroy a city to make some sort of point is idiotic."

"Then help me." Mason took a few deep breaths and

wiped the sweat off his brow. He wasn't about to lower his spells to avoid the small heat inconvenience, not until he was out of the building. There might be a few more thugs waiting to take their shot. "We know there's some sort of dark wizard plan going on."

Maybe there is nothing going on in Seattle and it's all in DC, but if there is, there's no way Raven hasn't heard at least some hint of it.

She stared at Mason with a heavy-lidded gaze. "You haven't told your Dark Princess about me, have you? Are you ashamed?"

He snorted. "I don't need to tell Alison about every woman I dated in the past."

"You don't need to, or you're afraid to?" A mischievous grin spread over the woman's face. "Too embarrassed to tell the little self-righteous Drow about the kind of women you've been with? Are you worried she'll think less of you?"

"I don't have time for this crap." He strode toward the door. "If I find out you knew something, I'll be back, and I'll be far less polite."

"Abel Ortiz," Raven called.

He stopped at the door and looked over his shoulder. "Who?"

"If there's something going on, he might have heard something. He had last time." Raven sighed, a bored expression on her face. "I don't care what the Galbrathians or any other dark wizards do to anyone else, but you're right. Destroying kemanas and freeing the Fremont Troll show a certain disregard, even indirectly, for my life." She lifted a thin blue vial and spun it around two fingers. "But I also try my best to stay far away from the kind of wizards who might attract the attention of overzealous Drow vigilantes and their pets. Abel might be able to help you, but you'll have to convince him to do so."

"And how do I do that?" Mason asked.

"That's for you to figure out." Raven stopped twirling the potion and pulled the top off the vial. She put it under her nose and inhaled deeply. "Worrying about the future is pointless, Mason. It might never come. You should enjoy the now." She upended the vial and gulped down the thick blue liquid inside.

A few seconds later, her eyes turned solid black and she gasped, shuddered, and moaned. A cerulean light suffused her skin.

He grimaced, hurried out of the room, and slammed the door behind him.

Hana leaned back in her office chair, her legs up on her desk. Alison might not let her do it in the conference room, but no one could complain about what she did in her own space. A girl needed a little leg-desk time in the morning. There was something powerful about using a desk as a footrest.

Is this what it means to be drunk on power? If so, it's not so bad.

Mason leaned against the back wall, his arms folded. "How is the kid doing?"

"She's fine. Tahir has her setting up a workstation in his

office right now. She's excited, even if she's still pretty nervous about us."

"Given what she's been through, it's not surprising that she doesn't trust adults."

The fox smirked. "Are you freaked?"

Mason looked confused. "Freaked by what?"

"Your girlfriend has a kid now." She cackled.

"Very funny." He allowed himself a smile before he returned to the reason he'd come that morning. "Did Tahir mention anything about Ortiz? He never responded to me. I wanted to talk to him, but you know how he can be when he thinks anyone but Alison is riding him."

Hana lowered her legs and straightened. "Oh, that's because he didn't need to. Sorry, I assumed we'd talk in the morning so I never sent you a message."

"What are you talking about?"

She smiled and shrugged. "I know Abel Ortiz—or know of him, anyway. I was surprised to hear he might be mixed up with dark wizards—although also not surprised at the same time."

"Why is that?" Mason pushed off the wall and stepped in front of the desk.

"He's a weirdo and runs a magical fight club. You're allowed to use inherent abilities or passive spells, but once the fight begins, no wands or spells are allowed. You're not supposed to try to kill the other person, either, but if a fighter doesn't kill too many people, he doesn't care if it happens now and then." Hana rolled her eyes. "He's really into the idea that you don't know a person's true nature until you've seen them fight."

The wizard snorted and looked away. "She could have mentioned that last night."

"She?" His companion grinned and leaned forward, her face alight with interest at the pronoun revelation. "You never told me that this contact of yours was a woman."

"What difference does it make? We all have many different contacts." His shoulders stiffened.

Hana studied him speculatively. "It makes a difference when you're trying to hold something back, and every instinct in me tells me that's what you're doing."

"I'm not trying to hold anything back." Mason's jaw tightened.

Why is he so tense just because I zeroed in on the fact that it's a woman? Oooh.

"We all have pasts, Mason." The fox smiled. "But here's a little friendly advice from a woman with a past. Alison isn't an idiot. She knows you've dated women before her."

He groaned. "How about we finish this conversation and go back to Ortiz? Do you know how to find him?"

"Abel? Sure. He's not exactly hard to find but I didn't do much fighting until I worked for Alison, so he's never someone I hung out around." She pushed out of her chair and straightened her cream top with a tug at the sides. "We'll need to change into outfits we don't mind getting blood on."

Mason gave her a confused look. "Do you think he'll attack us?"

"I think if we want to get anything out of him, we'll have to play in his little fight club." She shrugged like she'd merely suggested a trip to an ice cream parlor.

CHAPTER NINETEEN

Mason was surprised when he stepped into the massive gym and looked around. He'd expected something seedy and dark, not a brightly lit boxing ring surrounded by rows of chairs on every side. For an underground illegal fight club, the place looked remarkably innocuous.

Maybe it gets seedier at night.

Hana walked beside him. Even though he understood her reasoning for changing into gray sweats, it was hard to take her seriously when her sweatshirt had a giant cartoon unicorn with huge eyes on it and the caption, **I BELIEVE IN YOU**.

A bald, scarred man in a pinstripe shirt stood in front of the ring and watched two Kilomea trade quick jabs with a soundtrack of grunts. He frowned and shook his head after a few exchanges of blows.

"That's him," the fox whispered. "I've never talked to him before, but I've seen him from a distance at a few bars."

"He's a wizard. I doubt you'll be able to pull your charm without him noticing."

She shrugged. "Your ex-girlfriend is the one who sent us here. You take lead."

"I never said Raven was…forget it."

"Be careful in tonight's fights," Ortiz yelled. "I don't mind the occasional guy dying but killing people all the time makes things too predictable. It throws the betting off."

A Kilomea nodded with another grunt before he scowled in Mason and Hana's direction. The opponents folded their massive arms and glared at the newcomers.

Oritz looked over his shoulder at Mason. "Can I help you?" His gaze shifted toward Hana and he scoffed when it settled on her T-shirt.

"You're Abel Oritz, right?" Mason asked.

"Maybe. Who wants to know?" Abel fluffed his lapels before he withdrew a thin black wand from his jacket. He lowered it to his side and eyed Mason with open suspicion.

"My name's Mason Lind. And this is my associate Hana Sugimoto." He offered the man an easy smile. "I was told by someone that you could perhaps answer a few questions for me."

"You were told by someone I could answer some questions for you? That's interesting. Very interesting." Oritz pointed to locker room doors in the distance and then nodded to the Kilomea. "You two take a break while I talk with my new friend Mason. I'll call you if I need you."

The Oricerans nodded before they clambered over the ropes and jumped to the floor with an echoing thud. They headed away but directed the occasional scowl Mason's way.

The club owner waited until they'd stepped out of the room to approach Mason, his fingertips white from the pressure on his wand. "Who sent you? Tell me the fucking truth or we're done here—and it might get nasty even without those fighters I sent away."

Mason shrugged. "Raven."

"I should have known. That bitch." Ortiz snorted. "So why are Alison Brownstone's lackeys sniffing around me?"

The team exchanged concerned glances.

Ortiz scoffed. "You two are kidding yourself if you think people don't know your names by now. That's not a bad thing, necessarily, at least in my case. The Dark Princess kicks ass. She's proven her true nature again and again." He frowned. "The only thing I don't get is why she cares about what I do. I don't cause trouble with my fights. People die, but they know what they sign up for. There's no innocent blood spilled in my ring."

"This isn't about you," Mason clarified. "It's like I said. Raven said you could answer a few questions for us. If we come to some agreement, we'll leave you alone."

Some of the tension left the man's face. "What's it about then?"

"Raven said you might have information on dark wizards. We don't care where you got it or how you know it. We merely want it. Assuming you don't get in our way when we eliminate them, we'll have no problems."

The man looked from one to the other, a hungry curiosity in his expression. "And what will you give me for it?"

"We can pay you," Hana offered.

He shook his head and pointed at her. "No—you. I want you."

Mason tensed.

Hana rolled her eyes. "Please. You wouldn't know what to do with me if you got me, big boy."

"I don't want to sleep with you." Ortiz snorted. "I stopped having sex years ago." He tapped his forehead. "It's the only way a man can have true focus. He finds his soul in the ring and he gains a focus, and only then does he become a real man."

Hana furrowed her brow in annoyance. "Then what the hell are you talking about?"

"I've heard about you two," the club owner explained and his gesture encompassed them both. "The life wizard bodyguard and the nine-tailed fox. I bet if Lind fought here, he could become a champion, but you, little girl… you're merely some street-rat con artist Brownstone picked up. People say the only reason you can fight is because she gave you a bunch of artifacts. Being a fox means you're good at fucking with people's minds but not much more."

Her tails and claws appeared and the tails stood rigid. "I can do okay even without artifacts. Ask the Eastern Union."

A wide smile crept onto Ortiz's face. "That's what I like to see. The hunger. The desire to prove yourself in the only way that truly matters." He pointed to the ring. "Knock out one of my guys, and I'll tell you what you want. I have the perfect guy for you, Sugimoto. The only thing is I can't guarantee you won't get fucked up."

She squared her shoulders. "Bring it on."

He chuckled. "Good. Come back in two hours."

When they returned, a huge shoeless and shirtless man in boxing trunks stood in the center of the ring and chatted with Ortiz.

Hana's heart kicked up in anticipation. Her months of training with Alison were about to pay off in a way she'd never anticipated.

"Are you sure about this, Hana?" Mason whispered. "You don't have to do it. I'm sure I can convince him to give it up if I fight some of his champions or something like that."

The fox scoffed. "Have a little faith, Mason. I need the shields to survive getting shot, not a few punches. Alison's helped me become tougher, but it's not like I was never in a fight before I met her."

He withdrew a healing potion from his pocket. "I have a couple, just in case."

"Save them for the other guy." Hana gave him a thumbs-up. "I've definitely got this."

They closed on the ring. Ortiz climbed over the ropes and hopped to the ground, an almost jolly smile on his face. "This is my man Taylor. He's agreed to fight Sugimoto."

The fighter turned and narrowed his eyes on Hana. They flashed yellow. "They say you can turn into a fox."

A shifter, huh?

She smiled sweetly. "I can."

Okay, so it'll take more than a few punches, but I can still do this. I'll be faster than him.

Mason frowned but remained silent.

"Foxes don't last long in fights with wolves." Taylor sneered.

Hana rolled her eyes. "You've fought a nine-tailed fox before?"

"I'm talking about nature, little girl."

She grinned wickedly. "Stranger things happen all the time in nature."

Mason frowned. "This is only to knock-out or submission, right?"

"Eh." Ortiz shrugged. "Accidents happen. If she doesn't want to fight, that's fine. You can both leave, but if you want anything out of me, I want to see this fight."

The fox shook her head and approached the ring. "No, I definitely want to show Fido here a thing or two." She rolled under the ropes and summoned her tails and claws. "Unlike wolves, foxes were never domesticated."

"Last chance to give up, fox," Taylor announced. "After that, I'm gonna have to make you feel a little pain, first. Don't worry. I won't kill you, but I can't say I won't mess that pretty face of yours up." He looked at her unicorn sweatshirt. "And I'll get blood all over that unicorn."

"Good. He loves blood." Hana backed away from him and spread her legs slightly before she raised her claws. "Blood makes his horn grow longer."

"I know all about you, and you know what I think?" the shifter asked and raised his fists. "I think you're used to hiding behind the Dark Princess. I know your type. You think you're the shit because you hang out with the *big dog*, but you're nothing but a yapping little pile of shit." He charged and threw a few quick punches.

He was fast but not as fast as Hana with her tails. She ducked and weaved and effectively frustrated his attempts to land a strike.

What the shifter lacked in speed, he made up for in persistence. His advance was relentless and forced her back with each attack.

I need to find an opening. He's stronger than me, but I'm faster and there are no rules.

Hana turned to flank him and left herself open for a brief moment. A powerful left hook cracked her in the side of the head. Stars filled her vision as she crashed painfully and bounced on the ring floor with a groan.

Taylor slammed his foot into her stomach. "Does your unicorn like your own blood?"

The fox hissed in pain and clutched her stomach as her tails swayed. Her heart thundered and her vision swam.

"Hana," Mason yelled. He rushed forward but stopped at Ortiz's upraised palm.

"She can give up any time she wants. This isn't some Colosseum death match." Ortiz grinned and turned toward the ring. "Do you give up, Sugimoto? No dishonor in admitting someone's stronger than you. The fight is what's important, not the victory."

Taylor snorted and stepped away. "Some shifter. You're pathetic."

Hana growled and pushed to her feet. "I'm not a damned shifter. I'm a nine-tailed fox." She crooked a claw. "Let's see what you've really got, wolf boy."

"Fine, bitch. I've been nice, but if that's what you want."

He shifted instantly into a huge wolf and lunged at her but a quick sidestep saved her from his massive jaws. She raked his side with her claws and he howled with pain as his blood sprayed in a quick red arc.

There we go.

The wolf rounded on her and blood dripped from his side as he snarled menacingly.

Hana watched him intently. Her stomach and head still throbbed from the shifter's earlier blows. She'd managed an effective return attack, but the fight was far from over. "I don't need to be a shifter. I only need to be one hundred percent authentic Hana Sugimoto to beat your sorry ass."

Taylor bounded forward, but he stopped and changed direction after a few feet and caught her as she tried to escape his charge. The wolf bit deep into her side.

Fiery agony exploded from the wound and she screamed in pain.

Have...to...keep...focus.

She growled loudly but the wolf's large maw tightened on her. Somehow, she gritted her teeth, ignored the pain, and raked at his face to shred it with several quick slashes.

Taylor released her and staggered back, half-blind. He shifted into his human form and collapsed to his knees to hold his face and groan in pain

The fox lunged at him and her pulse pounded in her ears and pain seared through her body with each beat of her heart. She retracted her claws and launched a flurry of nearly blurred punches. Blow after blow thudded into the man's head until he finally fell sideways with a thud, unconscious.

I win, wolf.

She took a few steps before she fell to her knees and clutched her wound. Her breathing ragged, she blinked in an attempt to clear her vision, but darkness grew at the edges. She felt oddly nauseous and lightheaded.

Mason scrambled into the ring and handed her a healing potion.

She downed it and pointed to Taylor. "Give him one, too," she rasped. "I have a feeling Ortiz doesn't care what happens."

Her teammate nodded and fished out the other potion. He rolled the battered and slashed shifter over, opened his mouth, and emptied the healing potion down this throat.

The club owner chuckled. "He was going to die. What a waste."

Hana took several deep breaths as the pain ebbed and her wounds sealed. Taylor's injuries also vanished, but he remained unconscious. The only permanent casualty was her unicorn sweatshirt.

Ortiz clapped. "I didn't expect you to win, Sugimoto. Well done."

Several other fighters emerged from the locker room, including the two Kilomea from earlier. They frowned when they spotted Taylor on his back.

"Come back tomorrow morning at 9:00, and we'll chat about what you're interested in." Ortiz gestured around the room. "There are too many people here right now to talk, and what we need to discuss should remain private."

The Brownstone team made their way out of the ring. Neither spoke until they were almost out of the building.

"I miss my shield artifacts," she muttered. "That hurt

like hell." She touched her exposed side gingerly through the hole in her sweatshirt.

"That was a dangerous gamble," he replied. "If you were killed there, Alison would probably have burned this whole place down, starting with me."

Hana winced. "She has a lot on her mind. If we get something useful from Ortiz, maybe we don't tell her how we got it."

Mason looked over his shoulder as the one of the Kilomea threw Taylor over his shoulder and glared at them. "I think that's a good plan."

CHAPTER TWENTY

Alison strolled down the hallway toward Luke's office. Two Capitol Police officers stood on either side of his open door and both watched her with suspicion and their hands on their guns. She raised an eyebrow at the anti-magic deflectors around their necks.

Apparently, they've taken the threat seriously. That makes me feel a little better, at least.

She smiled politely at the two men. Among other things, she'd inherited her father's respect for law enforcement and the difficulties they faced in a world where so many criminals now had access to magical power. Being more common didn't make magic easier to handle, and even in the centuries ahead when the gates fully opened, there would still be more non-magicals on Earth than magicals.

What we do now will set everything up for the future. If I live as long as Myna, how weird will things seem in only a hundred years?

"Come on in, Alison," Luke called from behind his

massive desk. He studied something on a tablet in front of him.

The guards relaxed at his acknowledgment and their hands drifted away from their guns.

Alison nodded at both of the officers before she stepped inside the office. A large American flag hung on the wall with framed pictures on the other side. Most seemed to be Luke with packmates, family, other congressmen or politicians, and even a few actors and singers who had supported his campaign. There was one where he smiled beside Nadina, the two worlds' highest-profile Light Elf pitmaster.

More pictures sat on his desk, including a small framed one of Izzie. From the look of it, she was probably seventeen in the picture. It was a keepsake of a simpler time when they were all still together.

Oh, Luke.

"Please close the door," he asked. He set the tablet aside.

Alison did so and took a seat opposite him. "Thanks for agreeing to see me. I'm sure you're busy with all the crap related to the assassination attempt." She chuckled darkly. "No one cares when people try to kill me. Then again, I tend to kill those people. Self-correction, I guess."

"Exactly. If dark wizards show up, it makes sense to ask you to come, not push you away." He managed a playful grin. "And we both know this isn't the first time I've been in danger."

"That makes too much sense." She thought it over for a moment. As much as she was worried about Seattle, nothing involving dark wizards had happened there for two months, but Luke had just been attacked. "Has

Senator Johnston talked to you about our phone call last night?"

"Senator Johnston?" He frowned and shook his head. "I've talked to him a few times about some of the anti-dark-wizard funding measures I've tried to push, and I know he's knee-deep in many projects that people like me aren't even allowed to know exist, but we don't talk much otherwise. Why? Does he know something about what's going on?"

Alison drew a deep breath. "He's the reason I originally came to DC. He called me a few days ago—or, at least, I thought he did."

"I don't understand."

"The thing is, it turns out the call I thought was from him didn't come from him. Someone pretended to be him. Whoever it was even suggested I meet you."

Luke frowned. "What? I don't get it."

"I think dark wizards purposefully tried to bring me here and put the two of us together." She shrugged. "My tech guy has done his thing and he traced it to a burner phone left at a hotel in Georgetown. The PDA has already recovered the phone, and a contact of mine in there has let me know it's a dead-end, even with magic. I'm sorry, Luke. I didn't mean to drag you into a mess, especially when you're still getting established as a congressman."

"You have nothing to apologize for, Alison." He leaned back, his attention focused on his desk for a few seconds before he looked up. "Blaming yourself is crap, and you know it. We've both fought dark wizards in the past, and I've made getting the FBI and PDA resources to fight them one of my main causes in Congress. You didn't drag me into anything, Alison. I jumped in while howling, and I knew full well the kind of attention and enemies I might bring down on myself."

She laughed at the image of Luke leaping into a pool while he howled and waved an anti-dark-wizard banner. "If you say so."

"I do." Luke shook his head. "The thing is, I wish I could actually jump in."

"How so?"

He pointed to his suit. "I wear the nice clothes all the time. I go to meetings and I talk with staffers. We all sit around and try to craft law to make this country a better place. That's useful, of course, but it's constraining." He sucked in a breath. "When the enemy pokes me in the eye and challenges me directly, it makes me want to shift and go after them. I want to fight against them directly like the old days, but I'm a respectable member of Congress now, not some young shifter who can do whatever he wants. I'm also fully aware of how bad a reputation shifters have in general among the non-magical. It doesn't matter if it's not fairly deserved."

"They have the FBI, Capitol Police, and PDA all looking into this," Alison assured him. "You don't need to handle it yourself. That's one of the advantages of being one of the men in power, right? You don't have to get your hands dirty."

"I've read about your company. You have employees, yet here you are, looking into it."

"It's not that I'm looking into it." Her laugh was a little nervous. "I'm simply not...not looking into it." She nodded, satisfied with her not so brilliant response.

"Even though you don't have a client?" Luke raised an eyebrow. "You're not law enforcement. You're not obligated to look into someone trying to assassinate a congressman."

"First of all, I never claimed to only care about money. Second, this isn't any random assassination attempt. It's a dark wizard conspiracy. Third, you're my friend." Alison shrugged. "So I'm sniffing around a little with the help of my people, both here and in Seattle. I even might call that bounty hunter. I hope she didn't get arrested. I haven't tried to contact her yet since I wasn't sure how I would handle this situation."

He shook his head. "They released her with no charges and thanked her for her intervention, from what I heard, but unfortunately for her, it wasn't a dead-or-alive bounty, so she won't get any money out of it. Apparently, she wasn't that happy."

"I can imagine. That sucks for her, but it's not the end of the world. If she gives me some useful information, maybe I'll pay her a finder's fee or something. She saved a lot of people's lives, including yours. I'm not sure I'd have been able to throw a shield around you quickly enough."

A wistful look crossed Luke's face as his gaze dropped and focused on the picture of Izzie. "Any assassination attempt you can walk away from can't be that bad."

Alison waited a few seconds before she flicked her hand in the direction of the picture. "That's an interesting decoration."

"Things have changed since those days." He raised his eyes. "Pictures help me remember things, especially when I get busy and trapped in political bullshit. Daily reality quickly stacks up. I only took office in January, and it already feels like I've done this for years."

She shrugged. "A little focus on the here and now isn't a bad thing."

"Sure, but sometimes, I wonder if I should have tried to go with Izzie—maybe met up with her later."

Alison sighed. "You can't beat yourself up like that. She didn't want everyone around her to be on the run, too. No one knew she would run like this for so long, but she did what she did both to protect herself and to protect the people around her." She clenched her hand into a fist. "The more we can find out about dark wizards and not let them call the shots, the closer we get to Izzie not having to run anymore. They involved us in this fight years ago, and that's on them. They should have stayed the hell away from Izzie and the School of Necessary Magic."

Luke nodded slowly. "You're right. It doesn't matter what I wanted in the past. It matters what happens now. I have to do my best in the position I'm in, including my speech."

"Speech?" Alison searched her memory and came up empty. "I haven't really paid much attention to the news lately. What speech?"

"I have a speech coming up at the Lincoln Memorial. It's on magical and anti-magical unity. They want me to cancel it because they're worried about another assassination attempt, but I refused. If we give in to fear and let the dark wizards control our actions now, we might as well give up and let them run things. I might not be able to go off and have adventures with you like when we were teens, but I can certainly give a damned speech. We both know I can be good at running my mouth off when I need to."

She grinned. "I'll do everything I can to help track these guys down, Luke. You have my word."

"Thanks. I'm glad to have you back in town, even if the circumstances are obnoxious."

I swear to you, Izzie. I might not be able to end this right now, but between this and the Fremont Troll, I know we need to start taking the fight to the dark wizard families. We need them to be the ones running and hiding.

CHAPTER TWENTY-ONE

Hana examined the blue metal door in front of her. A. ORTIZ was stenciled in dark letters near the top on a brass nameplate. When they'd arrived at the time he'd suggested, they didn't find him in the ring. Instead, a janitor directed them down the hallway to Ortiz's office.

The place seemed deserted, and she was a little disappointed that Taylor wasn't around for some post-fight trash talk.

Would that have caused trouble? I don't know, but at least that wolf will know not to think he's automatically better than a fox the next time he runs into one.

Mason looked back and forth down the hallway. "If this was intended as some sort of trap, they would have sprung it already. I was a little suspicious that he didn't talk right away, which is why I set up all the spells."

The fox knocked on the door. "Everything I've heard about this guy says he doesn't screw people like that although he's a nasty fighter himself when he wants to be." She glanced at the crystal ring on her hand for reassurance.

"Who's there?" the club owner called from inside.

"It's Hana and Mason," she responded. "You didn't say anything about us calling ahead."

"Come in. Let's make this shit quick. I'm in the middle of something."

Hana opened the door.

His office was spartan with a few metal chairs set up around a green metal folding table. A few locked cabinets reeked of strong magic, and Hana wondered what might be inside. The fight promoter sat at the table in front of an open laptop, a slight look of annoyance on his face.

I wouldn't mess with us too much. I kicked your guy's ass, and Mason's ready to go.

"Close that shit behind you." He drew his wand slowly from his jacket. "We need to make sure there are no eavesdroppers unless you have a problem with that?" He narrowed his eyes and looked at the other man, perhaps sensing the spells on him.

Mason closed the door behind them and shook his head. "That's fine with us. We don't want any trouble. We merely want to know what you've heard."

Hana shrugged.

Ortiz murmured the spell and made a few quick movements with his wand. The walls shimmered for a brief moment. "Fucking Raven. She acts like it's no big deal to open her mouth about what I might know. I thought she knew to keep her mouth shut."

The fox suppressed her smirk. She had no idea if Ortiz knew about Mason and Raven's shared past, but that explained why she might give him information she might otherwise be more inclined to keep to herself.

"Well, she told me," Mason responded. "And you made a deal. Hana complied with your terms. Will you back out now?"

"My word is my bond, bodyguard boy." Ortiz's lips curled in a sneer, and both men stared at each other in silence for several seconds before the promoter pointed at Hana. "But before we get into that shit, I wanted to ask you if you're interested in fighting at all. There's good money to be made by a hot chick who can fight well, especially when she can tear people up like that."

"I'm not a big fight club kind of gal." She shrugged. "I didn't even want to hurt your guy that much, but he tried to bite me in half and forced me to."

"You could have fooled me the way you shredded him. That went beyond trying to get away." Ortiz chuckled. "Trust me. I've done this for a long time. I know killer instinct when I see it. I don't know if it's because of that fox shit or not, but I liked what I saw."

"I kill people on jobs if I have to, but that's different. I'm simply not interested in fighting bouts for money."

"Your loss." The man looked genuinely disappointed. "If you're ever interested, give me a call."

She responded with a shallow nod and realized she had never thought much about whether she had a killer instinct. For most of her life, she tried to avoid open physical confrontation using her powers and personality, and when that failed, she ran.

It wasn't as if she'd never hurt anyone, but she couldn't remember killing anyone prior to having to deal with the Eastern Union.

Alison has turned me into such an ass-kicker I don't even think about it anymore. Huh.

She grinned at the thought. *Does borrowed killer instinct count?*

Mason frowned slightly at her before he turned to Ortiz. "We held up our end of the bargain. So now it's your turn. It's simple. We don't care how or why you have the information, but we need to know if you know anything about any dark wizard plans right now in Seattle."

"Fair enough." He closed his laptop and sighed. "Fucking dark wizards. It'd be better for everyone if they all moved to some island together so they can play at that superiority shit without blowing cities up around them and causing trouble. They used to merely be annoying." He scoffed. "I never took any of that shit seriously with Galbraith back in the day. I figured it was nothing more than heavy talk, but then they blew the kemana up."

"Do you know something or not?" Mason snapped.

"Patience, bodyguard boy. Too much stress is bad for the heart."

Hana grabbed one of the metal chairs and turned it. She straddled the chair and set her arms on the back. As an aware wizard, charming Ortiz would be risky, but if he didn't give up anything useful, she might have to take the risk.

He muttered something under his breath before he took a deep breath and looked from one to the other. "Okay. I have a friend who likes to deal in magical artifacts with a focus on a clientele that consists mostly of less than reputable people." He shrugged. "I'm not one to judge, and he does well for himself, so what can I do?"

"Do these less than reputable people include dark wizards?" she asked.

"Only respectable criminals, not self-righteous assholes. He told me once he doesn't like their attitudes."

The Brownstone duo chuckled.

"This friend apparently heard from another friend who has…less scruples, shall we say," Ortiz continued. "This other asshole does occasionally deal magical artifacts to dark wizards. They might be assholes, but they have access to a lot of money. And this friend of a friend, he said that the Fremont Troll was a big trick."

"How the hell was it a trick?" Mason blinked in surprise. "It wasn't only Alison there fighting that thing. AET was there, and there were hundreds of eyewitnesses on site and thousands of eyewitnesses from farther away, and that's before you even consider the drones. The PDA was involved in strengthening the containment spell. This wasn't some big illusion."

"You misunderstand me." The club owner shook his head. "I'm not saying a trick as in it didn't happen. I'm saying it was a huge distraction from something else they were doing."

Bile rose in Hana's throat, and her stomach flip-flopped. "Releasing an ancient Oriceran monster of mass destruction was only a *distraction?* What kind of crazy-ass plan involves using something like that as a diversion?"

"Yeah. The way he tells it, the problem is that these dark wizards hate having to keep things on the down low, especially these old family types who think they should run the world. It's easy to get them to talk if you give them a little encouragement. They want to rant and rave at you about how special they are—much like Scott Carlyle does during his trial." Ortiz snorted. "What a douchebag. Brownstone should have simply wasted his ass when she had the chance."

Hana nodded, not convinced the man was wrong.

Mason folded his arms. "Okay, so if the Fremont Troll was the distraction, it's as Hana asked. What's the actual plan?"

"I don't know that. I'm not a dark wizard." The promoter shrugged, an apologetic look on his face. "If I did know, trust me, I'd let you know so you could stop whatever stupid bullshit they're cooking up. All I know is that this friend of a friend, he said it's part of a long play—something they've worked on for a lot longer than anyone thinks. It has something to do with Seattle. He said the guy even hinted that it had something to do with why the kemana was destroyed."

Hana's jaw tightened. It was bad enough that her parents had been killed in the terrorist incident, but that the dark wizards still tried to benefit from the grandiose destruction and mass murder was like spitting on their graves.

"What else?" she asked, a slight tremble in her voice. "What else did he say?"

Ortiz narrowed his eyes with a slight frown. "That's it. I'm no info broker. I only hear a few interesting things now and again because of the circles I run in. I share them with a few people, but maybe I should share them less with Raven." His gaze flicked to Mason. "I'm surprised someone like you even deals with someone like her. I know Brownstone likes to play it fast and loose with some of the scum she talks to when hunting, but Raven's bad news. There's nothing worse than a person who doesn't give a shit. With her, it's not even about being the best she can be in the now." Disgust settled over his face.

The fox rolled her eyes. "You also talk with her."

"True, but sometimes a fighter is desperate," Ortiz explained. "He wants another edge. She can provide that. It's one thing to mess yourself up for no reason, but it's another to take a risk to reach your true potential."

What a load of self-serving crap.

"Even if it cripples them or kills them?" Mason scowled.

"Everyone dies in the end, bodyguard boy. Even the oldest little damned gnome will someday shrivel up and die. Ashes to ashes. Dust to dust. If a man wants to find his actual limits, who am I to judge?"

"And who are you to question someone who wants to make you a little more money?" Hana asked, the lightness of her expression not matched by her almost feral tone.

Ortiz laughed. "Damn. Brownstone has you both all twisted up, don't she? From what I hear, Sugimoto, you used to rip people off all the time. At least I don't lie to anyone and pretend to be anything I'm not. I give them a choice, and they know the consequences. I don't like Raven not because of what she gives people, but because of what she is."

"Whatever." The fox snorted. "Spare me the lecture about what a piece of trash I used to be. That's the old me. She died, and Alison has helped a new me be born."

Mason gave her a reassuring nod.

"Like I said. Brownstone has you twisted up." The man shrugged. "I have nothing else for you. I told you what I know, and even if you beat every man or woman in my little club, that would still be all I know."

"That's not true," Mason responded.

"Oh?" Ortiz cocked his head to give him a dismissive smirk. "Are you saying I'm lying?"

"The friend of the friend. Who is he? We'd like to talk to him. We won't tell him how we heard about him."

The club owner burst out laughing.

Mason frowned. "What's so funny? Just tell us where to find him."

The other man sobered. "Where?" Another chuckle escaped. "Which piece of him? You mean the few parts they found and buried or the rest of him? Because I don't even know if the rest of him is still around given how messed up what they found was."

Hana sighed. "He's dead?"

"Oh yeah." Ortiz shook his head. "He never came back from his last deal with the dark wizards, and eventually, someone found what was left of him in his apartment. I figured they killed him to make an example of him or maybe to cover their tracks. Who the fuck knows?" He shrugged. "The point is, he's dead and then some." He pointed to the door. "Like I said, nothing more to tell you. I respect the strength you showed in the ring, and I respect the Dark Princess's strength, but why don't you get the hell out of my gym?"

Hana stood and looked at Mason.

He nodded to her and opened the door. "Thanks for your help."

"For what it's worth," the man added, "I hope you find the dark wizards and let Brownstone do her thing."

"I should have known," Alison muttered into the phone. "My instincts were right. But a diversion? If that's what they did to distract us, I can't even begin to imagine what the actual plan is. Destroy the city? But if they go that far, they'll end up in open warfare with this country, if not every country. The only reason they get away with as much as they do is because most people don't understand the threat they represent."

"I don't know, A," Mason replied. He sat in his office at the Brownstone Building. Hana had gone to check on Sonya and Tahir. "It also might be that we killed enough of them during the Fremont Troll incident to mess up everything they had planned anyway. The PDA certainly seemed to think so."

"And the PDA is also still dealing with the fact that they had a traitor in their midst. I trust Latherby, but I think they are still behind the curve on this. Damn it." She sighed. "Here's the deal. I doubt they're done with whatever they intend for Luke. If they aren't planning to assassinate him at the speech, they'll strike somewhere else soon, and I think it's a good opportunity for me to eliminate them here. I want you all to push at your end and see what you can turn up but be careful until I get back."

"We will, but the same thing applies to you. If you end up getting killed in DC, I think your dad will come and rip me apart."

She chuckled darkly. "Don't worry. You'd have plenty of time to run while he's destroying DC."

Mason laughed but it trailed off as he wondered

whether she actually was joking. "What about the bounty hunter?"

"Yeah, I think I'll hook up with her and see if she has any leads. The FBI and PDA are crawling all over this right now, but if she's followed that guy halfway across the world, she probably has insight. Also, she might have chosen not to share it with the authorities since they won't pay her for the first kill."

"That sounds good." Mason looked up as Jerry walked past his office and gave him a polite nod. "If you need us, let us know. Even if we can't bring the support team quickly, Hana and I can use…alternative transport."

"I'm fine, and I'll let you know."

"I love you, A," he added. "Be careful."

"I know. Talk to you soon." Alison ended the call.

Mason tossed his phone on the desk and shook his head. "We're spending a lot of time and effort on a job that the company won't even get paid for. Oh, well, she's the boss, I suppose, and she's the one paying."

CHAPTER TWENTY-TWO

Alison summoned a shield after the first knock at her door. She expected the bounty hunter, but it wasn't as if she'd registered under a fake name. If the enemy wanted to find her, they would have no difficulty. A quick strike by the dark wizards might be part of the plan.

I'm assuming those assholes think they can kill me by surprising me in my hotel room.

She scoffed at the idea and headed to the door to look through the peephole. Drysi stood on the other side, her hands in her pockets. She looked like a different woman from the other night in her black leather pants, zipped-up motorcycle jacket, and dark boots.

A little more leather than I wear, but it looks like we have a similar fashion sense, anyway.

Alison opened the door. "Thanks for agreeing to come and talk to me." She gestured inside. "I think we can both help each other out."

The bounty hunter wandered in, slight confusion on her face. "That's strange."

"What?" She closed the door and looked over her shoulder for anything unusual. "Oh. You're probably sensing the shield I put up." She chuckled and released the spell. "Sorry. I was simply being careful. I wasn't sure if you were here to kill me."

"I feel sorry for the bloody bastard who has to try to kill you by himself." Drysi laughed. "No, it wasn't the shield. It's this room."

"What about it? It's a normal hotel room. There are thousands like this all over DC."

"Exactly, but you're famous and rich. You have your own security firm, and you're around my age." The woman gestured around the room. "But this place looks like the kind of place I'd stay in. I expected not merely nice but some fancy and right tidy luxury suite in a four-star hotel. You are the Dark Princess, not the Dark Middle Manager."

Alison shrugged. "I grew up in modest circumstances. That's stuck with me. My dad has a lot more money than me, and you'd be shocked by how non-luxury his house is —if you don't count the high-security door to the basement armory."

Drysi fell onto one of the beds, her arms stretched to her side. "It's a soft bed. I'll give you that. Much softer than the bed at my hotel."

"I'd like to get down to business. I'm not trying to be a rude bitch, but these assholes tried to kill my friend."

"It's fine. I didn't come here to compare hotels." The visitor sat and nodded. "I won't lie to you, I'm unhappy that I won't be paid even a reduced bounty on the bastard I killed. That aside, now that they're all stirred up about the assassination, I have a chance to get some organizational bounty bonuses, at least. That's the problem with dark wizards. They know how far to push without going over the line and end up with bounties on their heads. Sneaky little bastards."

The half-Drow nodded. "My DC contacts are far more limited, but I hoped you might have had some leads."

"Didn't you use to live here?"

"Yeah, but me and DC never got along." She shrugged.

"I see." Drysi frowned. "I have nothing against you, Brownstone, but why should I lead you to my payday? I know you have an active bounty hunting license. I read about it. I came here to see what you might have to say, but that doesn't mean I'll turn over everything you want because you ask me to."

Alison held up a hand. "I don't need or want bounties. I'm interested in eliminating the dark wizards for personal reasons. Think of this less as competition than as free backup from someone who is really motivated."

A huge grin spread over the witch's face. "The *Tywysoges Tywyll* willing to work with me for free? That's too bloody perfect."

She blinked and stared at her visitor. "What? What's a *Ty, Ty*...whatever it was you said."

"That's what you're called in Welsh, Dark Princess." Drysi winked playfully. "All right. I won't turn that kind of powerful help away. I might do this for money, but I fancy myself an expert in hunting dark wizards. It's a way to make good money and do good at the same time. And it just so happens that I do have a lead. I was supposed to meet an informant at a place called the Orange Room. I don't know it, but I do have the address."

"The Orange Room?" Alison grinned. "I know the place. I met a contact there back when I used to work in DC. When are you supposed to meet someone?"

"In two hours."

"Did they say anything about you coming alone?"

The witch shook her head. "No."

Alison smiled. "Perfect."

Drysi placed her motorcycle helmet atop her lean yellow motorcycle, an electric Triumph streetfighter. She folded her arms and waited for Alison to walk over from her car.

Did she have that shipped here for the bounty? Alison wondered. *Or did she get it on the train somehow? I haven't heard of a magic cargo train. I wonder if the magic to do that is more complicated.*

She waved, and the women crossed the street together toward a sign reading. **THE ORANGE ROOM** which hung over an orange wooden door in a nearby building.

Nothing's changed since I last came here.

Alison opened the door, unsurprised by the empty room lit by a single ceiling lamp.

Drysi frowned. "You met someone here?" She looked around. "It isn't what I expected."

"Close the door."

The witch grasped the handle with a slight frown and pushed the door closed. The light around them twisted and shifted, and the more familiar luxurious dining room appeared.

Nope. Nothing's changed at all.

Alison opened her mouth to make a joke to the frowning Drysi but closed it.

Wait.

No music played. All the tables she remembered with their elegant tablecloths were present, but there wasn't a single person in the room. No waiters and no diners. Only emptiness.

Yeah, that's different, but maybe we're the only people here?

Her heart rate kicked up and her stomach tightened. She'd like her guess to be true, but she doubted it.

Drysi unzipped her jacket slowly. She muttered something harsh under her breath in Welsh. Alison didn't need to know the language to recognize an expletive.

"Was this place as empty the last time you were?" the woman asked. "I get intimate and elite, but this is downright ridiculous."

Alison shook her head and summoned a shield and shadow blade. "No. It was filled with people. I had the feeling it would always be filled with people."

The Welsh witch retrieved her wand with her left hand and selected a throwing knife with her right from a row of sheaths connected to a light tactical vest beneath her jacket. She cast a quick shield spell over herself and turned slowly. "This place seems posh."

"You could say that."

"It's not the kind of place that scum would be, yes?"

Alison nodded. "It depends on how you define scum."

A pulse of heavy magic flowed through the air, followed by three others.

The half-Drow narrowed her eyes. "Did you feel that?"

"Yes." Her companion took a deep breath and raised her wand.

Four gleaming portals opened around the women. Monsters with quadruple arms and thick scaly hides, the hands tipped with sharp claws, stepped into the room and hissed.

Of course.

The women immediately stood back to back as if they'd worked together for years.

"I'll give you this one chance," Alison shouted. "Back off right now. I've never met one of your kind before, so I have nothing against you."

Drysi laughed. "That's why I love Americans. You're always so optimistic. Tamping bloody monsters."

"Tamping?" Alison gritted her teeth as more monsters stepped through. "These are Zain. My dad fought these years ago."

"No, no. Tamping isn't the monster. It means…oh, I guess you'd say it makes me extremely angry. Yes. Right. Livid." Drysi chanted a quick spell and red lines of energy crackled over her throwing knife.

The Zain didn't attack. Instead, they waited as more monsters emerged from the portal until the room was filled with the creatures. The portals behind them snapped closed, and the enemy growled and hissed.

"Get the hell out of our way or back off," Alison shouted. "If you fight me, you will die."

The Zain rushed forward with a loud screech.

That speech works so much better with gang members.

She ducked a blow and sliced one of the monsters in half before she blasted another in the head with a bolt of light magic. The creature wailed in pain but it didn't die until she stabbed it through the skull.

"Careful now!" Drysi shouted as she threw her charged knife past the closest Zain into a cluster of four directly behind the two that hurtled toward her. The blade exploded on contact and blew the monster into chunks. The shockwave ripped into those nearby to create a wave of organic shrapnel among the four that felled two others. She removed the head from the closest attacker with a fireball.

Alison blinked and glanced at her, surprised. Three of the surviving monsters on her side lashed out at her in an effort to shred her with their claws. Her shield held but pulsed with each strike and weakened far more than she'd expected. Their ferocious attack forced her back a step. Another slash penetrated her shield and ripped into her red denim jacket.

She sliced the arm off one of the Zain before she turned and decapitated a second. A quick backstep followed as she layered a shield of both light and shadow magic.

It's like they have anti-magic claws. I remember Dad saying he saw them cut through armor like paper.

Drysi annihilated a Zain with a fireball in its face before she yanked out another throwing knife and rattled off an enchantment. This time, blue light arced over the surface of the weapon.

Two more monsters sliced at Alison and her shield began to fail.

She threw a quick shadow line to the ceiling and vaulted up. After releasing her blade, she raised her palm to deliver several rapid white blasts of energy into their adversaries.

The other woman looked at her for a moment. "Stay there until my next attack is done."

"Why?"

"You'll see."

The witch tossed her knife into the air and dropped to the ground. The weapon traveled only a yard up before an azure shockwave erupted from the blade and struck the remaining Zain. They screeched and collapsed to their knees, where they twitched spasmodically.

The bounty hunter jumped to her feet and methodically blasted the stunned monsters with fireballs while Alison continued to rain her light magic death down from above. Soon, all the Zain lay dead.

The half-Drow released her line and dropped to the floor with a sigh.

Drysi kept her wand up as she surveyed the room slowly. "That wasn't much fun." After one more three-sixty check of the room, she put her wand away and jogged to collect her two throwing knives. As she leaned over to pick them up, Alison noticed they were inscribed with faint but intricate glyphs.

She frowned. "Someone doesn't like you very much to send that many Zain to kill you."

"Word must have got out that I killed their man in the restaurant." The witch crouched beside one of the dead creatures. "I'm surprised. Why would so many creatures work for dark wizards? They aren't exactly mates of the Oricerans."

Alison shook her head. "Zain are magical mercenaries.

They'll work for anyone who pays them." She frowned. "But I doubt they created the portals themselves. The wizards must have reduced manpower if they now rely on hired muscle."

"That's some right tidy news, then." Drysi smiled. "That might also explain why the bloody bastards only had one man at the restaurant." Her smile turned to a frown and she gestured around the room. "Do dark wizards own this place?"

"I have no idea." She shrugged and looked around. "When I was here before, it felt more like an Oriceran place than a wizard hangout."

Did they kill everyone here? But that doesn't make sense. A dark wizard or two can't come into a place filled with elves and gnomes and kill them so easily. What have I missed?

"There went our lead, then." Drysi kicked at the floor with her boot and cursed again under her breath. "I didn't even get the name of the informant. I only talked to him on the net and the phone. I don't know if he's dead or if it was a trap and a lie to begin with."

Alison pointed to the door. "Let's get the hell out of here. I'd have my tech guy try to trace your communications, but I imagine they have already covered their tracks too well."

Should I let Johnston and the PDA know? No. Johnston might be okay, but if the Seattle PDA can be compromised, there's no reason the local office can't either. We'll work this my way until I know for certain what's going on.

"And what now? Any brilliant ideas?" Drysi smiled a little shyly. "I know I was the one who provided the leads, but I'm back to scrounging."

"No, we have a lead." She gestured around at all the dead bodies. "This was another assassination attempt by someone with enough resources to clear this club out and portal in a bunch of mercenary monster assassins. We simply need to figure out who owns this place and go from there. If the owner wasn't involved, there is at least a good chance that they know who is involved."

"Do you know who owns the Orange Room?"

She shook her head. "No, but I know someone who might."

CHAPTER TWENTY-THREE

Dysi sat patiently, sipped coffee, and enjoyed the softness of the bed. Alison had waited to place the call until she was back at her hotel room.

Okay, let's see if he's still grateful.

Alison dialed the contact number she had for Mr. D, the client's whose job had sent her to Seattle, to begin with.

The phone rang three times before the call connected.

"I heard you were in town, Miss Brownstone," the gnome answered. The voice was the same as she remembered, including the strange odd vowel emphasis that made him sound slightly unsettling. "But I'm curious as to why you'd call me. Please don't mistake my confusion for lack of gratitude for your earlier aid."

Alison cleared her throat. "I'll cut right to the chase, Mr. D. I'm hunting some dark wizards together with a bounty hunter. She had a lead that took us to the Orange Room, but when we arrived no one was there and we were ambushed by a pack of Zain."

A few beats of silence ticked by before the gnome

answered. "I see. That's most unfortunate. Although I'm pleased with your survival, I don't quite understand why you would call to inform me personally."

"Not only was the place empty when we showed up, but there was no sign of a struggle. That makes me think it wasn't that a bunch of dark wizards showed up and killed everyone, but more that everyone was cleared out, including the staff. The way I figure it, the only person who could pull that off is probably the owner."

"I'll admit that's a valid deduction. It might not be true, but it does seem likely."

"So I need to know who the owner is and if you know where they live," she replied. "You strike me as the kind of gnome with enough pull to have that information. I don't think I have much time to poke around and investigate this myself."

Mr. D took a long, deep breath. "It's rather unfortunate that dark wizards chose to disrupt things at my favorite club. I will send you a text shortly. It contains the address for the owner—a Light Elf who, on Earth at least, goes by the name Sunshine."

"Sunshine?" Alison made a face. "Seriously?"

"If you met him, you'd be even more surprised. He's a dreary, dreary man. Please handle this with haste, Miss Brownstone. I would hate to have to find a new favorite club."

The address led Alison to a quaint and appealing split-level home nestled in the woods in Annandale. Drysi refused to ride along and insisted on taking her bike. Even though Alison gave her the address, the bounty hunter traveled directly behind her car the entire time as if she followed her.

Or is she trying to escort me?

She wasn't sure if she should be flattered or insulted, so she chose the former.

When she reached the property, she slowed and pulled into the long driveway and caught a glimpse of a shadow in the second-floor window.

Alison brought the car to a stop and put it in park. She took a deep breath and a moment to layer a light magic and shadow magic shield around herself. Even if the more obvious visual presentation tipped anyone off, it was better to be prepared. If they ran into more Zain, a few good strikes could seriously injure her otherwise.

She glanced at the tear in her jacket.

I'll fix that with magic later.

Drysi pulled up beside her and set out her kickstand. She hopped off the bike and removed her helmet as the other woman stepped out of the car.

Alison nodded toward the house. "I saw some movement earlier."

"How many arms?"

"I couldn't see. Only movement. It could be dark wizards, Zain, or simply Sunshine wondering who the hell we are." She shrugged.

"Do you think we should have called ahead?" The bounty hunter unzipped her jacket and retrieved her wand.

She shook her head. "No. If there are dark wizards in

there, I'd rather give them less time to prepare. Besides, Mr. D didn't give me the phone number."

The front door swung open. Both women peered at the house, but they didn't see anyone.

"Hello?" Alison called out.

Drysi stepped in front of the vehicle with a frown. "We don't want any trouble. We simply have a few questions, mate."

A huge fireball roared out of the front door and rocketed toward her.

Alison shoved the woman out of the path of the attack. The fireball missed them narrowly and slammed into the car. The resulting explosion launched the vehicle into the air and metal, plastic, and glass erupted into the sky. The blast knocked the women hard to the ground. They rolled several feet and new, smoking holes appeared in Drysi's pants and jacket, but most of her body remained untouched thanks to the half-Drow's quick reflexes.

The bounty hunter blinked several times and scrambled toward her wand. "Bloody fucking hell. That almost killed me." She sounded genuinely shocked.

Was that your first close call?

"Get a shield up!" Alison yelled and scrambled to her feet. She fired several white bolts into the living room in an effort to lay down some suppression fire against whoever had attacked them.

Drysi snatched her wand up and cast a shield spell.

Alison charged the front and alternated between a series of shadow crescents and light magic energy bolts. Several attacks struck one wizard who should have stayed behind the couch. They hurled him back and pinned him in the corner as each follow-up strike depleted his shield. A few more blasts proved too much and an energy bolt scorched his chest. He collapsed without a sound.

The windows upstairs slid open. Wizards stepped forward and pointed their wands at Alison. Fireballs and energy bolts rained down on her as she sprinted toward the front door. She ignored the occasional strike that strained her shield as she continued to hurl her own attacks. The barrage forced three more wizards to retreat into the kitchen and shut the door behind them.

It's easier to raid open-concept houses. No one ever talks about that on house-buying shows.

Drysi snapped her wand up and released her own fireball at the second story. It struck one wizard, but he stumbled back after a brilliant flash as his shield saved his life. The bounty hunter took the opportunity to draw a knife and enchant it with another stun blast. She flung the blade toward the open window. Her target wizard dodged to the side with a smug smile before the blue energy wave engulfed him and he collapsed.

Alison barreled into the living room and raced toward the kitchen door. She extended twin shadow blades and coiled shadow magic at her feet for a few seconds to release energy and fly toward the kitchen. Her shielded shoulder smashed into the door and slammed it open.

The three wizards still hid in the room. Two of them crouched behind an overturned kitchen table and popped up to fire cobalt-blue energy bolts which narrowly missed her. Alison rolled as she landed and found her feet quickly in front of the first man. Several slashes from her blades carved through his shield like the Zain had through her defenses. Her opponent wasn't even able to attempt another attack before she'd impaled him.

She spun out of the path of another volley of energy bolts and the attack blasted holes in the wall behind her and spat dust into the air. Without hesitation, she leapt forward and sustained two blasts at point-blank range that stung and strained her defenses before her blades encountered the wizard's shields. Although she didn't penetrate their barriers on her first attack, they scrambled backward with real fear in their eyes. That mistake gave her the time to follow up with several more assaults until her Drow shadow magic overcame their enchantments and her blades found their hearts.

A loud explosion upstairs shook the house and several men screamed.

Alison released one of her shadow blades before she kicked open each closed door on the ground floor. She encountered no more dark wizards, so she bounded up the stairs. Drysi waited at the top, her jacket covered with blood and her clothes peppered with new holes.

"I decided I'd go topside whilst you went bottom," the bounty hunter explained. She pointed her wand down the hallway. "I have one left alive there. What about you?"

She shook her head. "No one left alive downstairs. Did you find the elf?"

The woman sighed and slipped her wand into her jacket holster before she walked to a nearby bedroom and gestured inside with a quick nod.

Alison hurried to the door and peered into the bedroom. A cloudy-eyed Light Elf in a silk robe lay on the bed and a jagged incision ran completely through his chest.

Drysi pointed to three dead wizards on the floor. All had slightly bluish skin. "All right, these three were dead when I got in here, so at least Sunshine took some of the bastards with him."

The half-Drow sighed. "Damn. I had hoped we could save him. Let's see what we can get out of the survivor."

They marched down the hallway. The bulk of the outer wall had been blown away and fragments of smoldering wood and drywall littered the yard below. From what Alison had seen, the bounty hunter liked to go loud.

Several dark wizards lay on the floor in the room, all dead except for one man in the corner. He was propped up against a side wall and groaned in pain, his leg bent the wrong way. A few throwing knives lay on the floor near the bodies.

Drysi marched over to the wizard and drew her wand. She crouched beside him and pointed the wand at his head. "Let me explain it to you, mate. If Alison hadn't saved me, I'd be dead. After that, if I didn't have a healing potion, I'd be dead." Her tone was filled with angry resentment and surprise.

Is this the first time she's raided a dark wizard hideout? Maybe she's used to only going after guys who are alone.

The dark wizard spat blood in her face.

The woman sighed and wiped it off with her sleeve. "You'll tell us what we want, or I'll transfigure your fucking prick into a peanut."

The wizard sneered. "You won't get anything out of me, you pathetic lesser witch."

"Oh?" Alison stepped forward. "What? Are you compartmentalized?"

Drysi looked up. "I've heard of that but I've not run into myself."

The wizard chuckled and grimaced when he accidentally moved his broken leg. "You won't get anything out of me," he repeated. "I'm surprised you're still alive after all the Zain we sent after you."

Alison glared at the man. "What's the big plan? You might as well tell us."

"You think you're so powerful, Brownstone, but what's the worse you can do? Kill me?" The wizard snorted.

She squatted beside him and held her palm out. Writhing shadow tentacles appeared. "Oh, sure, I can kill you, but I can do it slowly and very painfully to prolong your agony."

The man's eyes widened. "That's a lie. You don't torture people."

"Who told you that? One of the guys I killed? Oh, wait. They couldn't because they're dead."

The wizard gritted his teeth.

"I spent some time on Oriceran." She moved the palm with the tentacles closer. "And the Drow taught me some *very* interesting things," she lied. "These little guys are so hungry, and their favorite meal is brains."

She was honestly surprised that she could keep a straight face with all the bullshit she fed the man, but his wide-eyed expression suggested that he believed her.

Drysi blinked and looked from one to the other before she holstered her wand.

The dark wizard's lip quivered as all his confidence drained away. "I don't know the whole plan."

"I don't have time to deal with truth spells and counter-spells to figure out if you're compartmentalized. Maybe I'll let it nibble a little brain and see what you say then, huh?"

"I'm not under that kind of spell," the man insisted. "I simply don't know. They split us up into different groups with different tasks. Our job was to take this place and slow the non-PDA people down. We took the elf hostage and made him call people to clear the club out, but he tried to escape and we had to kill him."

Drysi frowned. "What was all that about? You brought all those monsters to kill me?" Bitterness laced her voice.

"We had people watching the restaurant and saw that you were working with Brownstone. The damned Zain were supposed to kill you both, or at least slow you down." He laughed again. "And it worked even better than we thought. We might have lost men, but you came all the way here."

Alison moved the tendrils alongside his head. In truth, it was nothing but a parlor trick but it appeared to work superbly.

"I don't know the rest of the plan," the man shouted. "All they told us was to ensure that you were kept busy even if you weren't killed today."

Drysi frowned. "What's so important about today?"

"Of course. Luke's speech at the Lincoln Memorial." Alison shook her head. "He has protection. Your people will never get to him. He's expecting an assassination attempt."

"Oh. That explains it." The wizard grinned and winced again as he jostled his leg.

"Explains what?" She leaned forward to glare at him.

"A few non-magicals with deflectors won't be enough.

I'll go ahead and tell you because your shifter friend is probably already dead. A wizard with the right artifact is more than a match for whatever pathetic guards he has." The wizard stared at her, wild-eyed. "And do you really think no one planned for the AET? I know there's a team working on them, too. There's one more team. This one will humiliate you."

"Meaning what, exactly?" Alison released the shadow tentacles. The man sounded like he wanted to talk, if only to brag.

"Come forward, and I'll whisper it into your ear."

Alison leaned forward. She leapt to the side on reflex at some quick movement out of the corner of her eye and summoned a shadow blade but frowned as she realized that Drysi had thrown a knife into the man's throat.

"Why did you do that?" She released her blade and stood.

Drysi pointed at his hand. He clutched one of her throwing knives.

"Sorry, instinct. And you saved my life earlier, so I owed you." She blinked a few times.

"I still had my shield up."

"Those aren't merely some off-the-shelf thing I bought at Costcutter. They're good at penetrating shields, too."

Alison shook her head. "It doesn't matter. I let these assholes lead me around by the nose thinking they had something bigger planned, but it was all about Luke in the end." She pulled out her phone and dialed her friend.

"What is it, Alison?" Luke answered. There was a hollow, echoing quality to his voice over the phone.

"Where are you right now?"

"The Lincoln Memorial. I have a speech to give in fifteen minutes. I only answered because it's you."

She groaned. "You need to get out of there. They've sent assassins who are probably already in the crowd."

"I can handle a few dark wizards," he replied, irritation in his voice. "I won't leave."

"I think they're enhanced with artifacts somehow," she explained. "And from what I've heard, AET might not show up. Damn it. I should have stuck by your side."

"It's hard to know with these slippery bastards. Fine. I'll have the police clear the area, but our best bet is for me to stay here."

Alison blinked. "What? No. Didn't you hear what I said? It won't be one disposable guy. I've seen this kind of thing before—artifacts that can dramatically enhance a wizard's power, and I'm not talking about some sort of kemana-sucking thing. If they got their hands on several of those, they'll be able to take you out easily. Anti-magic deflectors can be shattered with enough magic. I should know. I've done it."

"I'm tired of people having to run from them. They should have to run from *us*. Every time one of us runs, it increases the risk and makes them hungrier. All it does is make them think they can win," Luke protested. "They won't win, and we'll fight back."

"Of course we will, Luke, but you can't fight back if you're dead."

"If I'm here, we at least know exactly where they'll attack," he retorted. "I remember when you first came to the school. You could barely use your magic, but your power grew and grew. I was proud of you then, just like I am now. And today, I want to go back to the way things were. For today, I want to fight these bastards head-on. I have to go, Alison. I need the police to move all the people out."

He ended the call.

Alison groaned. "Damn it. Why does he have to be so stubborn?" A soft breeze blew through the open wall.

Distant sirens sounded.

"The cops are coming soon, Drysi," Alison explained. "Can you explain the situation to them?"

Her companion responded with a shallow nod. "It won't be fun, but I'm sure once I get the PDA involved, it'll sort the mess out for me. Why? What about you?" She pointed to the burning wreck of the car in the driveway. "Where do you plan to go without your car?"

Alison tapped in a quick text message to Mason and explained the highlights of the situation. Shadow wings sprang from her back. "On a little flight to the Lincoln Memorial."

CHAPTER TWENTY-FOUR

Mason, Hana, Tahir, and Ava sat around the conference table, concern on their faces. The idea of their friend and boss charging into battle without them at her back didn't sit well. Depending on what trap the enemy had set up, Alison could end up in major trouble.

"Shouldn't we go to help her?" Hana asked.

"If you're thinking about the magic train, you still have to travel to the appropriate location, take the train—which is fast but not instant—and then travel from the exit location to the Lincoln Memorial," Ava explained.

Hana, Mason, and Tahir looked at her, no one really surprised that Ava knew about the train even if she wasn't a magical.

"Perhaps we could contact Myna?" Tahir suggested. "She could open a portal there."

"I don't have her number," Hana admitted. "Do any of you?"

Everyone shook their head, even Ava.

Mason sighed. "It doesn't matter. Alison's message told

us to pay attention to Seattle. The dark wizards have stretched themselves thin, but they'll probably pull something here soon. Tahir, you should focus on emergency services reports, that kind of thing. We can take the helicopter and get to wherever they cause trouble quickly that way. Whatever they have planned, I assume they planned it with the idea that they could pull it off while Alison was out of town."

Ava folded her hands in front of her. "And Mr. Ortiz gave you no actionable intelligence?"

"Not enough. Only enough to know that more trouble will come."

The infomancer's phone chimed, and he bristled. "I told Sonya not to bother me for the next few minutes. This had better be important." He pulled his phone out. "I gave her a simple practice assignment to filter drone feeds. It shouldn't be something she has trouble with." He brought the message up, and his face twitched. After a quick flurry of typing, he hissed. "That's unfortunate."

"What?" Mason asked.

Tahir looked up and entered a final command on his phone.

Red lights flashed and a shrill klaxon sounded.

"*Alert! Alert!*" Ava's pre-recorded announced voice over the intercom system. "*Brownstone security is under attack. All non-field personnel are to shelter in a panic room immediately. Alert! Alert!*"

A resounding thud echoed in the distance.

Everyone bolted to their feet.

"What the hell?" Mason shouted.

"It's the front security grill." Tahir almost looked

pleased. "Sonya double-checked on a van that has sat several blocks away for some time. She flagged it during a drone test. Several men just stepped out of it, all with wands. Four other vans are rapidly approaching." The wizard frowned. "Ever since you met with Ortiz, I half-wondered about this possibility. Perhaps it was the residual influence of when my apartment was attacked, but it seems my paranoia was warranted in this case."

"Damn it." The other man gritted his teeth. "They have four vans of reinforcements, but Jerry's team won't be back for another hour. Maybe AET?"

"Not that we shouldn't contact the authorities, but I'm tempted to believe that if the dark wizards have mounted a daylight assault on Brownstone Security, they've taken measures to ensure their delayed arrival," Ava pointed out. "Didn't Alison's message suggest as much?"

Mason frowned. "I thought she was talking about DC, but either way, you're right."

Tahir headed toward the door. "I'll set up with Sonya and contact the police. I've wanted to test the security bots in a more realistic setting. This will do."

The ex-bodyguard slammed his fist on the table. "Shit."

Ava smoothed her skirt. "Might I suggest, Mr. Lind, that we hurry to the armory. The support staff have been trained for this exact scenario, and I'm confident they'll be fine, but I'd rather not have to explain to Miss Brownstone why her building was destroyed when she was away."

Her companions nodded and they rushed to the door.

Don't worry, A. We'll defend this place.

Mason slammed the outer armory door shut. Tahir had killed the alarm now that all the non-field support staff were safe in a heavily armored panic room.

Hana drew the *tachi* from its sheath and tapped her crystal ring three times to activate her shield. Mason summoned his own defenses, while Ava activated the bronze pendant.

The administrative assistant adjusted her glasses before she removed a magazine of anti-magic bullets from the tactical vest she now wore and slapped it into her assault rifle.

"We have six wizards near the front and waiting," Tahir explained via their ear receivers. "Thirty other men with anti-magic deflectors and rifles have deployed from the vans. They've broken into three teams of ten. One seems to be prepared to support the wizards. Another is running around the back, and a third looks to be preparing for a breach on a side entrance. Sonya and I have directed security bots toward the rear."

Ava stepped out of her heels and started down the hallway. She patted a few grenades clipped to her tactical belt. "If Mr. Arain could spare a few security bots to provide covering fire, I'll take care of the men attempting the side entry."

"I'll have Sonya help you with that," he replied.

Hana grinned. "So, it's me and Mason to hold the front, then? Six wizards and ten heavily armed men?"

"I'm sure you'll find it quite boring," Ava called over her shoulder. "If you can, please attempt to not cause too many explosions. We have barely finished painting this place."

Mason gave her a quick mock salute. "We'll do our

best." He rushed down the hallway toward the front entrance.

Hana hurried after him. "These guys must really hate Alison."

"Pretty soon, they'll really hate us, too."

He considered sending a text to Alison but decided against it. She was about to go into battle and the last thing she needed was to be distracted. It was time for the team she'd put together to show what they could do when their princess was away from her castle.

Loud explosions shook the front of the building. Hana and Mason arrived at the final intersection in the hall that led to the lobby. They stopped and peered cautiously around the corner.

A massive red beam cut through the front and inched slowly to the side.

"They're carving the front open," Mason muttered.

Hana shook her head as her tails manifested, her eyes changed, and her claws extended. "We've got this. You don't invite yourself into someone else's house."

He grinned and yanked a grenade off his belt. "Do you know what the problem is with many wizards?"

"What?"

"They forget how good regular old weapons can be." He pulled the pin and gripped the lever firmly. "Let's show these sons of bitches why they should never fuck with anyone who works for Brownstone Security."

The red beam made its final cut through the front wall and grill. A moment later, a loud roar sounded, and the entire front wall collapsed into the lobby in a massive cloud of dust.

Six wizards in dark robes strolled inside, surrounded by shimmering shields. Their ten mercenary soldiers with anti-magic deflectors walked in a line beside them.

"Oh, they're all dressed up," Mason murmured. "They want to put on the show. Well, let's give them the respect of a big opening. We make our move after the opening applause."

"Entry in the back," Tahir announced through the receiver. "Engaging the enemy. Entry in the side. The security bots there are under attack."

"I'm almost there," Ava responded.

"Everyone go radio silent unless you need reinforcements or you're on your way to reinforce," Mason ordered.

No one responded.

Does that mean they heard?

Without Alison, there was no clear chain of command for the primary field team. That was another thing they'd have to work out in the future.

"On three, two, one..." Mason hurled the grenade around the corner.

The wizards laughed when the soldiers scattered. It was too late. The grenade exploded and several who weren't killed instantly screamed.

He rushed around the corner, his body flushed with power. Hana hurtled in pursuit, not quite keeping pace with him but close.

The few remaining soldiers shook their heads to clear them and raised their guns to train on the approaching defenders. They fired a few rounds and the bullets streaked past the duo but didn't strike.

The fox bounded onto Ava's desk and launched herself

at a wizard, her sword held high. The arrogant man didn't even try to dodge, perhaps thinking his shield would be enough. The Masamune *tachi* cut through him with ease.

Hana kicked him toward a shocked wizard and stabbed another close by before he launched another spell. A fourth managed a dark bolt that knocked the woman back and stung, but the attack didn't deplete her shield. She rushed forward to slash and stab to end the lives of the men who dared to defile her friend's building.

Mason's speed and erratic movement successfully evaded the volley of slugs as he closed on the soldiers. He knocked a rifle out of a man's hand with ease before he yanked the man's head down and brought his knee up violently. Even if their anti-magic deflectors robbed him of his enhanced strength when attacking, the crystals couldn't do anything about his upper-body work in the gym.

The soldier's friends released another barrage of shots, and any hope the mercenary had of surviving vanished as he took their rounds when Mason threw him into the line of fire and ran on. He drew his pistol. Placing headshots from a few yards away was almost too easy. Their bullet-proof vests and anti-magic deflectors didn't offer protection from a bullet in the face.

Nice try, assholes.

He eliminated the final mercenary and spun to empty his magazine into the nearest wizard. The anti-magic bullets cut through his shield with ease and his body jerked with each strike before he collapsed.

It's an expensive way to defend this place, but I'm sure A will understand.

The security bots looked more like a glorified silver trashcan on treads than an elite last line of defense, but with stun bolts and stun rods, they provided a useful supplement to defense.

Tahir smiled as another invader fell to a stun bolt. He glanced rapidly at each of his three monitors. Six of his bots were left. The other four had been reduced to sparking, bullet-riddled messes. As for the enemy, almost every single man of the rear group now lay on the ground, stunned.

Sonya gritted her teeth at the station beside him and constantly shifted her attention between her screens. "I'm down to two bots. I'm sorry."

The infomancer shook his head. "Don't worry. Ava's already killed half of them."

The girl blinked. "Yeah, that's really weird, man. Isn't she the secretary?"

"That and so much more. I've tried to dig into her background, but it's extraordinarily well-hidden in terms of whatever she did before she came to the US. I found an image in a stray MI6 server that might have been her when younger, but that server was pulled offline only minutes later, so I didn't have time to push deeper. Alison has told me to not worry about it. She cares less about who Ava was before than who she is now."

"MI6? Isn't that like the British CIA?"

He nodded. "Indeed."

Ava ducked behind the destroyed remains of a security bot as she ejected a magazine and slapped in a fresh one. The advantage of fighting non-magicals was she could at least keep expenses down. Already, she had to fight the urge to tally the repair costs in her head.

Such rude and unfortunate timing. These gentlemen need to learn a little respect.

She popped up to fire a burst into an advancing soldier, only to have her gun jam. As if she'd planned it all along, she hurled the weapon toward the enemy and charged.

A bullet slammed into her vest and she hissed at the pain.

They're all using anti-magics, I see. The pendant is less useful than I would have hoped.

Her bulletproof vest might have saved her life, but she felt like she had cracked a rib. She'd worry about a potion when the rude invaders were handled.

Sonya's remaining active security bot eliminated another man with a stun bolt and he collapsed. The distraction combined with the twirling rifle that struck the soldier with a thunk allowed Ava to close. Her quick palm-strike to the throat sent him to his knees, where he gasped for air around the pain.

Ava dropped toward him, her elbow pointed, and slammed it right into the back of his neck. He fell forward and she whipped a knife out of a sheath and threw it into the head another man, who fell back, dead.

She took several shallow breaths as she looked at the bodies sprawled around her. Most of the men were dead, but they had a number of prisoners for the police and PDA.

Sloppy work, but acceptable.

Hana rested the flat of her blade on her shoulder and sighed. "I probably should have tried to keep one of the wizards alive. I simply got too into it."

Mason shrugged. "You have to do what you have to do in the middle of a fight. Besides, I bet these assholes have that compartmentalization shit going on anyway."

"The police are on their way," Tahir reported through their earpieces. "They claim there's some sort of glitch that has prevented AET from coming, but they have sent SWAT in case more mercenaries show up as reinforcements. We have a decent number of prisoners. Ava's started Zip-tying the ones who survived near her. I'm stunning the ones who awaken in the back until she can get there."

Hana frowned at one of the dead wizards. "Between the wizards and the anti-magic deflectors, they wasted a lot of people and money to accomplish not much more than us needing a little remodeling." She gestured toward the collapsed front wall. "Maybe a touch more than a little."

"Of course, because they made a big mistake," Mason replied.

"What's that?"

He glared at one of the mercenaries. "They assumed that if they removed Alison from the equation, we'd be easy to take down."

The fox bit her lip. "You still sure we shouldn't hop a train?"

Mason shook his head. "Ava's right. Even *that* train isn't that fast. We have to believe in Alison, just like she believes in us."

CHAPTER TWENTY-FIVE

With particular care to remain low, Alison flew directly toward the Lincoln Memorial and gained more than a few curious looks from people on the street. Some pointed, while others took pictures with their cameras and phones. Even at a time when many magical beings commingled openly with humanity, very few people would ever see a white-haired young woman swoop through the city with tenebrous wings.

I hope those damned dark wizards don't wake the Fremont Troll up again in Seattle. By now, Tahir's probably set some check on the cops to listen in for weird incidents. They probably didn't text me because they didn't want me to be distracted.

Much like I am now, I guess.

Months earlier, Alison's life had fundamentally changed in Washington, DC. In fighting terrorists, she'd used her wish to restore her sight and had been given a temporary boost that let her push past her limitations. Now, she didn't need to rely on ancient Drow birthrights to fight against a different kind of terrorist. She would show the dark wizards no more mercy than she'd shown the New Veil monsters who were ready to kill thousands in the name of their twisted and hopelessly pointless philosophy.

I only hope Luke's all right. They might have already made their move. That cocky bastard at the house certainly acted like it. If I lose Luke, I'll make those bastards pay.

Alison wasn't sure what to expect when she arrived at the monument. She was half-worried that she'd find a smoking crater, but as she closed on the marble columns and Great Emancipator statue, her stomach began to unknot itself. There was no crowd of innocent people waiting to be slaughtered, merely a small number of police. A few other police cars pulled in and their officers stepped out.

Alison frowned as she flew toward Luke, who chatted with a police officer. Several other officers drew their guns and ran toward her.

Oh, shit. Yeah, this doesn't look suspicious at all.

"Its Alison Brownstone," Luke shouted and waved his arms. "She's here to help. Don't shoot her."

The police halted and peered dubiously at her. After a few seconds, they holstered their guns and some looked visibly relieved.

The oppressive sensation of heavy magic filled the area, but Alison couldn't see any obvious spells or any unusual light.

Damn it. What does it mean? Do they plan to blow this whole area? They were prepared to level that restaurant and kill dozens of innocent people to get one target. They released a damned Mountain Strider in a major US city. It's not like restraint and avoiding collateral damage is high on the list of things they care about.

Fuck. Those crazy sons of bitches.

Alison released her wings, touched down lightly, and walked toward Luke. "Are you okay? Did anything happen?"

Luke nodded. "After your call, the police cleared the crowd out. Most of them should be well down the street by now. No one's shown up."

She looked around. A small number of the police had anti-magic deflectors, but there wasn't a single power armor or rail gun in sight.

"Is AET coming?"

"I honestly don't know. More police units are supposed to be on their way, but only a few cars have come." He shrugged.

Alison frowned and tried to locate any snipers, magical or otherwise. "The damned wizards have done something. They must have people on the inside with the local police and AET, or they've used a spell or something." She shook her head. "We should get out of here. Something's off. I have a very bad feeling about this."

Luke snorted. "Yes, something's off. Dark wizards are coming to assassinate me after they tried and failed once. I won't leave. You got here quickly, Alison. They're probably still on their way."

"You don't think they would have slipped in with the crowd?"

"I don't know." Luke tapped his chest. "Teddy Roosevelt once gave a speech after being shot in the chest. The least I can do is stick around and see if I can bait some dark wizards into showing up."

"I honestly don't like this." Alison's gaze darted around in search of something—anything—that might be off, but all she saw was cops, columns, and a giant Abraham Lincoln. "Depending on what the actual plan is, this could get too dangerous for everyone."

There had better not be any containment glyphs on that statue to prevent him from turning into a Mountain Strider. I think I'd have trouble bringing myself to fight a giant Abe Lincoln.

One of the police officers looked at her, a slight smile on his face.

Alison snorted. *I'm glad someone thinks it's his time to shine. Is this guy enjoying himself?*

The man dropped his hand to his pistol and yanked it out of his holster.

Alison summoned a shield and spun, expecting an enemy behind her. She grew a shadow blade immediately after.

Two shots rang out. The faint sensation of the first as it bounced off her shield made her turn again. She accomplished that at the same moment that Luke jerked and clutched his shoulder as he fell to his knees and grimaced in pain.

The police officer who had smiled earlier now sneered as he fired a few more rounds at Alison. Her shield absorbed them all before the man aimed his gun at Luke's head.

"Die, you shifter son of a bitch!"

She raised her arm to release a spell, but two other

policemen tackled the man and pinned him down. She rushed over to Luke as did several other officers. Blood seeped from his wounded shoulder.

"Damn it," she muttered.

Luke grimaced and stood, shaking his head. He clutched his shoulder. "I'm the one who was shot so I'm the one who should complain."

Alison drew a few deep breaths and resisted the urge to thrust a shadow blade into the assassin's neck. She turned toward the captive man who was now handcuffed by the other police cops.

"You're a cop!" she yelled. "Not only that, you're a cop who was specifically assigned to protect him. How could you? You took an oath to protect and serve."

"Stealing a uniform doesn't make me a police officer," the assassin snorted. "I'm no pathetic servant of mundane law. I merely borrowed the uniform from a foolish, foolish man. Don't worry, I made his end quick."

One of the cops who'd handcuffed him hauled him up roughly. "Thanks for the confession, asshole. Between this and trying to take out the congressman, I'm sure you'll get out of jail about the same time that there's a new king of Oriceran."

"I serve the true masters," the man insisted, "and they'll reward me for my loyalty and service." He nodded toward Luke. "That animal doesn't know it's place. Shifters are only useful when they serve the great families."

"You mean the dark wizard families?" Alison asked. "Give me a fucking break. You're so deluded it's painful."

"They are the only truly great families." He chuckled. "My masters didn't see fit to tell me all their grand plans, but I know that by the time this day is done, everything you've worked for will be dust, Alison Brownstone. Don't worry. I'm sure you'll be dead, so at least they'll show you mercy in their own way."

She shook her head. "You're a non-magical who is trying to help dark wizards take over? That's the stupidest fucking shit I've heard this week. Do you understand what they want to do? They don't think other magicals should have the authority they have, let alone regular humans. You're trying to help turn yourself into a second-class citizen."

"They will take over eventually," he intoned fervently. "And when they do, they will remember those who have been loyal to them."

Luke fell to one knee. He sweated profusely and his face was pale. "This hurts a lot more than it should."

Alison rushed over to him. "We should get you to the hospital."

"Something's definitely wrong," he responded through gritted teeth. "It's burning, and that sensation is spreading. I don't think that was a normal bullet."

The assassin laughed. "So you feel that, you traitorous dog? Those bullets were specially made to hurt you. If I'd hit you in the head or near your heart, you'd already be dead. The masters wanted you to suffer before you died."

Magic thrummed throughout the area.

Where is all this power coming from?

Alison helped Luke up and settled his arm over his shoulder. "Now can we get you out of here? I sense powerful magic, and I'm worried that they plan to blow this entire place up. You're not in the best shape to try to fight if they do."

The energy level continued to build, and several pulses of magic passed through her.

"Wait. Shit." Alison turned Luke's support over to a burly police officer. "I think we're about to have some company."

"Now, Alison Brownstone," the prisoner shouted. "You die."

She thrust her palm out and launched a stun bolt into the man. He shuddered and twitched before his head lolled forward. "Shut up already, asshole."

Focused once more, she re-summoned her blade and looked around. Most of the officers present didn't have anti-magic deflectors or anything more than handguns on them, and maybe a shotgun in their cars. They were hardly equipped to take on a handful of normal rogue wizards, let alone someone who was stronger than normal.

"Everyone should get the hell out of here," Alison yelled. "I'll handle things until AET arrives. Whatever is about to happen isn't safe."

Either I'm about to fight some huge monster, or this entire place will blow. In either event, I need to get everyone clear.

Ripples of magic shuddered through her.

"Here it comes," she yelled.

CHAPTER TWENTY-SIX

"They'll save me!" the assassin screamed. "You'll all die now."

"Pipe down," the officer guarding him commanded.

The prisoner spun and headbutted the man. The cop fell back and clutched his nose. Blood ran down his face while his assailant ran toward the memorial.

Alison brought her hand up, ready to blast the bastard.

"No, you don't," Luke yelled. He yanked his arm away from the cop helping him and shifted.

That's the way to do it, Luke.

The cops backpedaled as a huge wolf replaced the congressman, more surprise than fear on their faces.

Blood still dripped from Luke's shoulder, even in his four-legged form, as he howled viciously and launched himself at the fleeing lackey. He knocked the man to the ground and lowered his jaw in front of his face to growl menacingly.

Alison looked at the memorial, but she didn't see anything unusual.

What's happening? Will they portal in?

Two cops nearby hesitated for a moment before they exchanged looks and rushed toward Luke and the recaptured assassin.

"Uh, we'll take it from here, Congressman?" one of them offered and swallowed nervously.

Luke growled at the prisoner once more before he backed away and shifted to human form. He rested on one knee, grimaced, and clutched his wounded soldier. "Sorry. I'm simply tired of not having some skin in the game."

"You've been shot with an anti-shifter bullet, Luke," Alison yelled. "I think you've had plenty of skin in the game, but I'm not so much worried about him as I—"

A gargantuan spear of ice erupted from the inside of the memorial. Alison threw her hands up to spread lines of magic in front of the officers in the line of fire. Dozens of fireballs exploded from the memorial, accompanied by a blast of dark stone and lightning. The attacks smashed against her magical wall and cascaded in a torrent of rock, ice, and smoke.

Alison gritted her teeth as her wall strained under the onslaught. They'd either hidden inside or portaled in, but it didn't matter. The true enemy had arrived.

"Everyone get the hell out of here!" she shouted and raced toward the memorial as she fed more energy into the wall. "Whatever is in there isn't something you can destroy with bullets. Get the congressman out of here, too."

"I can help," Luke complained.

"Help by surviving," she countered.

The cops retreated hastily and two assisted Luke to escape. Another shoved the assassin forward. Some of the officers hesitated for a moment and glanced reluctantly back and forth before they joined the withdrawal.

Please tell me Lincoln didn't just try to kill a bunch of cops.

A robed wizard strode forward and stood between the memorial columns. A blue nimbus of energy surrounded his body, and a cerulean glow infused his eyes. Another man stepped forward, this time cloaked in red. A third man surrounded by white energy advanced. The final enemy was a woman covered in a green energy field. Each of the new arrivals wore a jewel on a silver chain around their neck with a matching color.

Some sort of elemental power artifacts, maybe? Great. That's a shit-ton of power radiating off them. Too much. This shit won't be as easy I would have liked, but at least it's a statue of a president.

But the dark wizards have already lost a lot of men. A little intimidation won't hurt.

"Now this isn't fair," Alison called out. "I can't tear up the Lincoln Memorial. This is straight-up an asshole move, but don't think that means I won't stop you. It's time you dickheads realize that you have no place in the modern world. Time has passed you by, and you'll never get what you want."

"Behold," the blue wizard shouted and his voice boomed, amplified by magic. "Alison Brownstone, today, we will prove how weak you are. Your interference in our plans ends. You might have saved a few lives temporarily, but once this day is over, we'll proceed with more plans than you can possibly imagine."

She released the magical wall but kept her hands raised, ready to throw a few spells. "I'm sorry I didn't bring a neat necklace. Nobody called ahead to tell me I needed to coordinate with the Fashionable Four."

"Your quips won't save you," the wizard sneered. "Everything has proceeded according to plan."

"As far as I can tell, you tried to assassinate a congressman, were stopped, and then tried to kill the people who were investigating that and were stopped again." Alison laughed. "It must hurt to know that when I show up, you assholes lose. The fact is that I've eliminated dark wizards since I was a kid."

The blue wizard floated in the air on a translucent column of pulsing blue energy. "That will make killing you that much more satisfying, but we can give you a choice." He pointed to the sky. A half-dozen drones circled above, most likely news drones.

"What?" She peered at the drones. "You want me to blow them up?"

"On your knees," he ordered.

"Excuse me?" Alison stared at him, more confused than annoyed.

He flourished his wand. "The world is watching. If you fall to your knees and beg our mercy, we'll consider letting you leave this place alive."

She laughed. "Do you seriously think I'll agree to that?"

"Our power is far greater than the other wizards you've dealt with before."

"Oh, you don't understand me at all if you think that will scare me. If anything, it will at least make this more fun." She fired two quick white orbs at the wizard.

The man threw his arms up and grunted as the orbs

exploded against him. "This is the so-called power of Alison Brownstone? Pathetic."

"Oh, now it's on," Alison shouted. She extended a shadow blade and raced toward the side of the memorial to draw their attacks and give Luke and the police a chance to complete their escape. The wizards and witch hadn't fired on the police after their first attempt, so Alison concluded that her loud mouth had successfully drawn their focus. "Let's see what you have, assholes."

All four of her opponents swiveled to point their wands at her. The resulting storm of ice spears, fireballs, rocks, and lightning kaleidoscoped around her. The impact strained her shields and knocked her off her feet, but it also made sure that their attention remained away from the wounded shifter and the officers. Even the men with anti-magic deflectors wouldn't be safe against a volley of magic with the force and power these carried.

I need to get those bastards away from the main memorial, too. This is a little different than trashing a bridge, and the last thing I need is my face all over the news as the woman who destroyed the Lincoln Memorial. They'll start calling me Alison Booth.

Once she'd layered a new shield, Alison sprinted down the steps that led to the main memorial as the enemy continued to rain elemental death to scorch and blast the grass and concrete around her. The cacophony deafened her, and she had to fight to hold her focus.

Alison turned and continued to run across to other stairs rather than risk damage to the reflecting pool. Repairing the grounds and stairs would be far easier than replacing the marble monument, and she had no idea what kind of damage the pool could take.

The elementalists floated away from the main steps, all carried by their own stream of energy beneath their feet.

Now we're talking. Yeah, keep taking the bait, assholes. It's close to time for me to fuck you up.

Alison spun suddenly and threw her arms out to hurl shadow crescent blasts toward the enemy. She clipped the blue wizard and the green witch and their colored fuels flashed for a brief moment. The only sign of injury was a slight grimace on their faces.

At least it wasn't like they were totally invulnerable, but here comes the answer.

The blue wizard shouted an incantation and a wall of ice sprouted from the ground and spread rapidly ahead of her to block her further escape.

"Nice try, but not good enough," she muttered.

She lunged up toward the wall and shunted magic to her hands and boots. Dark spikes extended from both, and she scampered up the wall with her magical climbing gear while she still managed to fire a few bolts of her own.

It looks like everyone else is clear and no AET will arrive. There wasn't enough support, to begin with. It has to be the dark wizards pulling strings.

Alison leapt off the wall as the red wizard crashed a huge fireball into the ice. The explosion shoved her hard into the tightly packed soil and she bounced a few times, thankfully with only a slight sting. Steam and ice filled the nearby air.

I need to land a good strike.

Four small bolts of electricity struck her and hurled her

back onto the grass-covered hill. She hissed and rolled for a few yards while she channeled power into both her legs and her shield. Dense ice balls and small white-hot fireballs pelted her.

I need to go on the attack. Those artifacts are feeding them so much power that if I sit here and take it, they'll eventually overwhelm me. But they don't constantly attack together, which means there's some sort of recharge factor that limits them. I can exploit that if I time it right.

Alison winced as her shield absorbed most, but not all, of the latest lightning strike. She twitched and fell to one knee when a burning sensation seared through her body. A few follow-up fireballs knocked her back.

"Time to change this around." She shoved to her feet, swayed slightly, and released her pent-up magical energy to launch her body upward. The sudden move gave her a few precious seconds as the wizards and witch's attacks landed uselessly around her previous position.

Another quick burst of magic launched her forward. Light and shadow magic pooled around her hands. She continued to channel more energy as she hurtled toward her four enemies, her minor burns and cuts pushed to the back of her mind.

They raised their wands to unleash a new torrent of abuse. All of nature's fury, from rock to lightning, slammed into her. Her shield wavered under the barrage and her wounds stung.

The attacks actually pierced her barrier in a few spots. Her clothes tore, and her skin burned and ripped. The pain seemed distant, a sensation buried in the back of her mind as if it were something that happened to someone else in someplace else. The need to channel more power for her attack was the only thing that mattered.

These guys don't deserve mercy. They don't give it to anyone else.

Alison yelled a challenge as her hands slammed into the ground and discharged her collected energy. A shockwave blasted from her and ripped into grass, stairs, and the enemy to form a bright column of energy for a few seconds. The closest attacker, the blue wizard, didn't even manage a scream as the powerful combination of light and shadow magic cut through his defenses and incinerated him.

The green witch managed to scream and remain intact, but her burned body pitched forward. Her light faded and her necklace turned to dust in the hot breeze.

The other two wizards were thrown off their energy cushions, burned and grimacing in pain but still very much alive.

Alison took several deep breaths to recover from the massively taxing spell.

The red wizard pointed his wand. An enormous flame burst from it and thrust him away like a rocket. The white wizard staggered to his feet, murder in his eyes, and lashed out at Alison with a lightning whip.

She threw her arm up and pressed more magic into her shield. The whip cracked and the blue-white energy danced across her magical barrier. Some leaked through and she hissed as her muscles spasmed.

These artifacts probably made these assholes about ten times stronger, but I can still do this.

"You won't win," the man screamed. "You can't win."

"Really?" She strode directly toward him, conjured a shadow blade, and decapitated him. "I win."

The red wizard finished his flight. He stood tall, his wand pointed at her. "We volunteered for this knowing we might fall but still wanted the chance to take down the great Alison Brownstone. You don't understand. Even if you kill us all, you haven't won."

"That's the very definition of winning, asshole." Alison laughed and stalked forward. "But I'm glad to hear you're volunteer assholes. That makes this even easier than it was." She released her blade and raised her hand to gather energy. A crackling white orb grew in her palm.

"Do you know what's happening right now?" the wizard shouted, his face a mask of triumphant glee. "Do you have any idea?"

"You're getting your ass kicked?" She continued to feed her orb. "You've lost seventy-five percent of your big, elite super dark wizard squad?"

"No." The man raised his head and squared his shoulders and pride gleamed in his eyes. "Our allies are slaughtering your friends in your pathetic little building. They're probably crying out right now, wondering why you're not there to save them."

Her eyes widened, and she gritted her teeth. "Bullshit."

"What good is all your power if you can't protect your friends?" he taunted. He released a couple of firebolts. Her shields held, even if the attacks stung. "True power extends beyond yourself."

Mason, Hana, Ava—

All the lingering fear vanished in an instant, destroyed by a real sense of pride.

Alison took a deep breath and a smile spread slowly over her face as she shook her head. "You don't get it, probably because you've done nothing but use people your entire life. That's all any of you little assholes can do. You throw all these explanations around and talk about tradition and loyalty, but it doesn't change the fact that you're a bunch of crabs that drag each other down to make sure no one escapes the bucket."

The wizard swung his wand and blasted a sheet of blue-white flame toward her. She pushed through the curtain of superhot fire.

"That's the way of nature, girl," the wizard sneered. "The strong should rule over the weak. Complaining about it doesn't change it."

"If that's the case, then why don't you assholes rule?" Alison countered. "Why is this planet ruled by normal people and not a council of dark wizards?"

"Because of lies—because of Oriceran!" he shouted.

"Or maybe because you are not as special as you think you are." She released her orb. It rocketed away from her hand and exploded against the wizard's chest.

He catapulted back and his body thudded against the already scorched stairs. His eyes remained open in a death stare at the sky but his necklace turned to dust.

She winced and fell to her knees when some of her injuries finally caught up with her. Thankfully, when she fumbled in her jacket for her healing potion, she found it still intact. She swallowed it and waited for the pain from her injuries to fade.

At least I made the dark wizards really go all out. Four power artifacts, huh. I bet that took a long time for them to collect.

Alison's survey of the area elicited a sigh. The stairs running up the hill and much of the grass now stood blackened. Small craters dotted the area, but at least the main monument remained untouched.

Good. America won't hate me. That's always nice.

She retrieved her phone and shook her head. It was a cracked, half-melted slab. "Well, that's wonderful. Thanks, assholes."

Slowly and a little stiffly, she walked down the steps toward the reflecting pool, her gaze on the line of police in the distance. There was no hint of AET dropships in the air, even though various police drones had joined the news craft to circle the area.

"It's time to borrow a phone."

Alison jogged toward the police, no worry left in her heart. She didn't care what the wizard said. She knew her friends, and she knew there was no way they would let a few dark wizards destroy them.

CHAPTER TWENTY-SEVEN

Hours later, in Luke's office, Alison rested her hand on his shoulder as she finished her incantation and let the healing spell do its work. When she'd stepped into the office, he already looked far less pale than he had at the Lincoln Memorial, but he did wear a sling.

I need to add healing magic to the long list of things I have to improve. She wondered why she hadn't thought of it before.

"That's good, I think," Luke confirmed. "It doesn't hurt anymore."

She raised her hand and nodded before she moved to the other side of the desk to take a seat.

Drysi Jones sat on the other side of Luke, a smug look of satisfaction on her face. She tapped a rhythm to a song only she could hear on her leg. The witch had been patient since she'd arrived with Alison.

Luke pulled the sling off his arm and threw it on his desk. He rotated his shoulder. "Thanks for the healing magic, Alison. You know me. I would have healed up fast, but it's nice to be back to full strength, especially when I will have meetings and press conferences coming up concerning this incident."

"You might want to have a dedicated healer look at that," Alison replied. "My healing magic still isn't anywhere near as good as my ass-kicking magic, and they did say it was some sort of special anti-shifter bullet."

"I'm fine, but I'll go to someone if it starts feeling worse. The hospital seemed to think I'd be okay with time and rest." He shrugged.

"That's good to hear."

Drysi nodded. "I would have hated to know I had saved your life, Congressman, in such a perfect manner before-hand only for you to go and die later."

"I do like to avoid wasting people's time." Luke grinned.

"That's a good thing to strive for, but why are we here right now?" the bounty hunter asked. "You specifically asked for us to come."

"Right. Let's get down to business. I wanted to thank you both. Not only did you save my life, but you did a great job of protecting innocent people. The damage around the memorial isn't that bad—mostly cosmetic and some mild landscaping work. The news has already stressed the lack of serious damage to the main Lincoln Memorial itself. The murder of the elf is more of a concern, but we're already in contact with the Oriceran ambassador about that as well. These dark wizards have pushed too hard in attacking people like that."

Drysi cleared her throat. "I won't lie, I'm happy to help take down some bad guys, but I don't honestly care that much about your American monuments. The police tell me I can't claim any bounty money for anyone I eliminated.

They say most of them didn't even have bounties, and the few who did were not dead-or-alive. This was a tidy job, and I deserve to be paid." She gestured passionately with her finger. "Saving people's lives might be its own reward, but that doesn't cover my expenses."

She reminds me of how Dad used to be back when I first met him. It's funny. She acts so hard, but I bet her soul's beautiful on the inside.

"Understood." He waved a hand. "Don't worry. I can make sure you receive a reward, considering your role in saving so many lives. There are certain special funds out there for exactly this kind of thing." He scratched his cheek and motioned to his computer. "You'd be surprised how much. Congress came up with many different ways to handle the chaos following the gates opening, even if this country—and most countries—all ended up settling mostly on bounty hunters."

"But I'll get compensation?"

"You'll get your money, Miss Jones. It's the least I can do for all your help."

"Thanks, mate." Drysi sighed. "I don't want to be on TV or anything like that. I'm not interested in fame. It's actually bad for my job." She glanced at Alison. "Not all of us want to be James Brownstone."

"Don't worry. Even my dad doesn't always want to be himself." Alison smiled. "I'm sure, between Luke and Senator Johnston—the real Senator Johnston—we can keep any mention of your involvement to a minimum. I've been involved in some crazy stuff that most people don't know about."

The witch nodded with a satisfied expression. "Thanks.

I don't want to be difficult but it's too much bloody trouble, and I don't have a whole team to back me up like you do, Alison."

Luke looked at Alison with concern. "Did you have a chance to check in with your people? It's been so crazy over the last few hours, I didn't have a chance to check the news to see if anything happened in Seattle, and no one mentioned anything to me. I've assumed they're okay, but maybe that was wrong."

She snickered. "Yeah, something happened. Dark wizards attacked the Brownstone Building with a major force."

Drysi blinked. "And you think that's funny? You didn't strike me as so twisted, Alison."

"The dark wizards had their asses handed to them," she explained. "The PDA, Seattle PD, and the FBI are interrogating some non-magicals who were with the wizards, but they seem to simply be mercenaries. It might still lead to follow-up captures, though."

"The PDA around here did nab a few dark wizards a couple of hours ago," Luke confirmed. "From what little I've been told, they're connected with the cell involved at least in the DC operations."

Alison frowned. "They had another plan besides killing me and you?"

Every time I think I've caught up, some other damned cockroaches scurry out from beneath the oven.

He shook his head. "No, the two the PDA caught were responsible for magic that disrupted some of the local police communications and AET vehicles. That's why AET didn't arrive in time to help you and why the police response was so staggered and haphazard. The two dark wizards waited for an all-clear from the rest of their team from what I heard, but they didn't get one and they got complacent, which allowed a PDA wizard to magically trace their location."

"AET didn't arrive in Seattle, either," Alison commented, her brow furrowed. "I wonder if they pulled something similar. I don't know many of the details yet."

"Probably. There are still too many pieces to put together, but it seems like their big plan was to assassinate me as a high-profile shifter and make you look bad, if only to weaken you in the public's eyes and your organization by attacking your building. But they didn't get me, lost to you, and your building and people are fine. It sounds like they went zero for three. There's getting beaten, and then there's getting your asses completely handed to you."

Alison chuckled. "I am an expert at handing dark wizards their asses." She folded her arms and leaned back. "But I still wonder. These bastards have plans within plans. There might be something we've missed. Maybe there's something more to the events here and in Seattle."

"Maybe, but we've won for now. I think they got too cocky and, in some cases, we were lucky, but you know what they say. Luck is where opportunity meets preparation." Luke pointed to his shoulder. "If that was my head, I'd be dead now, and they must have been convinced they could take you as long as they used those artifacts to aid them." He gestured broadly with his hands. "All of what has happened has really kicked everything into overdrive. The entire government is now very interested in countering the dark wizard threat. But if you weren't here, Alison, we would have been screwed and I'd be dead." He turned to Drysi. "And you as well, Miss Jones. I also owe you my life, and I promise I'll make sure you get paid."

The bounty hunter laughed. "I'll hold you to your promise, even if you are a politician."

Luke chuckled. "I hate to cut this short, especially given how much the both of you already helped me, but I have many people I need to talk to and a ton of scheduled meetings in my future. Call my office tomorrow, Miss Jones, and we'll arrange your reward money."

Drysi stood. "Thank you, Congressman." She headed toward the door.

Alison smiled. "I have to get back to Seattle, anyway. My assistant has a long list of things she wanted to talk to me about, and my boyfriend isn't exactly comfortable when he's not around to help me beat people down." She leaned forward to give Luke a hug. "It was good to see you again. Next time, let's hang out without the assassins, and let's make it a lot sooner than a year."

He hugged her and pulled back. "That sounds like more fun, and I agree."

She sighed and gave him a final nod before she turned to the door.

Luke spoke as she was about to step out. "Alison."

"Yes?" She looked over her shoulder.

"Next time you see Izzie…" He sighed. "Let her know I was thinking of her. I always am."

She smiled. "I will, but she already knows that." She turned and left and after a few seconds, jogged to catch up with Drysi who was about to enter another hallway. The woman still drummed her fingers against her leg.

"What's next for you?" Alison asked and matching the bounty hunter's stride. "After you get paid, of course. More dark wizards?"

"Back to Wales." Drysi shrugged. "I specialize in dark wizards, but they aren't my only bounties. I actually might take a break from the bastards for a while."

"Trust me, I know the feeling." She drew a deep breath.

This is a good idea. At least, I think it is.

"And have you ever thought about applying your skills in a different way?" she asked.

"Like what? Becoming an MMMA fighter or something? Many of those magical leagues are still illegal in most countries." The woman looked confused. "I'm tough, Alison, but only when I surprise someone."

"No. Nothing like that." She shrugged. "I'm still expanding my company. It has a security focus, obviously, rather than a bounty hunting focus, but I pay well. Right now, I'm still interested in finding some quality magicals. I've slowed hiring in other areas, but we could definitely use another skilled witch. It's hard to find powerful people you can trust."

Drysi nodded. "That's true. It's why I don't have a partner. There are simply too many bloody idiots out there. I've almost been killed by people I've worked with before."

"So, are you interested?" Alison asked. "We've worked together. You see how I operate and you know the kind of things I care about. I'd like to think that I impress you with my skill and ability."

"You're very impressive, Alison." The woman stopped and sighed heavily. She stared at Alison in silence and scratched her cheek. "I'm tempted. Very tempted."

"Then give in to that temptation." She grinned.

The bounty hunter shook her head. "But I don't think I'm a team kind of witch—not yet, anyway. I'm not saying I don't trust you to have my back, only that I'm not ready to answer to anyone else."

"I understand. It took me a while before I stopped doing the solo act. You have to do whatever's best for you."

Drysi winked. "I'll keep it in mind, *Tywysoges Tywyll.* Who knows what the future will bring?"

CHAPTER TWENTY-EIGHT

Alison gulped her champagne as she looked around the lobby at her gathered friends and employees. Light pop music played in the background. She gestured toward the silver trays on top of the long folding tables that had been set up in the area.

Everything from sushi to pizza was available. Several tables contained nothing but fruit of every color imaginable, even a few glowing Oriceran fruits.

Maybe I went a little crazy with that list I sent to Ava, but I wanted a quick party, not something that'd take weeks to put together. This isn't bad for a party I arranged in less than a day without Ava's help.

There was no real aesthetic or style to the victory party. She merely wanted to make sure everyone had something they would like to eat, and she didn't want the cafeteria staff to have to work, given that they had to go through the stress of the attack.

To her surprise, none of the non-field staff had quit following the raid, but Ava had made it clear that it did fall under the hazard clause of their employment, so everyone would receive a bonus. One of the junior administrative assistants had even joked about getting paid extra money to sit in a room and do nothing.

Should I train them, too? Or is it best to have them retreat to the panic room? But if I have that many attacks on my building, I'm doing something wrong. My guess is that the dark wizards won't try again—for a while, at least.

Alison poured herself more champagne and held her glass up. "I'm proud of you all," she called out.

The light din of conversation faded, and everyone looked at her.

"One of the reasons I was able to take down those bastards in DC is because I had all of you here to take care of everything," she continued. "I didn't feel like I had to watch my back."

Jerry averted his gaze, disappointment etched on his face. "I'm sorry we weren't here, Miss Brownstone."

"You have nothing to be sorry for." She shook her head firmly. "You were following up on something for the company. It doesn't matter. Other than a little remodeling and repair up front, we survived this well." She gestured toward thick tarps that currently covered the hole in the front where the wall had already been removed. "If dozens of men and six dark wizards had attacked any other company in this city, it would probably have meant many more deaths."

Ava snatched a champagne glass out of Sonya's hand. "A few years yet, Miss White."

The teen rolled her eyes. "Whatever." Her frown evaporated and was replaced by a huge smile, even if she kept her gaze mostly on the ground. "It's funny."

"What is?" Hana asked.

"I work for Alison Brownstone, and I got to help protect the Brownstone Building."

When Alison was around the girl's age, she'd been involved in dangerous things at the School of Necessary Magic and had gone on bounty hunts with her father. Somehow, the girl helping them fight off a dark wizard raid didn't seem as outrageous as it probably should have.

Sonya grinned at Tahir. "So the lie's become true."

He scoffed. "I suppose. Your performance in the recent incident was acceptable, but I'm eager to see what you can accomplish in the future with proper guidance."

She walked over to an ice-filled cooler to pull out a Dr. Pepper. "If I keep working here, I'll end up ridiculously badass." She popped her drink open and gulped down some of the soda.

"Speaking of working, we're taking the next two weeks off," Alison announced. "At full pay for everyone. Consider it a free vacation while we complete all the repairs to the building."

Jerry's disappointment vanished, along with that of the men and women of his team. They, along with the other staff, cheered.

"So, let's all have some good drinks and food and an even better time."

Ava sat behind her desk and tapped at her computer, a plate of fruit and a single glass of champagne beside her. She clucked her tongue. "I do hope we can at least go a few weeks in this building with it not in need of construction."

This was one party Ava couldn't skip out on. Too bad Myna

wasn't interested in coming. Next time, I'll hire a noodle cart for the occasion. That should get her here.

Weary and content, Alison leaned against the wall. She'd lost track of how many glasses of champagne she'd drunk. It'd been a long time since she felt she could truly cut loose, and with the dark wizard threat thwarted, it seemed like the perfect time.

A pleasant warmth had spread through her body, and her head was fuzzy.

I probably shouldn't try to do any magic for a while.

Hana attempted to turn the entire affair into a dance party as she swayed to the music with a red-faced Tahir in the corner. It was even more unfortunate because she tried to slow-dance to an up-tempo pop dance song.

Mason walked up to Alison, holding a slice of pizza. "Are you okay, A? You've been quiet for the last few minutes."

"Just thinking. And drunk. I should have known the Troll wasn't the last of this. I've wondered if I should have pushed harder." Alison set her glass down on a nearby table. "If I had, Luke wouldn't have been shot and that elf wouldn't have been murdered."

Mason shrugged. "You're one woman, A, and we're one company. There are entire government agencies trying to keep track of this kind of thing, and bad guys still slip through the cracks. The way I see it, the dark wizards constantly lose men and money on these little plans. Portaling Oriceran mercenaries in? Using not one, but four different high-end artifacts? They lost a load of men over the last few days, and their plans failed. Face it. We handed their asses to them, and they're probably sitting in some villa in the Alps shaking their fists about how badly they were beaten."

Alison nodded slowly. "You're right." She shook her head. "I didn't tell you something."

"What?"

"When I finished the fight, one of the dark wizards told me that they were attacking you," she explained.

"And I thought you called to let us know you were okay." He frowned. "Damn. I hope it didn't distract you."

"Not at all." She smiled warmly. "You're always telling me I'm not the only person fighting against assholes out there, and maybe I've begun to believe you. I didn't think for a second that you would be defeated, especially when you were already on alert." She frowned a little. "We need more glyphs and wards, though."

"I don't know how much that would have helped considering that they basically blew their way directly into the building." Mason glanced at the tarps. "At least it's not winter. That would have sucked."

"I want to be more prepared." Alison looked at the chatting, eating, and occasionally, dancing people in the room. "Sometimes, I think I should hire a huge internal security team, but at other times, I think it's best to keep things smaller while we establish everything. It's too bad Drysi didn't want to join us. I think she would have been a good fit for the team. I like her. She's, uh, spunky?"

He laughed. "Spunky? Now I know you're drunk."

"Oh, quiet, you. I'm only saying you were right about

the whole organic hiring thing." She patted him on the shoulder. "Don't let it go to your admittedly handsome head. Handsome head? Is that a thing? Face. That's it. Handsome face."

Mason took her hand in his and nodded toward Hana and Tahir. "Maybe they have the right idea. Don't worry about the company for one night, A. We won. They lost. You'll get who you need eventually. For now, we've done the eat and drink part. It's time to be merry."

She stared at him, her eyes narrowed. "You're only saying that because you're drunk."

He patted her cheek. "Look who's talking."

"Fine. Lead on." She smiled at him. "I like winning."

"Good." He tugged on her arm and led her toward Tahir and Hana. "You do it a lot."

Ava peered at them from her desk. She snatched her mouse up and clicked. The light pop music playing in the background changed to a slower song. Alison's hazy mind vaguely recognized it as the big love theme from a romantic comedy popular a few years back, *Manic Human Dream Girl*.

She always has my back, just like everyone else here.

Alison let Mason take her in his arms, and they swayed to the music. The dark wizards might still be out there with some other nefarious plan, but Mason was right. That week, the good guys had kicked their sorry asses.

Drysi bounced a few times on the soft bed. She was glad she'd switched hotels. Alison's hotel really did have much softer beds. Some people preferred a firm mattress, but she couldn't get a wink of sleep that way.

I suppose it's time to clarify a few things.

She retrieved a small crystal from her pocket and uttered the activation incantation.

"You have no reason to contact me," Conrad's curt voice said from the crystal. "Especially so soon after the incident."

"I bloody well do." Her hand trembled in anger. "Do you know how many times the others almost killed me?"

"We both knew something like that would happen, but you have to understand, Miss Jones, that almost all the operatives who were involved in these efforts had no idea who you were. If they had, survivors might have revealed your identity, just as you weren't informed about all aspects of this operation yourself." He snorted. "And that foresight has changed this from being a complete fiasco to merely mostly a fiasco."

Drysi released a stream of colorful invectives in Welsh. "I won't lie. Alison Brownstone's still alive and the shifter's still alive. That strikes me as a fiasco."

"Perhaps, but the fact that you've contacted me to complain shows that you're still alive."

"You're right. I didn't know about your plan to attack her building, but that was a miserable failure, too. Right now, the only thing in this entire bloody mess that has gone all right is that I've convinced Alison Brownstone that I'm someone to trust." She chuckled. "And I didn't even need the truth-bender. I don't understand why you didn't want me to join up with her right away, though. She was ready to hire me that evening."

"Some aspects of your background still need to be protected," Conrad explained. "And if you pushed to join her immediately, especially so soon after an incident, there was too much chance that some of those aspects would be exposed, but that's irrelevant for the moment. There's a more pressing issue."

"What issue?"

"Why are you wasting my time with your complaints about things that didn't happen? People *attempted* to kill you, but they didn't succeed." He sighed impatiently. "Please don't make me believe I've made a mistake. Your family has been loyal to mine in recent decades, and that's not a quality to be overlooked. I'm giving you a chance, Miss Jones, to serve our cause and raise the dwindling esteem in which your family is held."

Drysi furrowed her brow. "If other people kill me, I can't bloody well get in a position to take Alison Brownstone down when the time is right, now can I?"

"If you can't survive a few obstacles," he replied slowly and his tone dripped with condescension, "then what use are you? I had hoped she would die in DC in a public and embarrassing way, but we didn't anticipate her ability to withstand those artifacts. It's fine. That's why I prepared you as a backup plan." He scoffed. "Earn your rewards, Miss Jones. Keep in mind that every man killed during this operation was more loyal to other families than mine. I would have preferred that they killed Brownstone, but in all wars, there are sacrifices. A general cannot allow himself to weep for every soldier who dies on the battlefield."

"And am I a sacrifice, too?" she scoffed. "Merely another a soldier to die on your battlefield?"

"I provided you with information that revealed a much broader scope of my plans than given to any others," Conrad replied. "You were given the tools to survive and avoid detection by Brownstone. Just remember, you come from a proud lineage, even if recent generations have squandered your family's past honor and esteem."

Drysi could almost see the sneer on his face.

Someday, Conrad, when I've worked my way up, I'll make you pay for every insult, you fucking prick.

"I'm giving you an opportunity to make up for the fecklessness of your ancestors, Miss Jones," he continued. "And, yes, this will continue to put your life in extreme danger. After all, keep in mind that if Alison Brownstone ever discovers what you are, she will most certainly kill you." He released a long, weary sigh. "But I understand your concerns. In the future, I will endeavor to lower the unnecessary risk you're exposed to."

"Thank you. That's all I ask."

"Wait some time and don't contact Brownstone," he ordered. "I'll set up another situation that will serve as a useful excuse for you to encounter her."

"And then?"

"Wait," Conrad replied. "Patience wins wars as much as strategy. You're a potentially devastating weapon, Miss Jones, but you'll only be useful if we save you for the right time."

Drysi stared at herself in the mirror. She didn't remember ever looking so tired. "And when is that?"

"Just because you've been allowed to know more of the

plan doesn't mean you need to know all of it. You have your task. Rest for now. I'll contact you again when I've made the appropriate arrangements."

The crystal grew dark.

She stuck the artifact back in her pocket and laid her head on her pillow. She still remembered every time her great-grandfather would come over and tell her the stories of the ancient power and prestige of her family line. The man would know, considering how long he'd lived.

The world was cruel, and only those who took power would survive it. Her weak father and grandfather had squandered their wealth and power, and now, she was forced to hunt down magical criminals for scraps.

Drysi couldn't continue that way. She *wouldn't* continue that way. She was the only one left in her line. It was her responsibility to restore her family's wealth and influence.

Her breath caught. Alison's quick thinking at the house had saved the witch's life.

Why?

That was the nagging question. They'd just met, and it wasn't as if Drysi had claimed to have more information to offer about the dark wizard plot.

Quick thinking? No. She didn't even think about it. She simply acted. Her first instinct was to save the life of a woman she barely knew.

Drysi glared at the ceiling.

She's a naïve fool. Kindness and selflessness lead to your death. Magic is power, and Alison needs to understand that.

The witch rolled onto her side and her stomach churned. Conrad offered her a reward for service, but he made it clear that it was her responsibility to survive. She was no more than a tool to him.

It doesn't matter. I might be a tool to him, but he's also my tool. I can't let myself get distracted by a simple reflex action.

"No, Alison," Drysi whispered. "I'm not the fool. You're the fool."

The witch almost believed it.

The story is far from over. Alison's adventure continues in THE DARK PRINCESS.

FREE BOOKS!

Join the only newsletter hosted by a Troll!

Get sneak peeks, exclusive giveaways, behind the scenes
content, and more.
PLUS you'll be notified of special **one day only fan
pricing** on new releases.

CLICK HERE

or visit: https://marthacarr.com/read-free-stories/

The story is far from over. Alison's adventure continues in
THE DARK PRINCESS

AVAILABLE FOR PURCHASE HERE

Only 11 more days till I retire from the day job and play author full time. Those who know me well have been gently nudging me in this direction for some time. A lot of them remember the days of the Great Recession and how I managed to get down to a bed, a dresser, a tiny TV and three and a half chairs. Mix in that I'm a careful planner and it took some time for me to feel ready to leap into this new space.

But I'm good and ready. Budgets have been made and checked and rechecked. There's an ample reserve and bills are paid off and car already tuned. Health care has been worked out. Major purchases have been made and there's a plan going forward. I told you I was a planner.

And, most importantly, I'm okay with whatever comes next. Not only okay, excited. This has been a moment in the works for 30 years and has taken some inside work to get me here as well as all the hard work with others (like Michael Anderle) to build a successful career.

I had to really get it that whatever happens, the

universe has my back. That things reset to the positive and that the information that flows in is just data. If I make a decision and don't like the consequences, I'll make another one, and another, and another. I had to learn to ask a lot of questions of the right people and be willing to take the answers, sort through them, take what I like and leave the rest, and run with the info I did keep. To change the bar from 'if I can do it, I should do it myself' to 'do what you love, farm out the rest'. To trust in myself and know that this road isn't a narrow one – there isn't one right answer, or even a thousand right answers. Just keep going.

Soon, a dream comes true and even keeps evolving. That's another thing I've learned. There's really no such thing as arriving. It's more like another wild, wonderful step done with a lot of wild, wonderful people – like all of you – and then you get up and take another step and wonder where the journey will take me next. I'm hoping to the Italian countryside maybe... We shall see. More adventures to follow.

THANK YOU for not only reading this story but these *Author Notes* **as well.**

(I think I've been good with always opening with "thank you." If not, I need to edit the other *Author Notes*!)

RANDOM (*sometimes*) THOUGHTS?

So Martha and I were talking about new projects coming down the pike, and I was thinking about a fun adventure with some characters based upon some down-home country folk.

You know, the ones you'd like to have by your side when the @#$@ hits the fan? And yet, they are fun to hang out with when there isn't trouble.

My problem was trying to wrap my head around this type of character in the Oriceran Universe. Then, she nicely tied it up and delivered the idea to me on a platter.

Something simple, just one character (with friends, of course) that was a hunter...Maybe a bounty hunter, but maybe another type...

What we ended up with is a project we are calling the Monster Whisperer. Part good ol' boy wearing a baseball cap with a lure in it and part hunter who will stick a sawed-off 12 gauge up a creature's ass and pull the trigger to give them a lead enema.

But (and this is stolen from my brother-in-law John) we'll start a story with, "So, my friends and I were drinking…"

Damn, I can't wait to get started on this series!

AROUND THE WORLD IN 80 DAYS

One of the interesting (at least to me) aspects of my life is the ability to work from anywhere and at any time. In the future, I hope to re-read my own *Author Notes* and remember my life as a diary entry.

Las Vegas, NV

This one is short and sweet. I'm eating at Chin-Chin's (NYNY Hotel) in Las Vegas writing my author notes and eating beef fried rice.

However, I wanted to eat in the Aria at Javier's. Unfortunately, the Aria has a metric-@#@#-ton of convention attendees all wearing suits and talking business.

These fine folks have created lines long enough to make me want to get in the car and drive somewhere.

So, I walked over here after cutting through the PARK and I'm waiting to get me some vittles.

See, just thinking about the Monster Whisperer is causing my Texan to come out.

;-)

FAN PRICING

$0.99 Saturdays (new LMBPN stuff) and $0.99 Wednesday (both LMBPN books and friends of LMBPN books.) Get great stuff from us and others at tantalizing prices.

Go ahead. I bet you can't read just one.

Sign up here: http://lmbpn.com/email/.

HOW TO MARKET FOR BOOKS YOU LOVE

Review them so others have your thoughts, and tell friends and the dogs of your enemies (because who wants to talk to enemies?)... *Enough said ;-)*

Ad Aeternitatem,

Michael Anderle

CONNECT WITH THE AUTHORS

Martha Carr Social

Website: http://www.marthacarr.com

Facebook: https://www.facebook.com/
groups/MarthaCarrFans/

Michael Anderle Social

Michael Anderle Social
Website:
http://www.lmbpn.com

Email List:
http://lmbpn.com/email/

Facebook Here: https://www.
facebook.com/TheKurtherianGambitBooks/